He had managed to have the last word!

Tracey gazed at the door, jumbled thoughts running through her mind, not the least of which was annoyance with herself for finding Ryan Alexander so attractive when she knew she hated him. And she hated the idea of being under his guardianship.

Then she gave a small, contented smile. From his last comments, it didn't sound as if he was overly enthralled with the situation, either. Tracey would make sure that he regretted his insistence that she accompany her sister to the old family home.

Ryan had called her "Red," hadn't he? Well, he didn't know the half of her redheaded persistence yet!

OTHER
Harlequin Romances
by KERRY ALLYNE

The Wool King

by

KERRY ALLYNE

Harlequin Books

TORONTO • LONDON • NEW YORK • AMSTERDAM
SYDNEY • HAMBURG • PARIS

Original hardcover edition published in 1978
by Mills & Boon Limited

ISBN 0-373-02205-0

Harlequin edition published October 1978

CHAPTER ONE

TRACEY ALEXANDER paced stormily across the carpeted floor of the small lounge room, hands thrust moodily into the back pockets of casual jeans and a mutinous scowl descending on to her normally smooth forehead.

'Well, I don't intend to go and that's all there is to it!' she flared heatedly at the wall in front of her, although the words were clearly directed to the second occupant of the room, her sister—or more correctly, stepsister—Lynette.

At twenty, Tracey was the elder by three years, but the difference in age wasn't the only dissimilar thing about them; in looks it could almost be said that they were the complete antithesis of one another. Whereas Tracey was tall and slender, with shoulder-length copper coloured waving hair, grey-green eyes outlined by long curling lashes and a generously expressive mouth above a small but determined chin; Lynette was of less than medium height and inclined to plumpness, with short straight fair hair, hazel eyes surrounded by spiky lashes, and a cupid's bow mouth that was set in a rounded chin that couldn't by any means have been called decisive.

At the moment Lyn was twisting her hands together nervously as she perched on the edge of the dark blue sofa, watching her sister's every move anxiously, her eyes wide and apprehensive.

'But, Tracey, we'll have to go ... it—it's a condition of the will,' she stammered weakly.

'Damn the will!'

Tracey started pacing once more, only this time with her arms wrapped across her ribs as if in an effort to contain some of her anger.

'I don't see why it had to include me at all! I'm not an Alexander by birth, only by deed poll—and as for needing a guardian until I'm twenty-three ... whoever heard of such a lot of rot!' she demanded, finally coming to a halt in front of the sofa with her hands resting belligerently on slim hips.

'I guess Dad must have thought we did, what with the money from the estate and all, otherwise he wouldn't have made that condition. I don't think he ... he liked the idea of you going out with your boss so much,' Lyn offered hesitantly.

'There's nothing wrong with Boyd Wilcox!'

'He *is* married, Tracey,' Lyn felt she had to remind her, albeit not very forcefully.

'Separated!' came the quick retort. 'And there's quite a difference between those two states, as Dad well knew.'

'But Boyd's almost forty-five,' Lyn's tone mirrored her own appalled thoughts. 'Dad wanted you to find someone of your own age to go out with.'

Tracey's winged brows rose even higher. 'I knew that,' she admitted with disgruntled mockery, throwing herself on to the sofa beside her sister and clasping her hands together at the back of her head. 'But I just don't happen to like men of my own age, they always seem so ...' she brought one hand forward and waved it in the air explicitly, 'so ... immature! Boyd's not a raw youth any longer, he knows what he wants from life and he's not frightened to go after it, he's ...'

'Experienced?' supplied her sister with an unusual amount of acidity.

'*Adult* was the word I was thinking of!' Tracey's return was unnecessarily sharp, but at Lyn's almost tearful look of reproach she smiled remorsefully. 'I'm sorry, I shouldn't be taking it out on you like this, I know it's not your fault. It's just that it makes me so mad to think that Dad could do such a thing to me. I've been earning my own living for over two years now, and then to suddenly find myself landed with a guardian—well ...' she heaved a sigh, 'I'm just not wearing it, that's all!'

'Mr Gatehead, the solicitor, said we don't really have any choice if we want to participate in Dad's entitlement from the family estate,' recalled Lyn with solemn persuasiveness.

'*Your* family, not *mine*!' she was corrected swiftly.

'But you were included too!' her sister wailed plaintively.

'Mr Gatehead was most specific on that point, you know he was, Tracey. Either we both inherit, or neither one of us does.'

'And for that dubious honour we have to suffer the guardianship of some cousin of yours until we both turn twenty-three. No, thank you very much!' Tracey rejected the suggestion immediately.

'Well, originally it was to have been Dad's brother as our guardian, but of course, after our uncle died then the will had to be changed and so Dad chose his eldest nephew,' Lyn explained, unnecessarily seeing that her sister knew the facts as well as she did.

'Uncle, cousin ... what's the difference?' Tracey shrugged uninterestedly. 'As far as I'm concerned, the Alexanders can keep their precious money, and their guardianship. I'm not about to accept either of them.'

'But I'm not as confident and independent as you are,' Lyn commented in a small voice. 'I feel more secure when I have some family about me and I think—I think I'd like to go.'

The wistful words brought Tracey up short and she eyed the girl next to her understandingly. For so long now Lyn had been the cosseted baby of the family that the tremendous shock had affected her more deeply than it had the more resilient Tracey when they had received the terrible news that their father had been killed by a passing car when hurrying across the street on his way home from work one spring evening some weeks previously.

Theirs had always been a close-knit little family—Tracey not even knowing her own father, who had died before she was born, and only being able to recall the soft and reassuring presence of Ben Alexander who had given her all and possibly more than her natural father could have done, even to the gift of his own name. And as their mother had died early in their young lives—Lyn had only been seven at the time—Tracey and her stepfather had always done all they could to protect and cushion the sweet-natured youngest member of the family from any of life's more unpleasant aspects. Upon her stepfather's death, however, it had been brought home to Tracey that they might perhaps have safeguarded Lyn too much, for she was still very young for her age and less than prepared to make any effort to stand on her own two feet.

'Well, I expect you'll still be able to go out there if you want to,' Tracey now attempted to bolster her sister's morale with a carefree showing of confidence. 'I'm sure they'll understand the circumstances once they've been explained fully.' She squeezed Lyn's hand comfortingly. 'You'll see, everything will turn out for the best.'

Not doubting her sister's ability to pave the way for her on this occasion as she had so many other times, Lyn responded with a lightening of her worried countenance and a hopeful, 'But wouldn't you like to come too, Tracey? I mean you've always said you'd be interested to see how they run some of those big properties in the outback. I thought you'd like the idea.'

'Uh—uh!' accompanied by a definite shake of the head. 'Not under the circumstances Mr Gatehead was talking about. It will probably suit you—after all, they are your relations—but I'm not the type to take kindly to having some stranger saying yea or nay to any of my plans. That's not my scene at all!' Tracey smiled wryly.

'But I would have liked us to stay together.'

'So would I,' Tracey nodded her head emphatically. 'But not at the expense of our personal freedom. Besides, I enjoy going out with Boyd and can see no good reason why I shouldn't be allowed to continue to do so.' Then, on seeing her sister's downcast expression, 'Cheer up, Lyn, you'll be okay once you arrive at Wirrabilla, or wherever their property is.'

'But I'll worry about you,' Lyn murmured disconsolately, scuffing the toes of her tartan sneakers together in her anxiety.

'You'll worry about *me*!' For the first time since seeing their family solicitor, Tracey found something to laugh about and it even brought a rueful smile to Lyn's lips. 'At least it might stop you fretting over how the rest of the Alexander's will receive you.'

Lyn's head nodded up and down thoughtfully, although Tracey was pleased to see her lose some of her tenseness and settle back more relaxedly on the sofa.

'It was quite a surprise discovering that Dad was one of *those* Alexanders, wasn't it?' Lyn said quietly. 'I only remember seeing an article in the papers some months ago when one of them got married. Apparently it was a very gala affair.' She paused and a perplexed crease furrowed her brows. 'I do find it strange that Dad never ever mentioned them at all, though, or why they never bothered to contact him since he came to Sydney all those years ago. You don't suppose he could have been the black sheep of the family and was kicked out, do you?' worriedly.

Tracey lifted one shoulder indifferently. 'Could be,' she agreed, kicking off her sandals and tucking her feet beneath her, and grinned at the horrified expression that settled on her sister's face. 'Although I doubt it, knowing Dad,' which had Lyn relaxing once more. 'More like a case of the younger son not wanting to follow in his father's footsteps, so he cleared off to do his own thing.'

'That still doesn't explain why they never wrote to each other, though, does it? Why, it wasn't until we saw the solicitor that we found out we've got two aunts and uncles, and a whole host of cousins that we've not even met yet.'

'Sounds as if you'll be inundated with family from the moment you arrive,' grinned Tracey. 'You should feel safe and secure enough with all that many around. As for them not writing to each other,' she shrugged expressively, 'Well, you know how it is with some families, they don't feel the need to be in constant touch.'

'But that's hardly a reason for Dad not to mention them.'

'Oh, hell, Lyn, how should I know? You know as much about them as I do. Perhaps there was some bad feeling between them at one time for some reason or another. All I know is that Dad made sure he tied us to them pretty tightly when he made out that damned will, so whatever happened in the past he obviously didn't intend for it to continue for ever.'

'Mmm, maybe you're right,' concurred Lyn as she eased herself from the sofa to begin humming musingly as she made her way into the kitchen. A few seconds later she stuck her head back round the door jamb. 'Are you going out with Boyd again tonight, Tracey?' she asked.

Tracey stretched both arms high above her head and

breathed deeply. 'Not tonight,' she replied. 'We're going out tomorrow instead.'

'Tomorrow!' Lyn was back in the room as fast as she could make it. 'But you can't!' she protested, aghast.

'Why not?' with imperturbable calm.

'Because that's when ... Mr Gatehead said ... that's when our guardian is coming here to meet us, that's why not,' squeaked Lyn in her effort to get the words out as quickly as possible.

Her sister swung irritably away from the sofa and went to stand looking out of the window over the small suburban garden. 'And as Mr Gatehead also said that our guardian,' with unmistakable sarcasm, 'would be in town for over a week, I can't see why I should have to dance attendance on him the first time he deigns to call at this house,' she flung over her shoulder angrily. 'Besides, Boyd's managed to get tickets for that new show at the Domino Theatre. for tomorrow night and I don't want to miss it. I'm sure there'll be plenty of other occasions for me to meet your cousin—what did Mr Gatehead say his name was?—Ryan?'

'Something like that,' Lyn conceded dispassionately before hastening back to what was causing her so much concern. 'But couldn't you put it off until some other night, Tracey? I'd feel much better if you were here with me,' she pressed in a woebegone manner.

Partly from a niggling sense of guilt, and partly through impatience, Tracey turned back from her unseeing contemplation of the view beyond the window to snap, 'Oh, come on, Lyn, it isn't the end of the world! He's only coming here to meet you, not to seduce you!'

'And you're only saying that because you don't want to meet him yourself!' countered Lyn in a hurt voice.

With a wry grin Tracey admitted to herself that perhaps her young sister hadn't been too wide of the mark with that statement after all. For some unknown reason she wasn't looking forward to meeting Ryan Alexander and the knowledge of that reluctance was making her short-tempered. For the second time that afternoon she apologised with a sigh.

'I'm sorry, love, I shouldn't have said that, but I really don't want to miss seeing the show. How about I promise faithfully to make myself available to meet your cousin any time you nominate after tomorrow night? Will that do?'

'I suppose it will have to,' with a dismal sniff.

'Well, it's not really my fault,' Tracey felt obliged to point out reasonably. 'It might have been better if your cousin had made enquiries to find out whether it was convenient for him to call tomorrow night. For all he knows we might have been planning a private bacchanalia to which he wasn't invited,' she grinned engagingly.

At least her facetious words had the effect of rousing Lyn from the depressed state she had been working herself into, for she suddenly laughed and exclaimed, 'You are an idiot, Tracey! I shall miss you so when I have to leave. Are you certain you won't reconsider and come with me?'

Tracey shook her head, firmly. 'Not on your life! I'm my own mistress ... and I plan to stay that way!'

It was late, well after midnight, the following evening when Boyd's new brick red Centura pulled up outside the small house that the Alexander family had shared for so long. Tracey could see through the misting car window the yellow glare of a light shining from the lounge room, indicating that Lyn was waiting up for her, ready to be regaled with a full recounting of her sister's evening entertainment, and sighed even as she hugged a lacy shawl more closely about her shoulders as an unexpected chill touched her flesh. She turned to the man beside her with a slight frown puckering her forehead.

'I'd better not stay too long, Boyd, as Lyn's still waiting up for me. I expect she wants to tell me what her cousin had to say when he called,' she explained, a vague uneasiness making her restive. It wasn't like Lyn to wait till these hours to talk to her. Still, she shrugged away her misgivings, these weren't normal events they had been experiencing over the last few weeks and that probably accounted for it.

Boyd moved closer, his left arm sliding along the back of the seat until his hand reached her neck and began to

caress the soft skin. With a trim figure and his conventional
good looks to a large extent unmarred by his years, Boyd
Wilcox could feel the flickering tongue of desire mounting
within him as he gazed at the alluring face of his companion
turned towards him.

Drawing her closer, he gathered her into his arms, his
mouth trailing a warm persuasive imprint across her cheek
until he claimed her lips hungrily. For a moment Tracey
responded to the pressure of his demanding mouth, but
then she began to struggle faintly in his arms. Inexplicably
she was on edge tonight and Boyd wasn't his usual urbane
self either—he had never been this passionate before—and
she dragged her lips from his to protest breathlessly, 'No,
Boyd, I ...' but his mouth silenced her roughly while his
hand pushed aside her protective shawl and slid the fragile
shoe-string straps of her evening gown from her shoulder.

Now his lips sought the exposed warmth of the soft
skin covering her throat as he murmured fervently against
the sweet smelling flesh, 'Tracey darling, I want you so!
I wish you'd ...'

What he wished was never voiced, for the next moment
Tracey nearly died of shock as the door on her side of the
car was wrenched open to reveal in the intermittent street
lighting the dark outline of an extremely large man as he
bent towards them, grinding out the question, '*Tracey Alexander?*' in a scarcely controlled tone of flaring anger.

The two in the car could only raise their heads in
stunned astonishment at the stranger's appearance until
Tracey nodded wordless confirmation of his query, whereupon he leant into the interior, steely fingers gripped her
upper arm and he bit out bleakly, 'I'm Ryan Alexander ...
your *guardian*!' while he almost literally dragged her bodily
from the vehicle to stand beside him on the pavement,
shaking with embarrassment at what he might have seen or
heard, and fury at what he had done.

Boyd's somewhat blustering, 'Now, look here!' was
almost completely drowned by Tracey's more vehement,
'How dare you!' but her guardian paid no attention to
either castigation as he bent to the car once again and advised grimly, 'I think you'd better be on your way, Mr

Wilcox. I understand you have quite a distance to go before you make it home,' which left Tracey with the distinct idea of choking her sister for having been so expansive with regard to her private life during the evening's meeting with her cousin.

'No, by God, I'm not leaving!' Boyd made to move out of the car after Tracey, but one look at Ryan Alexander's threatening stance had her rushing forward and assuring him, 'No Boyd, I'll be all right—I can manage it,' with more confidence than she felt before there was a chance for the confrontation to develop into anything more than a verbal one.

Her brave-sounding words had her guardian's lips twisting mockingly, which only served to bank the fires of her temper even higher as, after Boyd's one last doubtful, 'You're sure?' she snapped, 'Of course I'm sure!' before biting at her lip contritely and continuing in a softer tone, 'I'll—I'll see you in the office in the morning. Okay?'

Boyd made a gesture of defeated acceptance and moved back behind the steering-wheel as Ryan Alexander slammed the passenger door closed with little consideration for the lock mechanism. No sooner had the Centura pulled out from the kerb than a hard hand had hold of Tracey's arm and she was being propelled rapidly through the front gate and up to the steps leading into the house, accompanied by a savage, 'Get inside, you little ...!' he bit off an expletive with grim intent. 'You look like some cheap tramp who's had an overly busy night!'

After her initial gasp of furious indignation that he should dare to make such a comparison, Tracey retorted swiftly, her temper beginning to get the better of her.

'And you'd know, of course, having no doubt had a great deal of experience with the type!' she flung at him, bowing her head sarcastically in deference to his unconfirmed greater knowledge.

Apart from a tightening grip on her arm there was no answer forthcoming to her gibe as with cold deliberation she was pushed past the open front door, which thudded resoundingly closed behind them—presumably with the aid of a well aimed foot—and forced down the dim hallway

and into the lounge. At last, after one final move that sent
her into the middle of the room, Tracey's arm was set free
and she stood silently, rubbing absently at the painful red
marks caused by his ungentle grasp while she took stock of
her antagonist.

Right from the first she had known that he was a big man,
but in the glare of the overhead light it struck her forcibly
that he was even larger than she had imagined and seemed
to tower over her in the small room. Swiftly her mind
harvested the salient features; judging him to be around
thirty-two self-assured years old; broad-framed, but supple
—no superfluous weight there, she decided; dark hair curling towards the collar of his smoothly expensive pale fawn
suit; clear blue eyes that were accustomed to mirage-
wavering horizons; a deeply tanned skin that could only
have come from continual exposure to a relentless sun; a
finely moulded nose above a challengingly curving mouth;
and a resolute chin with a noticeable cleft in the centre to
emphasise its determination.

Tracey groaned inwardly. Here was someone she didn't
want to tangle with. He was too male ... too impregnable
... too dominant! She flushed deeply under his derisive
scrutiny and dropped her wrap on to the sofa in order to
pull her dress strap hastily back over her shoulder—something she hadn't been given an opportunity to do before—
and, as much as she would have liked to outstare him, she
abruptly began to doubt her ability to do so and looked
around the room quickly.

'Where's Lyn?' she enquired with an attempt at hauteur,
but without quite meeting his gaze.

'She went to bed hours ago. The same place you should
be, instead of making love in a parked car!' he informed her,
coldly contemptuous.

'If you don't like what you see, then you shouldn't look,
should you?' Tracey retaliated hotly in an effort to alleviate
the embarrassment that was once more sweeping over her
at the thought of the scene he had witnessed in the car,
and stalked over to the low coffee table to extract a cigarette from the packet lying there. Lighting it with fingers
she was annoyed to find decidedly unsteady, she blew

the smoke aggravatingly in his direction.

Ryan's lip curled detestably. 'Hardly a case of having to look when you conduct your affairs in the middle of a public thoroughfare for all and sundry to witness!'

'Hardly that either!' flashed Tracey. 'Except for the car on the other side of the street there was no one else around.'

'I was.'

'Ah, yes, Lyn's cousin from the bush,' she acknowledged him derogatorily. 'And might I be allowed to enquire just why you're still here at this hour? I thought you would have been long gone by now,' she inadvertently let slip her inner thoughts.

'No doubt,' with strong overtones of mockery. 'But unfortunately your little ploy for avoiding me didn't work, did it?'

'You think I didn't come home until now just to keep out of your way?' She uttered a lightly jeering laugh. 'I'm afraid you have an inflated sense of your own importance if you think I was worried about meeting you!' she deliberately refrained from dignifying him by the use of a name. 'I couldn't care less what you do—you've got no control over me!'

With insufferable satisfaction he put a large tanned hand to the top pocket of his jacket. 'And I have a document here that says just the opposite,' he goaded.

Tracey's chin lifted a degree higher as she eyed her opponent rebelliously. Once and for all Ryan Alexander had to be made to understand her position. She was not leaving Sydney!

'I don't care what the document says,' she told him carelessly. 'I have no intention of leaving town to go and live on a property in the middle of nowhere—as I expect Lyn's already informed you—and I can't see why you're so determined that I should.'

'The Alexanders look after their own.'

'But I'm not an Alexander,' she smiled sweetly up at him.

'Your name makes a liar of you with that statement.'

'In which case, I'll change my name! I'll—I'll marry Boyd!' she announced somewhat grandiosely.

Mocking eyebrows rose. 'Lyn tells me he already has one wife.'

'He's—he's getting a—a divorce,' Tracey stammered, none too certain of the facts she was relating. Boyd had certainly said he intended getting one, but up until now she had never seen or heard of any evidence to support his statement. Her doubtfulness wasn't lost on the man opposite her either.

'Not quite sure of that, though, are you?' he commented with obvious pleasure at her discomfiture, seating himself leisurely in one of the two matching armchairs beside the fireplace where he rested his elbows on the arms and his fingers came together in a steeple beneath that unyielding chin.

'Judging by his behaviour tonight, I wouldn't have said it was marriage that lover-boy had in mind right at the moment,' he drawled with a lazy, knowing smile.

For a time that smile threw Tracey completely off balance, but then she gulped hastily and determinedly ignored the quickening of her pulse as she roughly stubbed out her cigarette and swung back to face him with a challenging look in her eyes.

'Either way, it's no business of yours,' she flouted daringly.

Ryan's reaction was to again tap the pocket of his coat confidently. 'The document ... remember?' he refreshed her memory.

'What's that got to do with me getting married?' she queried in surprise.

'Because from now until you turn twenty-three you have to have my consent before you can marry.'

'What?' Tracey could hardly believe her ears. 'You've got to be joking!' she glared at him furiously, her eyes green and angry. 'Mr Gatehead said nothing about that. Why should I have to have your consent?'

'Because I happen to have been appointed your legal guardian and the trustee of your income from the family holdings for the next two and a quarter years—a fact of which you are already very well aware,' he reminded her imperturbably, clearly well pleased with the predicament in which she found herself.

Not so Tracey. She had a definite premonition that she was being forced into something over which she had absolutely no control, and she fought against it blindly.

'A fact which I also intend to ignore,' she shook her head slowly in an effort to convince him of her sincerity. 'I refuse point-blank to accept you as any sort of guardian and, short of keeping me permanently under lock and key, you can't make me do otherwise,' she told him, not a little smugly.

His head tilted to one side consideringly. 'You think not?' he quizzed softly, ominously. 'What about Lyn?'

'Well, what about her?'

'So you would deliberately stop her from inheriting under her father's will just to satisfy your own selfish whims,' he suggested with a scornful glance.

'I'm not being selfish,' Tracey defended herself resentfully—he was putting a decidedly wrong interpretation on her lack of compliance with her stepfather's wishes. 'I can't see why I have to be included at all—I wasn't born an Alexander.'

'The will states both of you agree to the terms therein, or else neither one of you will receive anything from the estate.'

'That's blackmail!'

'But it is what your stepfather wanted,' he reminded uncompromisingly.

Didn't she know it! She had always known that Ben Alexander hadn't been in favour of her seeing so much of Boyd, but that he should have gone to such lengths in an attempt to break their relationship was something she couldn't fully appreciate. Of course he would have known that, if there was no other way open to her, she would always stand by Lyn, but that didn't make her position any more tolerable.

'I'll—I'll contest it in every court in this country,' she now threatened with more bravado than she was feeling in a last-ditch effort to defeat him.

'Then not only will I make sure that the cost of such an action takes every last cent you own by the time the case is heard, but you can also be certain that should you by some unforeseen chance happen to succeed in having the will set aside, then I will have you in court so often replying to appeals that you'll be closer to thirty-three before a final verdict is handed down,' his voice cut across the room with such deadly assertion that Tracey couldn't doubt that he wouldn't do all, and quite probably more, than he had predicted.

'How fortunate for you to be wealthy enough to ensure that everyone falls in with your wishes,' she gibed mutinously.

His agreement was a smoothly complacent, 'It has its advantages,' which had Tracey immediately casting about frantically for some other obstacle to place in his way, and eventually came up with a defiant, 'Boyd will help me!'

'Perhaps.' Ryan sounded extremely dubious on this point. 'I know his impassioned words tonight were to the effect that he wanted you, but somehow I didn't quite get the impression that he would be prepared to wait at least another two and a quarter years before he could have you, *Tracey darling!*' with a merciless mimickry which had her colour deepening uncontrollably and her hands clenching impotently at her sides.

'And you have no idea what Boyd is, or isn't, prepared to do for me,' she finally managed to throw at him.

His head nodded sagely. 'No, that's true,' he conceded with such agreeableness that Tracey was immediately alert. 'So why don't you ask him tomorrow, at the office, hmm?' That lazy smile of superior knowledge came into play again. 'I'll be very interested to hear what he has to say.'

Tracey whirled on him indignantly. 'Why? Do you think it's so unlikely that he would want to help me?'

Ryan withdrew a cigarette packet from his inside pocket and lit one with the flickering flame from a gold lighter before leaning back relaxedly in the chair and assessing her every feature with narrowed eyes.

'I wouldn't exactly say that,' he ultimately let his thoughts be known. 'Rather, let's say that I think it very unlikely that he wouldn't want repayment for his aid, and one doesn't have to rack one's brains very hard in order to surmise just what sort of compensation your Mr Wilcox would have in mind.'

Would that be a condition attached to any help she might receive from Boyd? That she live with him without the benefit of marriage? Tracey really did find that hard to believe, although, now she came to think of it, he did always skirt the subject of matrimony very carefully. Before she had always believed he was just reluctant to become involved again after suffering one unhappy union, but Ryan's insinuations were beginning to make her wonder now if, after all, it wasn't just a case of him wanting to have his cake and eat it too!'

However, she wasn't about to let this overbearing relative of Lyn's see that he was causing her to have doubts regarding Boyd's loyalty, so she opened her eyes wide to advise insolently, 'I shouldn't judge everyone by your own standards, if I were you.'

'I'm not—that's why I'm keeping an open mind regarding yourself at the moment. From the exhibition I witnessed this evening it wouldn't surprise me to find that you're already complying with any conditions Boyd Wilcox might care to impose,' in a tone of cool arrogance.

'Oh, boy, you really are the living end, aren't you?' Tracey lashed back with despising scorn. 'First you bring my enjoyable evening to a very abrupt finish; then you drag me in here and start laying down the law as to what I'm supposed to be allowed to do for the next couple of years; then you proceed to cast unfounded aspersions on Boyd's character and, for a finale—just to top it all off—you're now accusing me of God only knows what!' she cried stormily, trembling with resentment and an overpowering sense of inevitability. 'Now, if you consider you've caused enough of an upset for one night, would you mind leaving? I don't think there could possibly be anything else for us to say to each other—besides which, I'm tired and I'd like to go to bed!' she concluded petulantly.

Taking his time about putting out his cigarette, Ryan rose to his feet with the lithe action of an active man and moved slowly towards her. After one wary step backwards Tracey stood her ground nervously, not wanting him to guess just how uneasy she was in his presence. When he halted before her his hand came up to span her chin, tilting her head back unhurriedly, but she refused to hold the blue gaze and curtained her eyes with dark lashes to obliterate him completely from view.

A warm thumb smoothed hauntingly against her chin and she shivered involuntarily under his touch even while she heard him commenting, as from a distance, in resigned exasperation, 'If you kept more reasonable hours you wouldn't feel so tired,' and it was with an unreasonable kind of reluctance that she felt his hand leave her jaw to slide gently across her cheekbones. 'And nor would those be making an appearance,' he said.

Feeling she had to make some gesture of individuality, Tracey took two quick steps backwards, away from his unnerving presence which was ridiculously making her quite breathless, and now her eyes opened fully.

'Are you implying I've got dark circles under my eyes?' she questioned in astonished disbelief.

'Not implying ... telling!' Ryan corrected her explicitly with scant regard for her feelings as he headed for the door, and leaving Tracey to trail behind his tall figure indignantly. Upon opening the front door he stepped out on to the porch, then turned back with a satisfied look on his face.

'Don't forget to let me know what Boyd's views are on the matter, will you, Red?' he remarked with such an aggravating smile that it was nearly impossible for Tracey to stop herself from actually hitting out at him physically. 'I shall be very interested to hear what—er—proposals he has to make.'

Then he was striding down the path with a rapid tread and across the road to the car parked opposite, leaving Tracey with only time for a swiftly shouted, 'And don't call me *Red*!' before he had disappeared from sight inside the vehicle.

For only a moment she stood in the hallway, watching as the powerful engine of the midnight blue Charger roared into life, but before it could move away she had shut the door, leaning back against it wearily until she heard the sound of the engine fade in the distance, then walking slowly back down the hall to switch off the lounge room light and head dispiritedly for the bathroom.

Tracey didn't sleep at all well that night, alternately
waking throughout to find herself first burning hot and then
shiveringly cold, while her disconnected dreams had her
tossing and turning restlessly for those periods when she
did actually manage to doze off.

CHAPTER TWO

IT was nearing seven-thirty when Lyn crept into her sister's bedroom the following morning and gently shook her awake with the warning, 'You're going to be late for work if you're not careful, Tracey.'

One slim-fingered hand moved vaguely against the covers in reluctant acknowledgment and Tracey rolled on to her back, trying to force open eyelids that felt as if they were sliding over a bed of sand.

'Thanks, Lyn,' she whispered with a throatiness that wasn't normal, and although she swallowed and tried again, the result was the same. Levering herself upright, she put a hand to her aching head and murmured faintly, 'Oh, heavens, I feel ghastly. I must be coming down with the 'flu or something.'

'Perhaps you shouldn't go to work today, then?'

Abruptly the events of the night before came flooding back and Tracey shook her head feebly but determinedly. 'No, today of all days I can't stay at home,' she declared positively. 'There's something I have to discuss urgently with Boyd.'

'Couldn't you phone him instead?' suggested Lyn anxiously.

'Uh-uh!' Tracey vetoed the idea immediately as she struggled from beneath the bedclothes while Lyn handed across her gingham housecoat. No, this was something she had to do face to face, if only to prove to the insufferable Ryan Alexander just how wrong his denigrating suggestions had been.

By the time she had washed, dressed and had breakfast—during which she had only half listened to Lyn's narration of her meeting with her cousin the previous evening and had replied even more hazily to any of her questions, and all the while trying to force half a slice of toast, a cup of tea and two aspirins past her lips—Tracey felt more dead

22

than alive. Her head felt like an overblown football, her eyes were watering annoyingly, her throat was sore, her legs felt like rubber, and she ached in muscles she hadn't even known she possessed.

Going up in the elevator of the building where she worked she sneezed three times—once for each time the doors opened to allow other passengers to alight while letting in a draught of cool air—and discovered Boyd hovering impatiently nearby when she arrived at her desk. He didn't give her any more time than to slide her bag into the bottom drawer of her desk and remove the cover from her typewriter than he was beckoning for her to follow him into his office.

'Come in here, Tracey, and then we can talk without being disturbed,' he urged.

With a quiescent nod she followed him into the tastefully furnished room, and no sooner had Boyd closed the door behind them than he attempted to take her into his arms, but Tracey wrenched herself almost irritably from his embrace and moved across to the leather chair in front of his desk where she sank down on to its padded comfort weakly.

'I'm sorry, Boyd,' she murmured hoarsely on seeing his hurt expression. 'But I really don't feel at all well this morning.'

Immediately he crossed to her side, a worried look on his face. 'Why? What happened last night?' he demanded almost curtly.

'Last night?' Tracey stared up at him with a puzzled frown, then realised just what he was referring to and smiled ruefully. 'Oh, that!' she dismissed it negligently. 'No, I was meaning that I seem to have caught one of those viruses somewhere along the line and I feel, to be quite honest, lousy!'

Perching on the arm of the chair, Boyd put a sympathetic arm around her shoulders and hugged her to him gently. 'Poor darling,' he consoled tenderly. 'You shouldn't have come in today. You would have been better spending the day in bed.'

Tracey lowered her head, nodding as she watched her fingers smooth the pale pink material of her dress nervously across her knees. She wasn't too sure how best to begin and she cleared her throat unhappily. 'I probably wouldn't have come except that,' a deep, steadying breath, 'except that there was something I had to see you about,' she managed huskily, and not all of it brought about by her illness.

'See me about?' Boyd echoed with a slight frown.

She nodded again, not wanting to look at him, and keeping her eyes on the fingers that were now curled defensively around each other in her lap.

'Yes—you see, Lyn's cousin,' her eyes met his for a moment, 'the man you—er—met last night, is quite adamant that both Lyn and I are under his guardianship and that we both have to move on to the Alexander property at Wirrabilla until his responsibility is concluded in accordance with Dad's will.'

'I see,' Boyd greeted her information darkly, leaving her side to pace around the desk and lower himself into the swivel chair on the other side. 'I should have known he was going to make trouble, from his attitude last night! That's what's wrong with these wealthy squatters—they've been a law unto themselves for too long, they run their properties like feudal baronies and expect everyone else to bow and scrape to their wishes the minute they open their mouths,' he sneered, though to Tracey's way of thinking there seemed to be slightly more than a touch of envy in his words as he uttered them. 'Isn't there any way you can get around that stupid condition your father made?' he asked.

Tracey's shoulders hunched broodingly. 'I don't know. I—I did say I'd take it to court,' she told him hesitantly.

'And?'

'He said that if I did he would see that it cost me every cent I own and that I would be closer to thirty-three before I received a final judgment.' She looked at him questioningly. 'Could he really do that?'

Now it was Boyd's turn to shrug his shoulders. 'I suppose he could if he really wanted to,' he sourly deflated any hopes she might have had. 'Legal work is never cheap and the wheels of justice turn slowly at any time, so I guess if someone felt inclined to stall the system for as long as possible, it could take years before the matter was finally settled.'

That sense of the unavoidable was back again in full force, making Tracey appeal to him a little desperately, her hands opened wide. 'Then what can I do? I don't want to leave Sydney.'

Boyd's eyes narrowed a little and his lips pursed thoughtfully. 'I might perhaps be able to help you to some degree,' he proposed softly.

'How?' sitting forward eagerly. 'Will you help me with a court case?'

'As Alexander has already told you what his intentions are regarding that form of retaliation, I hardly think it would be worthwhile throwing good money after bad in an attempt to thwart him that way,' Boyd once more unthinkingly squashed her ascending optimism. 'No, that wasn't exactly what I had in mind. I was thinking more along the lines of,' he coughed—rather uneasily, Tracey thought, 'of me taking care of you.'

Tracey sat there staring at him, pleading inwardly that he wasn't about to confirm Ryan Alexander's suggestive comments, but try as she might she couldn't keep the flatness from her tone as she enquired tightly, 'In what way?' on a deeply held breath.

He leant forward enthusiastically, his arm outstretched towards her over the desk between them, but Tracey refused to respond by putting her own hand in his as his proposition came tumbling forth.

'Well, I do have a large house with plenty of space. You should know you can always rely on me to provide you with a roof over your head, Tracey,' he told her fervidly, his eyes shining, but at the look that came into her own eyes, 'There's no strings attached, darling,' he was swift—too swift—to disclaim. 'It would just afford you a breathing space, that's all. Somewhere to give you a chance to decide exactly how you're going to fight this man's claim,' he smiled reassuringly.

Tracey sank back wearily into her chair, a hand to her pounding head. So Lyn's domineering cousin had been proved right in the end. Oh, Boyd might assert that there were no strings attached, and she had no doubt that he might even believe this to be true at the moment, but after his passionate embraces of the night before it didn't take much imagination on Tracey's part to foresee just how tenuous her position would be if she took him up on his offer of assistance. With a slight shake of her head she rose slowly to her feet.

'I'm sorry, Boyd, it just wouldn't work out,' she refused his invitation listlessly.

With a muttered exclamation, Boyd thrust back his chair and strode to the front of the desk, catching hold of one of her hands and pulling her close. 'Tracey, Tracey, you're reading all the wrong thoughts into my suggestion,' he tried to impress his innocence on her. 'I thought by offering my protection it would be giving you a way out of this mess,' he insisted, but couldn't quite succeed in keeping the possessive glow of self-gratification from his eyes, and Tracey shook her head again, disbelievingly this time.

How could she have missed seeing that look on his face before? Boyd had never had any intention of getting a divorce, and she had been a fool to have believed otherwise. It had taken her six months to discover what Ryan Alexander had been able to detect from one very brief, very pungent meeting. And the fact that Ryan had been right wasn't in any way helping her to become reconciled to the fact! Determinedly she twisted out of Boyd's hold and headed for the door, trying hard not to let her disappointment show.

'I think I will take the rest of the day off it you don't mind, Boyd,' she said, head held high and her gaze holding his bravely.

'Tracey . . . !' he called after her imploringly, but she ignored the plea and when he made a move towards her she resolutely opened the door and stepped through into the main office.

Pausing only long enough to retrieve her bag from her desk and replace the cover on her typewriter, Tracey hurried between the long rows of desks, returning the called greeting from other members of the staff with only a lacklustre smile and a casual wave as she passed them on her way to the elevator shaft.

Outside it was beginning to rain lightly and she looked up at the overcast sky with despairing eyes. That was all she needed—to get soaked to the skin before she could make it to the bus stop!

The light was fading between gunmetal clouds by the time Lyn arrived home that afternoon, her arms clutched about two large bags of groceries. On her way through to the kitchen she noticed Tracey's shoulder bag lying on the couch and hurriedly deposited her purchases on one of the cupboards before rushing along the hall to her sister's bedroom. Quietly she turned the handle and slipped inside.

'Are you awake, Tracey?' she called softly to the head of bright hair just visible above the line of covers on the divan bed.

The tousled hair moved and Tracey's grey-green eyes came into view as she pushed herself a little higher on the pillow. 'I think so,' she smiled wanly at her sister's small, worried face. 'Not that I'd expect anyone to be able to tell, because I certainly feel half asleep most of the time.'

Lyn stepped further into the room. 'Would you like me to call Dr Hamilton for you?' she asked.

Tracey moved her head negatively. 'No need—I called in to see him on my way home this morning and he wrote me out a prescription for some vile concoction, as well as some capsules, which I dosed myself with at lunchtime. I won't need another lot now until after dinner.'

'Would you like me to get you something, then? A cup of tea ... or coffee?'

About to refuse, Tracey changed her mind. 'I think I might like a cup of tea, if you don't mind, Lyn.'

'Coming right up,' the younger girl returned with a smile. 'No trouble at all.'

After her sister's departure, Tracey lay for a while watching the still falling rain running down the glass of her window, until suddenly her ears pricked on hearing the muted sound of voices coming from the kitchen and then the sound of Lyn's laughter. She relaxed again. It must be one of their neighbours calling in for a tide-over cup of sugar or some such requisite.

She was almost asleep again when her bedroom door opened and, expecting Lyn with her promised tea, she prepared to lever herself up on the pillow, but on seeing the tall male presence enter the room, dressed in dark blue flared pants and a white silk knit shirt which showed bronzed and sinewed forearms to advantage, she gasped and sat bolt upright, for the moment unmindful of the brevity of her own lace-embroidered nightgown as she stared at him accusingly.

'What—what are *you* doing here?' she spluttered. 'And, more particularly, what are you doing *here*?' with one slim forefinger expressly indicating her bedroom.

Lazy blue eyes roamed leisurely over her rebellious face, taking in the over-bright and glittering green eyes and flushed cheeks—all ready symptoms of her virus—and a smile caught at the corners of his fascinating mouth which had Tracey dragging the blankets almost to her chin in a vain attempt to defend herself against the totally alien feeling of helplessness that was sweeping over her in the face of Ryan's almost palpable virility. His dark head indicated the cup of tea he was carrying in one tanned hand and which he placed on her bedside table before thrusting both hands deep into the pockets of his pants to stand gazing down at her with a dark fathomless look.

'I brought your tea to save Lyn the trouble,' he explained levelly. 'And maybe I just wanted to assure myself that your illness was fact ... and not fiction,' he went on with an enquiring quirk to one slightly crooked eyebrow.

'Why wouldn't it be?' Tracey asked, eyes wide with surprise.

'I thought you could, perhaps, have been avoiding me again.'

'Avoiding you?' she echoed. 'How could I? I didn't even know you were coming!'

'Didn't Lyn tell you?'

Tracey's forehead creased with concentration. Lyn might have mentioned it that morning at breakfast, but she hadn't really been paying attention to anything her sister had said at the time. Now she shrugged off-handedly.

'She could have done,' she admitted nonchalantly. 'I can't remember.'

'Had other, more important matters on your mind, did you?' he drawled.

'Such as?' Tracey rounded on him artlessly, knowing full well what he was meaning and dreading the derisive mockery she was certain would be forthcoming.

Again that look of subtle shrewdness that had her fuming inwardly as Ryan folded his arms across his chest and suggested, 'Such as, what ideas Boyd Wilcox could devise to extricate you from my guardianship.'

Determined to evade answering him for as long as she could, Tracey gave a deliberately secretive smile and dropped her gaze annoyingly from his. 'Maybe he didn't need any ideas,' she hinted intriguingly. 'Maybe I've just decided to disappear ... some time when your back's turned,' she smiled provokingly up at him now.

His reaction was swift and inexorable. Before Tracey even had time to realise what was happening his arm had snaked out and she found her wrist grasped in an inflexible hold while his head lowered several feet closer and his eyes shed a cold warning.

'I wouldn't recommend that you put me to the trouble of conducting a search for you,' he advised in an implacable tone. 'You might find the repercussions to such a heedless action extremely unattractive!'

'They couldn't possibly be more unattractive than the present situation!' The words burst forth hotly from Tracey as she tried ineffectually to break his grip on her arm. 'Boyd was right on one count at least this morning—you squatters have been a law unto yourselves for too long! It's time someone stood up to you and told you where to get off!'

To her utter amazement Ryan began laughing in undeniable amusement. 'And you're going to be that someone, are you, Red?' he asked lazily, giving her a taunting look that sent nervous tingles down her spine.

Torn between her desire to remonstrate with him over the nickname he had used, or to take up his mocking challenge, she eventually chose the latter.

'Don't be too ready to write me off as an opponent, Ryan Alexander!' she at last managed to call him by name, but only because it came in the form of a warning. 'Just in case you haven't already guessed, I'll tell you right now ... I have no intention of blindly obeying every damned decree you care to hand out over the next two years or so!' She slanted her chin at him defiantly.

To her chagrin he didn't even appear to consider her proposed opposition worth commenting upon as he casually released his hold on her and unhurriedly asked in an ironic voice, 'From that, am I to understand that you've finally accepted the terms of Ben's will and are now ready to submit to being my ward?' with brows raised in a baiting manner.

Hating his easy self-assurance and struggling vainly against what she knew to be a stacked deck, Tracey let her voice contain all the insolence of which she was capable when she retorted scornfully, 'A squatter's ward! Big deal!'

Ryan's eyes took on a chilling hue. 'A word of warning, honey,' he cautioned with a threatening shake of his head. 'Don't try venting your frustrations on me just because Romeo Wilcox happens to have feet of clay, or you could find yourself in the middle of a brawl you haven't a hope of winning!'

There was complete silence for a few moments as Tracey digested his galling representation of Boyd, the truth of which, unfortunately, she couldn't in any way dispute, and then he gave a maddening smile of discernment.

'Tell me,' he continued sardonically, 'what plans did your beloved put forward this morning for your—er—liberation? Is he going to back you to the hilt in a gallant and humanitarian defence of your freedom? Or did he, after all, have other less—shall we say, savoury?—ideas in mind?' with so much loaded sarcasm that it had Tracey clenching her fists in fury and her eyes flashing like lightning as she hurried into speech.

'Whatever they were, with your guardianship as my only other alternative, I might agree to them,' she blazed recklessly at him, knowing quite well she had no such plan in mind but, just as perversely, determined that he should think otherwise. 'It could turn out to be quite ...' she paused piquantly, 'interesting at that.'

The narrow-eyed glance he directed towards her was so

bleak that Tracey could almost feel the ice forming from the shivers that beset her, and when he leant forward to place his hands, knuckles downwards, on the edge of her bed she inched nervously away from him, her own eyes wide and wary in her flushed face.

'Yes, you'd better back off if you know what's good for you, Tracey!' he endorsed her apprehensive movement starkly. 'You're doing your damnedest to goad me to the end of my patience, but,' with a frosty glint, 'I don't think you'd care for the aftermath very much if you were successful. So take care, or I might feel inclined to make my guardianship even more onerous than you already imagine it's going to be!'

Tracey returned his gaze mutely. She would dearly have loved to add a warning of her own to that autocratic statement but, she realised with strict honesty, at the moment she just didn't quite dare! Instead she made do with a gibing, 'I wouldn't have thought that was possible!'

Ryan straightened and rested his hands on surprisingly slim hips for such a muscular man, his curving mouth catching and holding her attention hypnotically, his head inclined with mockery.

'Wouldn't you now?' he questioned at last in a slow drawl. 'Then it's just as well I warned you, isn't it? Otherwise you might have been persuaded into believing it was possible for you to defy me at will and escape unscathed, mightn't you?' he laughed down into her slightly bemused face before turning on his heel and heading for the door.

Her trance broken, Tracey glared stormily at his retreating figure, searching desperately for something—anything—that would cut him down to size. When nothing suitable came quickly to mind she contented herself with a truculent, 'Oh, why don't you go to hell!' as his hand reached for the door handle.

Turning, he gave her a long level look. 'Don't worry, honey,' he assured her in an ironic tone, 'with the thought in mind of living in close proximity with you for the next couple of years, I'm sure I very soon shall,' and closed the door before she had a chance to reply.

Tracey slumped resentfully back on to her pillows. So

he had managed to have the last word after all! She gazed
at the pastel green door powerlessly, all types of jumbled
thoughts running through her mind, not the least of which
was annoyance with herself at still being able to find the
man so very attractive when, at the same time, she just
knew she hated him! And she was hating the idea of having
to spend so much time under his guardianship. But then
a small pleased smile began to pull at the corners of her
mouth—from his last comment it didn't sound as if he was
overly enthralled with the idea either—and that thought
started to engender a feeling of complacent satisfaction. If
it was the last thing she ever did, she was going to make
sure that Ryan Alexander regretted his insistence that she
should accompany her sister to the family property. Instead
of everything being to her disadvantage, she was going to
find some way to make sure some of the setbacks went his
way, and she smiled openly, her even white teeth gleaming.
He had called her 'Red', had he? Well, he didn't know the
half of her redheaded persistence yet, she chuckled delightedly, reaching for the tea that Lyn had made her, but
after one mouthful replaced the cup and saucer on the table
with a grimace. It was stone cold.

She snuggled down beneath the bedclothes, musing. At
least she would have to admit that Ryan was stimulating
company. For the period he had been with her she had been
able to totally disregard the unpleasant effects of her 'flu,
but now they were returning in full force and, as if to prove
their uncompromising vigour, they soon had her sneezing
aggravatingly.

Later that evening, after Ryan had returned to his hotel,
Lyn hurried back to her sister's bedroom and parked herself
on the edge of the bed, looking at Tracey sympathetically.

'How are you feeling?' she asked.

'Okay,' Tracey hunched one shoulder indifferently. There
were other subjects she wanted to discuss and she launched
into her first question immediately. 'How come your cousin
was back here again tonight?'

'Because I invited him,' Lyn answered in surprise. 'I
told you this morning that he was coming. 'Don't you re-

member?' And without waiting for a reply, went on, 'Of course I didn't know last night that you wouldn't be feeling up to it, but I thought you would want to discuss all the arrangements with Ryan before we left Sydney.' A happy smile made her eyes shine. 'It's terrific that you've decided to come after all.'

'Yes, isn't it?' Tracey returned with a light mockery which, fortunately, she noticed was lost on Lyn. *She* had decided, had she? As far as she could see, Ryan Alexander had never considered she had a decision to make! From beneath dark lashes she eyed her sister suspiciously. 'And just what arrangements were there to be discussed?' she wanted to know.

Lyn waved her arms in the air in an all-embracing gesture. 'Oh, you know the sort of thing,' she replied, pulling a face. 'Giving notice at work, packing all our things, putting the house up for sale ...'

'What!' broke in Tracey forcefully. 'Whose idea was that?' As if she had to ask!

'Ryan's. As you know, Dad made him the executor of his will as well as everything else, and he said that as we wouldn't be living here there was no need for us to keep the house,' Lyn explained a little doubtfully at the expression that was making its way over her sister's face.

'Well, I might have something to say about that!' Tracey retorted indignantly.

'But—but—I thought it sounded quite reasonable,' Lyn offered hesitantly in a placatory voice. 'After all, we won't be living here, will we?'

'Not for the next couple of years, no.' The admittance was still hard to make. 'But I don't plan to live in the bush for—for *ever*!'

'But as Ryan is the executor, we don't really have any say in what happens to the house, do we?' with an enquiring tilt to her fair head.

Tracey's lip curled bitterly and she heaved a disgruntled sigh. No, they probably didn't. Not when Lyn's high-handed cousin was in charge of all their affairs. She looked interestedly at the younger girl.

'You don't mind the house being sold?' she puzzled. It

wasn't like Lyn to take a change of circumstances so readily.

Lyn shook her head casually. 'Oh, I expect I shall miss the old place,' she told an increasingly astonished Tracey. 'But after what Ryan's been telling me about Nindethana ...'

'Where?' with a frown.

'Nindethana,' Lyn repeated obligingly. 'That's the name of the family property. It means "ours".'

Tracey's smile was scornful. She should have guessed *his* ancestors would have given the place such a proprietorial appellation. She was only surprised they hadn't changed the Aboriginal into English so there could be no doubts whatsoever left in anyone's mind as to just who owned the station.

'And just what was—Ryan—telling you?' she asked.

Lyn's face became quite animated as she relayed her store of information. 'It was mostly about the rest of our family—our grandfather, aunts and uncles, and cousins. By the way, it was Glen, Ryan's younger brother, whose photo we saw in the paper when he got married. Oh, and yes, one of our aunts—I think Ryan said it was Nancy—has a daughter, Carol, who's eighteen—which puts her in the middle of the two of us. Isn't that terrific?'

'Terrific,' agreed Tracey with a reluctant grin, but pleased to see Lyn so enthusiastic about meeting her long-lost relations when previously she had been so nervous of the coming reunion. 'But don't tell me they all live on the one property. It must be horribly crowded if they do.'

'Oh, no,' Lyn was quick to reject the assumption. 'Only our grandfather still lives on Nindethana with Ryan now that Glen's married. The others all run separate holdings around the place. I can't remember now exactly where they all are, though,' she frowned.

'Doesn't matter,' Tracey made a negative movement with one hand. 'But am I supposed to presume from that remark that our dear guardian hasn't, as yet, provided us with any kissing cousins of his own?'

'I hope not,' giggled Lyn shyly. 'He isn't married.'

'Isn't he now?' Tracey's lips pursed in silent thoughtfulness. Not that she should have been surprised, because to her way of thinking there was more than a touch of untrammelled independence in Ryan Alexander's flagrant maleness which bespoke of the unfettered bachelor rather than a contented spouse. 'So it's an all-male household we'll be moving into,' she went on in the same abstracted way, then, 'Aren't there any women on the place at all? What did you say the name was? Ninde ...?'

'... thana,' Lyn supplied with a smile before going on. 'Well, I know of at least one, that's Mrs Gray the house-keeper, but I should think there would have to be some others. After all, I suppose it's a fair guess that some of the stockmen would be married.'

'How many have they got?'

'Stockmen? Goodness, I didn't think to ask how many staff they had, Tracey, although ...' with a considering gaze, 'I should imagine it would be quite a few because, whichever size it was, it sounds awfully large. At least, to me it does,' she qualified.

Tracey's brows drew together in puzzlement. 'Which-ever size it was?' she repeated.

'Mmm, I did ask Ryan how many acres they had, but I wasn't too sure whether he said eighteen or eighty thousand, and I didn't like to ask him again in case he thought I was a bit dense for not having understood the first time,' Lyn confessed self-consciously.

'Goose!' her sister grinned up at her. 'It was eighty thousand.'

'Oh, did you ask him too?'

A wry smile curved Tracey's soft lips. 'No, I didn't ask him—and he didn't tell me. Let's call it ninety per cent intuition and ten per cent guesswork. I just can't picture your cousin being satisfied with anything less than vast!'

'*Our* cousin,' Lyn corrected her uncomfortably.

'Oh, no,' Tracey refused to accept any such kinship. 'He's no cousin of mine, and even though I don't appear to have any choice but to agree to his being my guardian, there's no way anyone can make me acknowledge him as a relation too!'

Lyn looked as if she was about to say something more on the matter, but changed her mind and began talking

about something else instead, deeming it more prudent in
view of Tracy's obvious antagonism towards her cousin,
and it wasn't until a while later that Tracey herself brought
the conversation back to their pending departure with a
sarcastic, 'And just when are we expected to take up resi-
dence in the great outback?'

'We'll be leaving a week from next Monday,' Lyn informed her quietly, but without being able to contain all
of her unexpected excitement, and apparently more than
content now that she knew her sister would be travelling
with them. 'You know, I didn't think I would, but I'm—
I'm looking forward to it,' she glanced at Tracey to gauge
her reaction.

Tracey made herself smile in response. She was happy
for Lyn's sake. Happy that she was accepting this sudden
change in the mode of their lives without her usual reluctance to approve anything that might take her away
from what she had been accustomed.

As for herself? Tracey sighed. She would have been content to have forgone any of the Alexander money that might
be coming her way and to have stayed in Sydney and found
a flat of her own, or shared one with some other girls, but
she wasn't going to be given the chance to rule her own
life any more. She now had a guardian to decide all that
for her. A guardian! How that word infuriated! It just
wasn't in her to accept Ryan Alexander's autocracy with
any equanimity, and she found herself twisting in the bed
irritably at the thought that he would have the power to
control almost every move she made until she turned
twenty-three. And it had started already, she chafed inwardly. The orders had been given. They were leaving
on Monday week! There had been no consideration called
for on her part—none asked, in fact—it was simply an
issued command which they were supposed to spiritlessly
observe. Nor could she look forward to the following
months when it was clear that more of the same would be
forthcoming! She sighed again, but rebelliously this time.

CHAPTER THREE

IT was a cloudless afternoon when the streamlined Charger pulled away from the only home Tracey and Lyn had ever known and carried them inexorably through suburbia to Bankstown airfield where Ryan's Piper Arrow was waiting to take them on the long journey to Wirrabilla.

Once there, it seemed to take only a short time before arrangements had been made for the vehicle to be collected by the car hire firm; their luggage to be safely stowed aboard; and Ryan to check the final details of his flight plan with the control tower.

As Tracey sat in one of the rear seats of the plane—she had steadfastly refused to take the front seat that Lyn had offered her—she watched the outskirts of the city sliding away rapidly beneath them once they were airborne and gradually fell into musing over the happenings of the past week and a half since that eventful day when she had come down with the current virus; discovered Boyd's unreliability for herself; and been subjected to a discomfiting attack of Ryan Alexander's dictatorship.

There had been her notice to hand in when she returned to work and more of Boyd's pleas and persuasions to avoid. Arrangements had had to be made for their furniture and household possessions to be stored in anticipation of the time when they might wish to put them to use at some future date; and prospective buyers to show over the house at all sorts of odd hours as well. And all the while there had been Ryan's forceful personality to ignore—or at least, she amended ruefully—attempt to ignore. She doubted very much whether it would be possible for anyone to completely exclude him from their calculations, his was such a magnetic commanding character.

Slowly but inevitably the days passed; farewells had been said and instructions received to, 'Write and let us know how you're getting on,' from friends and workmates. Boyd

37

had repeatedly asked Tracey to reconsider his proposal, he had even gone to the lengths to swear faithfully that he would file for a divorce, but she had adamantly vetoed every suggestion he made and for the last couple of days the atmosphere between them had become very tense and strained.

As the hour wore on Tracey slipped dark glasses on her nose for protection against the glare and looked down to the widespread plateaus of the Great Dividing Range—that almost unbroken line of mountains which stretched from Queensland in the north to Victoria in the south, and which separated the coastal from the inland plains with such dedication that it wasn't until twenty-five years had passed after the first settlement had been founded at Port Jackson that the early explorers' attempts to cross them were finally successful.

Now the land began to spread away beneath them; fertile plains dotted with matchbox houses; country towns basking in the glow of a life-giving sun; and every so often the glint and reflection of a winding river or meandering creek. Lyn was talking desultorily to Ryan, but not wanting to join in their conversation, Tracey laid her head back against the padded rest and closed her eyes. It was only her second time in a plane—last year she had flown with two girl friends to Surfer's Paradise in Queensland for their holidays—and she was finding now, as then, that the constant drone of the engine, together with the increasing heat, was making her drowsy.

When she finally awoke some time later it was to hear Ryan saying, 'There's Bourke,' and gesturing through the perspex to that lowland town on the banks of the Darling which for most Australians denoted the beginning of the outback. Combing a hand through her hair, Tracey looked skywards. Oh, God, she really was going 'out the back o' Bourke'! It hadn't been some ghastly dream after all. Out to where 'the crows fly backwards to keep the dust out of their eyes', and into the land of the Never-Never and the Black Stump. She, who had never felt any need to complain about the aspects of city life, was about to be unceremoniously brought to ground in the middle of squatter territory where properties were few and far between; water was a precious commodity; the sun would fry eggs on the open ground; and senseless sheep outnumbered the human population in a ratio that didn't bear thinking about! She scowled at the dark head in front of her for being the cause of all her discontent and closed her eyes again. She was damned if she would look at those red soil plains any more often than she had to!

It was a change in the sound of the engine which brought her eyes open the next time and, realising they were losing height, she glanced downward with an unwilling but uncontrollable interest stirring her sense. As the plane banked smoothly the homestead and associated buildings—the name of the property painted heavily over the roof of the largest of them—swung into her line of vision and she couldn't help but give an astonished gasp at the size of the complex. She wasn't sure quite what she had expected but, if what she could recall reading was anything to go by, then that group below her would probably constitute a greater number of structures than was usually erected in some outback towns.

Swiftly now the ground was looming up to meet them and a disciplined thump heralded their return to terra firma as clouds of red dust swirled behind them and the young man waiting beside the small hangar at the edge of the airstrip clutched his hat to his head as they sped past. Rolling more slowly now, Ryan taxied back to the small building and cut the engine while the girls stretched cramped legs and emerged into an alien but strangely breathtaking terrain where they could feel the heat beating up from the ground through the soles of their sandals and the still blazing sun above surrounded them with a furnace-like atmosphere.

'Help, isn't it hot?' breathed Lyn as the three of them began making their way towards the hangar and the car that was now visible behind it.

Tracey swept sun-bright hair behind her ears and grimaced. 'Yes, I shall probably end up looking like a lobster after a few days,' she returned tartly.

'I doubt it—you didn't use to.'

Ryan's coolly spoken remark had both of them turning to

him enquiringly, but before Tracey could put her thoughts into a question another voice had broken the silence.

'G'day, boss! How was the trip?'

'Good, thanks, Doug.' Ryan directed a cursory look towards the homestead in the distance. 'How have things been here?'

'Running pretty smoothly—old Justin saw to that,' with a wry grin.

An answering smile touched his employer's mouth before the girls were introduced to Ryan's brown-haired and brown-eyed senior jackaroo, Doug Horton, and while they waited in the slanting shade of the building for their luggage to be collected from the plane their eyes automatically strayed to the oasis of green that surrounded the homestead some half mile or more away.

Not that they could make out all that much from where they were standing, but it was possible to discern graceful palms outlined against the washed blue sky, willow-like drooping myalls and broad-leaved bauhinias among the buildings, and away to the right a sporadic line of magnificent river gums followed the twisting trail of a slow-moving watercourse.

The slam of the boot as it closed over their cases advised their imminent departure and both girls clambered into the back seat of the car while Ryan took the wheel with Doug beside him. The journey across the intervening ground was accomplished quickly and after alighting to open the wide steel homestead boundary gate, Doug lifted a hand to the brim of his hat in a casual salute and the car continued on without him towards the large, sprawling white house with its wide shaded verandahs completely enclosed with flyscreens.

No sooner had the vehicle pulled to a halt before the front three steps than two figures emerged from the house and, pushing open the screen door, hurried down the stairs towards them. The first to reach them was a woman in her middle fifties, her once dark hair showing decided streaks of grey, but she possessed a pair of warm brown eyes which surveyed both Tracey and Lyn with a maternal affection, and a sweetly smiling mouth that radiated a welcome as she held out a hand to each girl.

'Ben's children here at last,' she sighed happily, her hands tightening on theirs warmly. 'I'm Nancy Denham—you father's sister—and this is,' turning to bring forward the young girl who had followed her from the homestead, 'my daughter Carol, one of your cousins,' she smiled.

The family resemblance between the two younger girls was quite noticeable, for, although she was taller and slimmer than Lyn, Carol Denham's fair hair and hazel eyes were almost identical to Tracey's stepsister's, and Carol's laughing comment on the fact once the introductions had been acknowledged broke the ice as far as a nervous Lyn was concerned.

'You had a good flight?' Nancy's enquiring look encompassed all three of them, although she spoke directly to Ryan.

'Well, it was certainly a quiet one,' he answered in a laconic voice, and Lyn explained with a shaky laugh,

'I was too nervous to talk much. It was the first time I've ever been in a plane.'

Tracey made no comment at all. Let Ryan think what he liked. It suited her just fine if he thought that nerves had been the reason for her silence during the whole of the journey.

'Oh, dear,' murmured Nancy consolingly. 'You really shouldn't have worried because Ryan is an extremely competent pilot, but never mind, you're here now and that's all that matters,' as she placed an arm around each girl's waist, urging them towards the verandah. 'Come along in, out of this heat, we can talk just as easily inside as we can out here.'

Mounting the steps, they crossed the cool verandah where small tables, loungers and long-armed squatters' chairs mingled with potted plants and ferns, and moved into the wide air-conditioned entrance hall where the deep red floor and panelled doors glowed with the patina of many polishings. Turkish rugs were laid almost the entire length of the passageway; the walls hung with a variety of gilt-framed paintings; and placed along one side were a pair of matching mahogany serpentine card tables with delicate inlays and satinwood friezes, decorated with strikingly colourful dried flower arrangements in pewter bowls, while an ornate grandfather clock took pride of place on the op-posite side.

The sitting room when they entered it seemed enormous by Tracey and Lyn's standards, containing as it did a wide arched fireplace, the mantel of which was adorned with shining copper plates of varying sizes and designs, a sec-retaire with glass-fronted bookcase, three padded and cushioned settees, as well as a number of wing chairs and occasional tables which had been placed harmoniously about the room.

A tray bearing fine bone china cups and a matching coffee pot which had evidently been ordered on the plane's approach was brought into the room by a smiling house girl who placed it on the table beside Nancy's chair and bobbed her head bashfully in acknowledgment of Tracey and Lyn's presence, then departed as quickly as she could with her dark curls bouncing.

Accepting a cup gratefully from Nancy's outstretched hand, Tracey almost let go of it again when that woman suddenly asked with a questioning smile, 'I don't suppose you would remember much about the place, would you, Tracey?'

'Remember?' Tracey echoed in a daze. For the second time that afternoon an inconsequential comment had her frowning deeply. 'Remember what, Nancy?' she probed, and omitting the formal 'Aunt' as they had been requested.

'You don't know? Ben never told you? Ryan didn't re-mind you?' Nancy gave a disbelieving shake of her head and looked closely at her nephew.

Tracey looked from one to the other bemusedly. What was it they were supposed to have told her? That she was to remember? She stared at Ryan suspiciously and anxiously wondered what it was that he had seen fit not to inform her.

He merely crossed one long leg leisurely over the other and grinned disarmingly back at his aunt. 'It appears we have the advantage over Tracey—she hasn't got a clue what you're talking about, Nancy,' he drawled.

Lyn, seated next to Carol on one of the comfortable set-tees, looked as blank as her sister did, but it was obvious her cousin knew what was going on, because she was smiling broadly in response to their baffled expressions.

'I really can't believe it,' Nancy continued in the same incredulous tone. 'That neither of them told you anything about the time you lived here, when you ...'

'When I lived here!' Tracey interrupted in as much stunned incredulity as her informant had previously displayed, her fingers gripping the saucer beneath her cup tightly. 'You mean I've been here before?'

'Oh, yes,' Nancy confirmed swiftly. 'You lived here from just after Ben married your mother until you were about two and a half years old. You knew Nindethana from front to back, and everyone on it,' she relayed with a smile.

'Good grief!' There didn't seem to be anything else to say and Tracey sank into her seat with a dumbfounded look on her face. Another thing her stepfather had kept secret from his family, but before she could start to even wonder why, Nancy began talking again.

'I'm sorry to hear that Ben cut himself off from us to the extent that he apparently never even spoke about his family or birthplace at all, but what I really can't understand is why Ryan didn't say anything to you either.' She turned again to her nephew curiously and teased, 'Especially when he and Glen—that's Ryan's younger brother who's still in Europe with his new wife, Pamela, at the moment—made such a fuss of you. Even though they were so much older, they used to take you everwhere with them.'

A responding glint appeared in Ryan's eyes. 'Mainly because she refused to be left behind,' he explained lazily. 'You had definite ideas about what you wanted even then, didn't you, Tracey?'

Dragging her confused thoughts together—she found it impossible to envisage a time when any demands of hers would have received anything but peremptory rejection from the man before her—Tracey's eyes glowed greenly as she viewed him over the rim of her cup and accepted the challenge.

'Don't we all?' she countered sweetly. 'It's just unfortunate that some of us aren't in a position to make certain our plans are never thwarted.'

'A pity,' he agreed with a goading look. 'But then it is suggested that it tends to spoil the character if we always get whatever we want, isn't it?'

'How true!' she returned his glance with one of defiance, and repeated with pointed sarcasm, 'How true!'

Not that her gibe appeared to have found its mark, for he only reacted with a complacent smile which showed strong white teeth against the bronze of his skin and had Tracey's pulses quickening traitorously so that she wasn't able to make a suitable retort before he proposed sardonically, 'It's good to hear that we agree,' and replaced his cup on the tray, continuing regretfully, 'Now, if you ladies will excuse me, I'd better have a word with Marty and catch up on what's been happening around here,' as he rose to his feet and laid an affectionate hand on his aunt's shoulder.

'Mmm, Father said he wanted to see you directly you arrived too,' Nancy told him, looking up fondly. 'But he went riding again this morning and now he's having to pay the price for his stubbornness in ignoring the doctor's orders by spending the rest of the day in his bed. See if you can make him see sense, will you, Ryan?' she entreated earnestly.

Under cover of his reply Carol whispered to the other two with an expressive lift of her eyebrows, 'That's Grandfather they're talking about. He had a bad accident some years ago and injured his back when his horse put its foot down a burrow and rolled on him. Now he's not supposed to go riding any more, but as you heard, he still does. I expect you'll meet him before we have dinner this evening.'

'He sounds very determined,' ventured Lyn nervously.

'Oh, he's that all right,' Carol laughed, and spared a sideways glance for her cousin as he left the room with a lithe stride. 'Although Ryan can be just as daunting as Grandfather is at times too.'

A worried look crossed Lyn's face at this particular piece of information. 'Is—um—Grandfather very intimidating?' she asked apprehensively.

'Sometimes,' Carol nodded in agreement. 'Even though they reckon he's mellowed a lot from how he used to be, I still find I'm often as nervous as a kitten when he's in one of his difficult moods.'

'Oh, dear!' Lyn looked at her sister with dismay. 'Ryan didn't mention anything about our grandfather being like that,' she murmured miserably.

Knowing how Lyn was likely to work herself into a fit of depression over Carol's unwitting disclosure, Tracey now spoke up brightly.

'Don't look so worried,' she encouraged. 'Didn't Carol also say that Ryan could be just as daunting if he chooses, and you certainly seem to get on well enough with him. Anyway, I hardly think we've been here long enough for your grandfather to find something to complain about.'

Lyn's obvious tension seemed to lesson somewhat, but only to the extent where she nodded glumly, and Carol, seeing the still worried expression, offered reassuringly, 'Hey, I hope I didn't give you the wrong impression. He's really not that bad! I think it's just that he's worked hard all his life and now that Ryan's running the company he's finding time hanging heavily on his hands and, in order to relieve the boredom, he enjoys being contrary.'

Cantankerous old buzzard, decided Tracey grimly, and she could feel her temper beginning to rise. Not only were they supposed to kowtow to one dictatorial Alexander, but they were also apparently expected to jump to the tune of a querulous one as well! She glowered at the idea. Well, she could give them fair warning that they had at least one person in their midst who wasn't prepared to accept everything they cared to hand out. She would like to remind them that she also had a will of her own!

After both Tracey and Lyn had politely refused the offer of second cups of coffee, Nancy suggested that Carol might like to show them to their rooms while she had a word with Mrs Gray regarding the final preparations for dinner, and taking their leave the three girls wandered down the passageway, talking amiably as they went.

Tracey's bedroom when they came to it was large and airy—didn't they have any normal sized rooms at Ninde-thana? she mused wryly—and was furnished in Victorian rosewood which Carol explained had been taken from the first Alexander homestead when it was demolished and the present building erected.

By the time Tracey had finished unpacking the cases which had been waiting in the room for her, made good use of the bathroom and changed into a chocolate-coloured linen dress, the keyhole neckline edged in frosty white, the delicate trails of golden clouds were turning vermilion in a turquoise sky that was assuming an apricot hue on the horizon in the last rays of a dying sun.

Knocking on Lyn's door, she entered to find her sister deliberating agitatedly between apple green voile and tangerine cotton, and promptly suggested with a grin, 'Wear the green voile—at least it makes you appear cool and collected, even if you're not!'

'And by the sound of what Carol was saying earlier I think I'll be needing every morsel of calm I can find. We seem to have inherited a grandparent who isn't one of the doting kind that you read about, don't we?' Lyn remarked gloomily.

'I shouldn't let that bother you,' Tracey returned with a reassuring show of confidence she was far from actually feeling. 'On a property the size of this one it shouldn't be too difficult to evade the presence of one old man for long periods of time.'

'I guess so,' conceded Lyn rather laboriously as she pulled at the short back zip of her frock before moving to the dressing table to begin a vigorous brushing of her short hair. 'It is a lovely home, though, isn't it?'

'Mmm,' Tracey agreed reluctantly—it went against the grain to praise anything that Ryan Alexander might own— but she couldn't help adding, 'Still it's not to be wondered at. In those days materials were plentiful, labour was cheap, and most of the early settlers grabbed more land than they knew what to do with.'

'Why wouldn't they?' shrugged Lyn in surprise. 'It was there for the taking—and I never knew you cared one way or the other before,' she accused her sister's reflection in the mirror with a frown.

A rueful smile caught at Tracey's mouth. 'Neither did I,' she admitted honestly. 'Perhaps it's because I wasn't given a choice as to whether I wanted to come out here or not. It was presented as an order—to come ... or else!' she recalled resentfully.

Lyn's hand stayed its brushing in mid-stroke. 'But I thought Ryan said you'd changed your own mind about coming.'

'Had it changed for me, more like!'

In the lull that followed, Lyn turned round and stared hard at her sister, her tone low and thoughtful when she finally spoke. 'You don't like him, do you?' she asked.

Tracey's thoughts churned. Like? Dislike? What anaemic words they were to use in regard to anyone as implacable and domineering as Ryan Alexander! Love or hate were the words that sprang immediately to mind—there could never be any half measures involved when it came to dealing with someone of his disruptive vitality—but for the present she didn't care to pigeonhole her feelings quite so neatly. Instead she lifted a shoulder offhandedly and replied, 'No, I don't ... like him,' in a flat tone.

'Why? Because he apparently made you come when you didn't want to?'

She didn't have to consider for long. 'Not only that, but because he's so arbitrary, so ...' 'attractive', her mind mocked, but she thrust the thought away determinedly, 'so ... self-assured!' she concluded with an emphatic nod.

'I—I think he's nice,' Lyn communicated her thoughts a little warily in view of her sister's antipathy.

Not that she needed to have worried, for Tracey merely grinned teasingly and conceded. 'He probably is—provided you obey his every command without question. But if you don't,' she held up a warning hand, 'then watch out, because our guardian squatter doesn't like having his authority flouted.'

Lyn's responsive smile faded a little as her head tilted to one side and she queried puzzledly, 'Why do you always call him that?'

'Call him what?'

'A squatter.'

Tracey grinned. 'Well, isn't he?' she replied mockingly.

'Not really—not in the strict sense of the word he's not,'

Lyn came shyly to her cousin's defence. 'A true squatter was one who marked off large areas of Crown land for himself and just squatted on it without paying anything for the privilege. These days, if their properties aren't freehold, the owners lease their runs from the government for a fee. So you see,' she spread her hands wide in an unconscious plea, 'he's not really a squatter at all.'

'As far as I'm concerned he is,' Tracey wasn't about to surrender to such logical reasoning. 'Maybe not on the land,' she allowed with a grimace, 'but he's still squatting on my right to independence, and that instantly makes me want to defy every single order he gives. A guardian, for heaven's sake!' Her eyes sought the ceiling in disbelief. 'I thought they went out of fashion with bustles and whalebone corsets!'

'Poor Tracey,' smiled Lyn sympathetically. 'Dad always used to say you had an uncommon love of personal freedom.'

Tracey rose to her feet and ran smoothing hands down the sides of her dress. 'In which case, it might have helped if he'd remembered that fact before including such a restrictive condition in his will.' She half smiled ruefully. 'A condition, I might add, that I still find myself doubting at times when I think of it.'

'Oh, it was there all right,' Lyn assured her earnestly, turning back to the mirror to apply a pale lipstick. 'Mr Gatehead wouldn't have made a mistake over anything as important as that, especially not after you nearly bit his head off when he first mentioned it,' she grinned at the memory.

'Yes, well, it was so unexpected. I just couldn't believe he hadn't made a mistake.' Tracey began moving towards the door and waited with her fingers on the handle for Lyn to join her. 'But I'm now reconciled—well, almost,' with a self-mocking smile, 'to serving out my time as a detainee of your most omnipotent relation.'

'Don't say it like that,' remonstrated Lyn diffidently, wrinkling her nose. 'It makes it sound as if you're some sort of prisoner.'

'Just telling it like it is,' retorted the unrepentant Tracey with a smile.

There was a man of almost thirty in the sitting room talking with Nancy and Carol when the two girls entered, and introductions were quickly performed. Marty Bradshaw, the station's accountant, was a pleasant-faced young man with a ruddy complexion and a pair of twinkling brown eyes, who immediately asked the girls what they would like to drink and cheerfully poured the sherries they chose as their aperitifs. Standing beside him, Tracey let her eyes wander round the room, noticing Lyn gravitating to where Carol was now seated on one of the settees, and Nancy crossing to speak to Ryan after he had followed them into the room and began pouring himself a drink.

'So you're Ryan's wards,' Marty smiled.

Tracey took a sip from the fragile glass she held and nodded. 'Makes us sound as if we haven't the brains to run our own lives, doesn't it?' she mocked.

'I wouldn't say that,' he contradicted slowly, thoughtfully. 'I would have thought you'd be pleased to have a capable man handling things for you.'

'Financially, maybe ... personally, definitely not!'

He gave a low chuckle. 'Don't tell me he's brought home one of those militant Women's Libbers!'

She never had been before, but Tracey had the feeling that was the direction her tendencies had been heading ever since she had come into contact with Lyn's cousin. Now she looked at Marty interestedly.

'And if I was?' she asked. 'Would it matter?'

'It might to you.'

'To me?' Tracey was surprised. 'How do you mean?'

Marty smiled and drained the remains of his drink before replying. 'Because you're off your head if you think the boss is going to let a female—any female—get away with disruptions around here. He's not the type to sit back tamely and tolerate a woman assuming any of his prerogatives in the name of emancipation,' he advised wryly.

Tracey's mouth curved with sweet reflection. 'Isn't he?' she murmured serenely, while from beneath the cover of silky lashes her gaze sought and held the object of their discussion contemplatively.

Head bent low as he listened to some remarks Nancy was making and dressed in pale grey pants that emphasised slim hips and long, muscular legs, and a maroon silk knit shirt, Ryan Alexander looked every inch the dominant male, and Tracey found herself wondering dryly if, perhaps, she might prove to be a little rash in considering taking on someone she already knew to be a redoubtable opponent on his home ground. Then she gave a small incorrigible chuckle. So what? If she became a deep enough thorn in his side, he just might send her back to Sydney, mightn't he?

She raised deeply green eyes to Marty's now speculative face. 'But then it's taking some men a lot longer than others to realise that the women of today don't intend to obey unquestioningly whatever the so-called master of the house decrees, isn't it?' she reverted to their conversation irrepressibly, her delightful smile bringing an acknowledged grin to his own lips, although this was immediately followed by an admonishing shake of the head.

'I'm thinking you're about to bite off more than you can chew if you're contemplating playing one-upmanship with the boss,' he smiled down at her in good-natured warning. 'The scales are too heavily weighted in his favour for you to have any success in that direction,' he added for good measure.

Tracey wasn't about to be put off so easily and especially not so early in the piece. 'That all depends on the yardstick you use to measure success, doesn't it? Sometimes it's better to lose a battle in order to win the war,' she quoted with such whole-hearted positiveness that Marty threw back his head and laughed aloud.

'What's the joke?' enquired Lyn as she came to join them, her hazel eyes going searchingly from one to the other.

A little dismayed by the fact that they had become the cynosure of all eyes in the room, Tracey tensed warily as Marty replied, her fingers tight about the stem of her glass, lest he should make public the gist of their conversation.

'Your sister was just expounding a theory of hers—on the role of modern man in today's changing world,' Marty explained ambiguously, one eyebrow lifting banteringly as Tracey let out a sigh of relief at his innocuous words.

Lyn's brows drew together. 'And that was funny?' she prompted, perplexed.

'It was the way Tracey tells it,' grinned Marty.

Lyn dismissed the remark with a shrug, not interested in pressing the point, and the next moment a tall figure appeared in the open doorway. Although getting on in years and, as a result of his recent obstinacy, having to rely heavily on a cane for support, Justin Alexander still retained a whipcord frame and a dark head of hair remarkably free from any signs of grey. As he offered a general greeting and lowered himself stiffly into a capacious chair, Tracey had the distinct feeling that those shrewd blue eyes in the craggy face had critically noted every relevant detail concerning the newcomers in their midst.

Ryan broke off his conversation with Nancy to provide his grandfather with a stiff jolt of whisky and catching Tracey's eye indicated with a movement of his head that Lyn and herself should join them. In turn she gave her sister a morale boosting wink and quipped, 'The wool king beckons,' before offering their excuses to Marty and, with Lyn keeping pace beside her, moved across the room to where the two men waited.

With the customary acknowledgments disposed of, Justin Alexander focused penetrating eyes directly on Tracey. 'You've changed,' was his first surprising dry remark.

'I should hope so—in eighteen years,' she responded swiftly, a half smile appearing at the corners of her mouth.

'Mmm, a long time ...'

For a moment Justin's eyes lost some of their keenness as his mind retraced those lost years, reminding Tracey that he hadn't seen, or even communicated with, his youngest child in all that time, and making her wonder once again what could possibly have created such a bitter rift between father and son.

'And you, Lynette,' his voice firmed almost immediately, 'were you agreeable to accepting Ryan as your guardian, and coming to live here?'

Lyn's head bobbed up and down affirmatively. 'Oh, yes, Mr Alexander, I ...'

'Nobody misters anyone in the outback, child,' he interjected brusquely. 'Either call me Grandfather, as most of your cousins do, or make it Justin.'

'Yes—Grandfather,' she agreed in a dutiful voice.

His attention came back to Tracey. 'You would still rather be in Sydney, though, eh?' he queried narrowly.

Accusing eyes flicked upwards to Ryan, which promptly drew a sardonic, 'He didn't have to tell me—there's nothing wrong with my eyesight—and you've a belligerent sparkle in those eyes of yours that doesn't suggest you're exactly overjoyed with your present circumstances,' from his grandparent.

Having been pushed on to the defensive, Tracey lifted her chin a little higher and answered defiantly, 'Who would be happy being landed with a guardian at my age? This isn't the eighteenth century, you know!'

'I'm well aware of that fact, young lady, but if it's any consolation to you, the men in this family don't receive the bulk of their inheritance until they're twenty-*five*! So be grateful for your two years' grace!'

'It isn't.'

'Isn't what?' he barked.

'Any consolation to know that,' she informed him heatedly. 'I didn't want the money in the first place!'

'Well, whether you want it or not, you've got it—but you can think again if you suppose I'm going to sit idly by and watch some young fortune-hunter marry you and get his hands on hard-earned Alexander money before you're old enough to know your own mind!'

'That's good,' she flashed back caustically. 'Because I wasn't planning to marry a parasite like that anyway!'

'And for the next couple of years Ryan's here to make sure of it,' he pressed home with an aggravating self-satisfied smile which irritated beyond words, but before Tracey could find a suitable retort he had called exasperatedly to his daughter, 'Nancy! Isn't that dinner ready yet?' and almost as if in response to his query one of the house girls appeared in the doorway and Nancy began to lead the way into the dining room.

It was sheer instinct which told Tracey that Justin Alexander wouldn't appreciate help to rise from his chair, knowing unconsciously that he would prefer to lever himself up even though it might take him seconds longer, but Lyn had only a gentle and soft-hearted nature to guide her and leant over impetuously to lend a supporting hand as her grandfather made stiff and somewhat imbalanced upward movements.

'Leave me be, leave me be!' he shrugged irascibly away from her touch immediately. 'I'm not so decrepit that I can't manage for myself!'

As always Tracey prepared to go to her sister's defence, Lyn's trembling lips and worried eyes as she hurried after Nancy bringing to the fore the glint of battle in eyes made emerald-bright with anger, but her censure was never made, for as Ryan passed her an inescapable hand gripped her upper arm and the next moment she was being swept along beside him.

One wrathful look back over her shoulder and she attempted to pull free, grating under her breath through tight lips, 'There was no need for him to be so rude! Lyn was only trying to help. It seems to me someone should tell him what a bad-tempered old barbarian he is!'

'Another squatter to be put in his place, hmm?' he mocked.

'Very funny,' she snapped sarcastically. 'You're a regular barrel of laughs!'

'And you're a hard act to follow, Tracey.'

'Which means ... what?' she frowned suspiciously.

'That it's time you stopped smothering your sister in a protective cocoon—let her start to make her own way in the world. It's bad enough with her having to follow in the footsteps of an older sister who looks like you do, but for God's sake, isn't it time you stopped fighting all her battles and left her to find her own feet? She's already got a damned inferiority complex the size of this station,' he charged incisively.

'What would you know about it?' she gasped, both angry and annoyed that he should presume to make such an accusation. 'After our mother died somebody had to look out for Lyn—or would you rather have had me ignore her altogether?'

Ryan's mouth levelled uncompromisingly. 'Don't use the

loss of your mother as an excuse,' he advised coolly. 'I
happen to have lost my own at an even younger age than
Lyn, but I can assure you, I felt no need to be coddled and
pampered like you have her.'

'I'm not surprised,' she gibed, eventually managing to
free herself from his hold. 'After all, you're a real chip off
old Rocky—the lump of granite without a heart—over
there, aren't you?' nodding her head towards the chair
Justin had occupied, only to find him standing less than
three feet away from them, and a steady flush of embarrassment began to climb her cheeks as she stammered, 'I—I'm
sorry, I shouldn't ...' only to be interrupted by Justin's
diverting laughter.

'So you haven't changed as much as I thought you had,'
he finally commented once his unexpected bout of amusement was finished. 'You always were a fiery little minx,
wasn't she, Ryan?' he looked to his grandson for corrobora-
tion.

A wry smile tilted Ryan's lips disarmingly. 'You mean
spoilt, don't you?' he taunted.

'Then you only had yourselves to blame if she was, because you and young Glen always saw to it that she got
whatever she wanted. The pair of you never could say no
when she started pleading with those big green eyes of hers,'
he chortled delightedly at his grandson's expense.

'Perhaps I should remember that,' put in Tracey dulcetly,
and earned herself a long, steady look of warning from
Ryan in response. 'Or do you think he's altered to such an
extent over the years that he's now immune?' provokingly
to Justin as they began moving forward once again.

'I should hope so,' he snorted in disgust. 'He wouldn't
make much of a guardian if he wasn't!'

An assessing glance from the cover of thick lashes and
Tracey sighed audibly. 'Don't worry, you can put your
mind at rest,' she advised with mocking overtones. 'From
what I've already seen of him, he's not only immune, he's
downright disparaging as well!'

CHAPTER FOUR

THE dining and sitting rooms were connected by folding panelled doors and the softly subdued décor of the former was enhanced by the gently mellowed Regency mahogany furniture; the skilfully carved sideboard which supported some exquisite pieces of crystal glassware; and the polished floors which, once again, were adorned with flawless hand-woven carpets.

Tracey was pleased to find herself seated next to Marty at the heavy white damask-covered table, although Justin's somewhat unnerving presence on her right had her devoting most of her attention to the delicious meal prepared by Mrs Gray rather than attempting to engage him in any casual conversation. It was while they were enjoying the last morsels of their cream-filled dessert that Nancy began talking about the barbecue that was to be held the following Saturday.

'I thought it would be as good a way as any of introducing you to the rest of the family—as well as everyone else hereabouts,' she said, her eyes sweeping from Tracey to Lyn and back again. 'I thought you would probably prefer an informal gathering,' she smiled.

Carol's expression was one of lively anticipation. 'Mmm, everyone's dying to meet you both—especially my two brothers,' she laughed. 'They wanted to come with Mum and me to welcome you, but Dad needed them at home, so they've had to wait,' she relayed gleefully.

'Will there be many here?' Lyn enquired on a doubtful note.

'Oh, loads!' Carol confirmed blithely. 'There's almost twenty just in the immediate family, and when you take in second and third cousins as well as neighbours, and friends, etcetera, it doesn't take long for the numbers to climb. The word is out, you see,' she grinned, 'the missing Alexanders have come back to the fold at last.'

Been ordered back, you mean, amended Tracey to herself, her resentful gaze scorching its way across the table to where Ryan listened courteously as Nancy filled him in with the arrangements she had made for the evening during his absence.

The coffee was already waiting on a small octagonal table when they returned to the sitting room after the meal was concluded and no sooner had Nancy poured the liquid than Ryan and Marty made their excuses and disappeared from the room with theirs; Carol and Lyn carried their cups out on to the verandah; and Tracey remained with Justin and Nancy—who was settled in one of the deep wing chairs next to the hearth, her crochet hook guided by nimble fingers flashing through the scalloped edging of a pastel pink silk jacket. As if sensing someone watching her, she looked up and smiled.

'I'm sorry we aren't able to offer you the same kind of entertainment you're probably used to,' she apologised. 'I'm afraid we usually have to make our own out here. I like crocheting, knitting and reading myself, but I expect you would prefer something a little less staid. There is a television and a stereo in the next room if you want to use them and, of course, there's always the library or the games room down there,' with a hand waving in the general direction of the hallway. 'They've got that set up for table tennis, billiards—or is it snooker?' she frowned to herself, then shook her head, 'I never can remember, and there's also a dart board hanging around somewhere usually. Of course, there's also that good old standby, a pack of cards, which someone always manages to produce once a few of the men get together,' she laughed indulgently, and momentarily surveyed the two on the verandah who were now conversing amicably as they stretched out on padded loungers. 'I'm pleased to see Lyn and Carol getting on so well,' she confided. 'I thought with their ages being so close they might have a lot in common—I just didn't realise how much. They're very similar to look at, aren't they?' she smiled.

'Very,' agreed Tracey, returning the older woman's smile with a vivacious one of her own. 'Lyn's usually rather reticent about making friends, but I have the feeling it could be very good for her here.'

'But not for you?' Nancy queried shrewdly, her brown eyes tolerant as they scanned the vital countenance before her.

Without wanting to hurt either her or Justin's feelings, Tracey dissembled. 'I—I don't know yet, Nancy. I haven't thought all that much about it. It's too early to tell.'

'Not too early for you to have had words with Ryan, though? I get the distinct impression you're not—er—terribly enthusiastic about having been placed in his care. Am I right?' she asked with one raised and questing eyebrow.

Tracey avoided looking at either of them, tracing a finger unhappily around the rim of her coffee cup, head downbent and seemingly engrossed in the dark liquid. Her eyes flickered up hesitantly and her shoulders hunched defensively.

'Yes, well, I'm sorry if I made it so obvious,' she murmured softly.

Nancy digested this in silence, her crochet hook speeding on its way. 'You didn't want to come with your sister?' she questioned after a few minutes.

'Not if she had to have a guardian, she didn't,' supplied Justin suddenly, his features giving no indication of what he was feeling.

'Ah!' The slight frown that had been creasing Nancy's forehead disappeared. 'Now we're getting somewhere,' she exclaimed with an understanding smile, although it was soon replaced by an intent look as she sought to impress, 'But that was your father's wish, Tracey. Ryan is only fulfilling the terms of Ben's will—he isn't the type of man to take such a responsibility lightly.'

'But he doesn't have to be so overbearing about it, does he?' Tracey couldn't help voicing the indignant question. 'I'm not a child any longer and I refuse to be treated like one. I told him in Sydney I was willing to forgo my part of the inheritance and I'm still finding it confusing that Dad should have made such a condition in the first place. He must have known I wouldn't accept it willingly,' she sighed.

'Yet he still made it,' Justin pointed out acutely. 'So one

could presume that he, at least, considered there were good reasons for it.'

'Perhaps,' acceded Tracey grudgingly, a faint flush staining her cheeks as her thoughts involuntarily returned to Boyd—a flush that didn't escape Justin's steady scrutiny.

'And that's what has put you at odds with Ryan?' he demanded.

Tracey placed her cup on a nearby table, stalling for time, and uneasily aware that it wouldn't be simple to put anything over this perceptive couple. Not that she had any real desire to, but at the same time, she didn't feel up to relating the whole of the story either. She cleared her throat nervously.

'Partly,' she acknowledged unwillingly.

'And the rest?' Justin wouldn't let it stop there.

'Can't we just leave it at that?' Tracey pleaded, moving restlessly in her chair. 'I should never have mentioned it.'

'That's as may be,' he conceded shortly. 'In the meantime, I'm interested to know what was wrong with this man you were seeing that neither my son nor my grandson approved of him.'

After swallowing her first shocked surprise at his sharp intuition, Tracey held his gaze determinedly. 'Neither of them knew him well enough to approve or disapprove,' she retorted.

'Enough to consider him unsuitable, though.'

During the pause which followed, Tracey sought valiantly for a change of subject, but Justin's demanding, 'Well?' gave her no opportunity to pursue her line of thought, and feeling as though she were being spotlighted in the middle of a darkened stage her expression turned rebellious.

'He was married,' she told them defiantly.

Nancy's disappointed, 'Oh, Tracey!' was overridden by her father's cane being thumped on to the floor with ominous force and Tracey immediately corrected, 'Well—separated,' in a less challenging voice.

'You think that makes it any better?' Justin roared, causing the two girls on the verandah to turn their heads to see what was happening and then shrink back out of sight again upon seeing the thunderous look on their grand-father's face. 'No wonder Ben wanted you with a guardian —he always was too weak to control the females in his own family himself,' he concluded somewhat scornfully.

The slighting reference to her adoptive parent had Tracey entering the fray once more. 'He wasn't weak—he was kind and gentle,' she replied vehemently. 'And for your information, women aren't *controlled* any more, like a . . .' she searched for an appropriate simile, '. . . a mob of sheep being pushed around by a snapping dog at their heels!'

'A good sheepdog doesn't snap . . . he encourages and guides by his mere presence,' Justine enlightened her with pungent condescension.

Tracey's mouth curved sweetly. 'Just like a good husband should?' she quizzed.

'Don't think you can sidetrack me with your impudent answers, young lady, I'm still waiting to hear what excuses you have to offer for keeping company with a married man!'

'Excuses! Why should I have any? I've already told you he was separated, and I didn't have to justify my actions to anybody.'

Nancy's fingers stayed their agile movements. 'Not even to Ben?' she queried with a frown.

'My God!' expostulated Justin in sheer disbelief before Tracey had a chance to reply. 'She's no different from her mother—her morals left something to be desired too! And to think a son of mine was feeble enough to let it happen a second time. What in hell was he thinking about?'

For the space of one whole minute Tracey stared at him dumbly, her mind in a whirl, then as her pulse began to accelerate with indignation, 'How dare you speak like that about my mother! You couldn't possibly know what she was like!'

'Couldn't I, by heaven? How I wish that were true! You seem to have forgotten that you and your mother lived here for nigh on two years when Ben first married her. Two years of waiting to see who she was going to set her cap for next. The bonds of matrimony meant nothing to her either!' he ground out contemptuously, ignoring Tracey's heated, 'That's a lie!' and continuing as if she had never spoken. 'In the end I had no alternative but to order her off the property before she had a chance to wreck my entire family.' His voice quietened and his eyes grew weary. 'From that day onwards I never saw or heard from my youngest son again—he cut himself off so completely that we didn't even know where he'd been living until that solicitor contacted Ryan after his death. And I have your mother to thank for that,' he informed her bitterly. 'An unprincipled, amoral little ...'

'Father! I think you've said enough!' Nancy interjected swiftly, her eyes leaving Tracey's white face to plead silently with her parent. 'It all happened a long time ago, and Tracey isn't to blame for her mother's behaviour.'

Outwardly composed, Tracey was a mass of churning, screaming nerves inside. Even without Nancy's tacit agreement with her father's statements, unfortunately there could be no doubting the pained vehemence in his revelations, and reluctantly she recalled from the dark recesses of her own mind angry words which had made no sense to her at the time, but which had penetrated the closed door of her parents' room on many occasions, and now began to fill what had once been puzzling gaps in her knowledge.

Whether Justin replied to Nancy she had no idea, because the throbbing at her temples was drowning all extraneous sounds and it wasn't until her blankly focused eyes became aware of Ryan as he bent to speak to the girls on the verandah that she was capable of willing any sort of movement back into her temporarily paralysed limbs.

'Tracey!'

Justin's commanding call had her shaking her head evasively and refusing to answer as she gained her feet unsteadily. 'It's been a long day, so if you'll excuse me ...' she murmured throatily, and walked stiffly to the hallway, leaving Nancy's distressed and exasperated, 'Now look what you've done!' and the testy response, 'Well, she was bound to find out some time,' hanging in the air behind her.

Once having reached the safety of her room there wasn't even time for Tracey to take a cigarette from the packet she had feverishly dragged out of her bag before there was a sharp rap on the door and, without waiting for an answer, Ryan stalked into the room with an angry stride, his eyes cold and his mouth taut as he slammed the door shut again.

'I want to talk to you!' he announced savagely, muscular arms folding across an even more muscular chest.

Tracey kept her face averted, seemingly absorbed with the cigarette packet she was fingering so studiously. 'Do you? What about?' she asked, and was amazed at the calmness of her own voice.

'About what's been going on this evening,' he grated through clenched teeth. 'The minute I walk into the sitting room it's to see you disappearing like some ghostly vision about to perform its nightly wanderings, and I get frantic head-noddings from Nancy to follow you. Suppose you start by telling me why?' he suggested sarcastically.

'Why Nancy suggested you follow me? How should I know? Perhaps you'd be better asking her that,' she returned with a swiftly brazen glance.

Ryan's long legs covered the ground between them before Tracey realised he had begun to move, and a heavy hand encircled one of her wrists tightly, pulling her roughly round to face him squarely.

'I'm asking you!' he ejaculated shortly. 'And I want an answer—now! I've had just about as much as I can take of your petulant and unco-operative behaviour. I'm not having Nancy and Justin putting up with it as well.'

His touch burnt like fire against her bare skin, and all the control Tracey had been striving so valiantly to maintain finally broke as she flared into resentment.

'Oh, no, that would never do, would it?' she gibed recklessly, his image blurring through the unshed tears that were hovering at the back of her eyes. 'Just because the Alexanders feel free to say what they like, there's no reason to believe the same conditions apply for me, is there? I should be a good little girl and remember I'm only here because you weren't given any choice in the matter. It must have caused you a great deal of annoyance when you discovered you couldn't have one without the other. How it must have gone against the grain to accept both of us!' she cried heatedly.

Ryan looked down at her with a frown. 'What the hell are you talking about?' he demanded arrogantly.

'As if you didn't know!' she retaliated bitingly, and had to catch her bottom lip between her teeth to stop its trembling. 'We were thrown off the place last time . . . remember? Apparently my mother was too much trouble to have around and, I don't doubt, the same was felt of her daughter! But my stepfather made sure I came in a package deal the second time, didn't he? Either you take both, or none at all. Or maybe that was just his way of getting his own back—to make sure I was foisted on his family whether they wanted it or not!' she stormed unevenly, her breath coming in deep, shuddering gasps.

'Of all the idiotic, pig-headed little morons . . .!' Ryan branded her mercilessly, bronzed hands clamping firmly on to her shoulders and accentuating each criticism with a shake Tracey wondered didn't break her neck. 'I might have known you'd come up with an interpretation like that! You distrust everybody's motives but your own, don't you?' He let go of her irritatedly and swept one hand around the back of his neck. 'It's never occurred to you that Ben really considered you as much his daughter as Lyn, has it? That, in his eyes, you were just as entitled to share in his inheritance as she was? No,' he answered for her coldly, 'all you can do is suspect his intentions. But, just so you don't continue to labour under such an unbelievable misapprehension, allow me to inform you that I could easily have side-stepped that condition in Ben's will had the family wanted me to—and without depriving Lyn of her legacy. As you reminded me once before, money does sometimes bring its own advantages. There are ways and means, Tracey!' he stabbed at her scornfully.

'Then why didn't you? You knew I would have preferred it that way,' she glared at him mutinously.

Ryan returned her look exasperatedly. 'For crying out loud, don't let's go through all that again! You know very well why—because Ben wanted you here, and because,' surprisingly his mouth shaped into the semblance of a wry smile, 'Justin gave orders that I wasn't to come back without you, that's why!'

After the previous disclosures she had been subjected to that evening, Tracey wouldn't have thought it was possible for anything else to shock her—but that did, and she enquired warily, 'Why would he say a thing like that?'

'If you weren't so preoccupied with declaring war on every Alexander you meet, you might have been able to work that one out for yourself,' he reproved uninformatively.

'It hasn't exactly been one-sided, you know!' Tracey immediately flashed back with indignation. 'You haven't quite been what I would call a benevolent guardian up until now, and your grandfather thinks I'm—I'm ...'

'Mmm ...?' he prompted, a dark brow lifting interestedly.

'It doesn't matter.' She hunched away from him moodily, her thoughts returning involuntarily to Justin's dogmatic statements and the shock they had inflicted. Dim memories of her mother conjured up an uncertain picture of a pretty, laughing blonde wearing a pale blue evening gown, hair beautifully coiffured, her eyes glowing with expectation, and she closed her eyes to shut out the scene.

Regrettably, she now knew the meaning behind her stepfather's reproachful, 'Another night, another party, Mary?' and the tinkling laugh which had preceded her mother's appeasing, 'Don't be silly, darling. You know I can't avoid these business functions.' To this her stepfather had retorted with unusual sarcasm, 'Can't ... or don't want to?' while her mother had laughed again, but not quite so merrily this time, as she shrugged, 'We can't all hide our lights under a bushel, Ben,' and had swept haughtily out of the room.

The feel of warm hands cupping Tracey's pensive face had the effect of bringing her eyes open once more and blinking rapidly under Ryan's enquiring gaze.

'From the expression on your face, I think it does matter,' he corrected softly. 'What does Justin think you are?'

Tracey's eyes clouded to a smoky grey. 'Why should you care?' she demanded bitterly. 'You implied the same the first night we met, and *he* likes jumping to the wrong conclusions too. He said my mother didn't consider marriage a barrier either!' gloomily.

'You told him about Wilcox?'

'Sort of,' Tracey admitted unwillingly, and dragged herself restively out of his reach when he began to smile, a lazy moulding of his attractive mouth which sent delicious shivers through her nervous system, but which at the same time had her unaccountably resenting the very vitality which attracted her.

'I'm glad you find it amusing, because I certainly didn't!' she snapped angrily.

If anything Ryan's smile widened. 'Well, what did you expect? A standing ovation?' he drawled mockingly.

'No—just to be left alone and allowed to run my own life! I was doing quite nicely until the Alexanders came along with all their rules and restrictions.' Abruptly she stopped and sent him a calculating glance from the cover of ebony lashes. 'But as everyone already thinks the worst of me, perhaps I should try following in my mother's footsteps. It might serve to relieve the monotony, and after all,' she paused and smiled provokingly, 'it did manage to get her thrown off the property and back to Sydney, didn't it? Maybe it will do the same for me too.'

'More like it will have Justin deciding it's time you were married yourself and providing you with a suitable husband,' blandly.

The sheer presumption of the proposal left Tracey gasping. She knew it wasn't unheard-of among some families of the squatocracy for particular sons and daughters to be conveniently brought together with such alliances in mind, but if they thought she would be a willing party to such a suggestion then they could think again!

'And is that the reason he insisted I came back with you?' she charged scornfully. 'To make sure I also became a pawn to be used for the advancement of the Alexander holdings? Wasn't Lyn enough? Are there two properties he wants to get his hands on?' she taunted.

The narrowed blue eyes and hard-clenched jaw warned Tracey she wouldn't like what was coming next, and she stepped back quickly, but nowhere near fast enough to evade Ryan's hand as it sank into her hair and dragged her head back roughly.

'No, you redheaded little shrew, that wasn't the reason,' he informed her tersely. 'Because in this family, as with many others out here, land is only inherited by the male line—chauvinistic of us, I know—but that's the way it is!' he goaded sardonically, uncontritely. 'So, should you happen to marry a grazier, you'll be taking Alexander money with you, but you won't be bringing any land in exchange! That's just not how the system works, honey!' with an emphasising tug at her hair before releasing her contemptuously.

With a tentative hand to her tingling scalp, Tracey glared back at him, a challenging angle to her chin. 'And is that why it's known as a man's country?' she jeered, heedless of the consequences. 'Because the females are treated as second-class citizens, easily bought out of their shares with a few dollars?'

About to open the door, Ryan looked back at her coldly. 'Never second-class, and very rarely a *few* dollars, Tracey! But don't let that stop you ... you keep hanging in there,' he commended satirically, his eyes sweeping over her derogatorily. 'With luck, I'm sure you'll manage to have every member of this family as dissatisfied with your waspish presence as you are!'

As the door closed loudly behind him, Tracey stood staring at its blankness, biting at her lip miserably, all the anger and resentment dissipating with Ryan's departure. It was the first time in her life she had ever been described as waspish, or a shrew, and she found the idea rather distasteful since her normal disposition was anything but. She wandered disconsolately back to the dressing table, lit her long-awaited cigarette and pushed open the doors leading on to the wide verandah, where she gazed for a few seconds through the protecting gauze at the moon-hazed landscape, listening as the gobbling call of a nightjar on the wing suddenly rent the unbelievable quiet, and then lowered herself with a sigh on to a convenient lounger.

A long time after her cigarette was finished her thoughts were still turbulent and disjointed. The house behind her was very silent now and she wondered if the rest of the household had retired for the night, but then soft footfalls turning the corner to her side of the verandah informed her that at least one other was reluctant to seek their bed that evening.

Tense as her eyes tried to penetrate the darkness outside the rim of light filtering from her bedroom, she relaxed on a softly expelled breath when it was Nancy's voice that queried from the shadows, 'Tracey? Don't you feel like sleeping either?'

As the older woman stepped directly into the light Tracey shook her head by way of confirmation, at the same time moving as if to rise, but Nancy put out a staying hand to her shoulder, saying, 'No, don't go. I'd like to talk to you, if I may,' as she seated herself gracefully in a cushioned wicker chair nearby.

Athough Tracey settled back compliantly in her own seat, her eyes were wary when they sought Nancy's face and her fingers curled together nervously in her lap as she broke into hurried, forestalling speech. 'It's—er—very quiet here at night, isn't it? On the coast we—um—usually only get this type of stillness when a storm's brewing,' she faltered, and lapsed into apprehensive silence again.

Nancy gave some thoughtful attention to twisting her wedding ring around her finger and then looked up with a half-rueful smile. 'Is that a respectful way of telling me you would prefer to restrict the conversation to safe, uncontroversial topics?' she quizzed.

Again Tracey sighed. 'If it was, I think it would be the first polite thing I seem to have said since I arrived,' she owned wanly, remembering Ryan's descriptions. 'You must think I'm very rude, and I'm sorry, because I didn't mean to be.'

'And we're sorry too, because we didn't mean to be quite so abitrary either,' Nancy smiled encouragingly. 'Father was very contrite for what he'd said once he'd calmed down.'

It was quite an effort for Tracey to put a halt on the sarcastic, 'Oh, yes, I can imagine,' that hovered on the end of her tongue—it being impossible for her to picture either of the Alexander males displaying penitence for anything they said or did—but in the end she managed it and merely gave a careful expression of understanding by way of a reply.

'You didn't know about your mother until tonight, did you?' Nancy now asked watchfully.

Tracey lowered her eyes to her clenched hands and took a deep breath. 'I'm not sure really,' she confessed slowly, huskily. 'I think I may have done subconsciously, but without anyone actually having put it into a definite statement before, there was no reason for me to deliberately analyse all the evidence ... if you know what I mean.' Her eyes lifted to Nancy's for a few seconds and then fell again as she continued. 'I knew, of course, that Mum and Dad weren't exactly what you would call a devoted couple in the last couple of years before she died. She was always going out and leaving Dad to stay home with Lyn and me, then when she did get home there would often be the sound of arguments coming from their room that woke me up because my room was next door. But when you're only nine or ten years old you unquestioningly believe it when your mother tells you it's part of her work as a buyer in a department store to attend so many night meetings.' She half shrugged fatalistically. 'I guess it's not until we grow older that we lose the naïveté and suspicions begin to creep in.'

'Yet when Father first mentioned it, you disputed the suggestion strongly,' Nancy probed gently.

'A spontaneous reaction, I suppose,' Tracey admitted wryly. 'Having been an ostrich with my head in the sand for so long, I didn't appreciate his digging it out for me. Maybe it's a weakness in my character—a dislike for facing up to unpalatable facts.'

'I doubt it,' Nancy squashed the idea firmly, reaching out to cover Tracey's hands briefly with one of her own. 'I couldn't imagine anyone being overjoyed to discover that one of their parents hadn't been as stainless as they would have liked them to be—and especially not when the discovery comes in such an unexpected and blunt fashion as my father delivers his apocalypses.'

'He is somewhat devastating when he gets wound up,

isn't he?' agreed Tracey ruefully. 'Although to be strictly fair, I suppose you can't really blame him when you take into account the fact that he lost all contact with his son because of my mother.' She stopped suddenly as a thought hit her. 'Your brother too, Nancy,' she recalled sorrowfully. 'It's a wonder either of you are prepared to accept me here when I must be such a reminder of everything you would rather forget.'

Nancy's head shook vigorously in negation. 'Never think that, Tracey,' she commanded earnestly. 'I was upset when Ben left—we all were, of course—but fortunately the loss abates over the years, and once Father had shed his grief at knowing he would never see Ben again after the solicitor advised us of his death, then he was, quite frankly, thrilled to learn that Ben had made that condition in his will and that you would be coming back to us with Lyn.'

'But why?' Tracey had to ask in puzzled wonderment, especially when Ryan had intimated much the same. 'I'm not really his grandchild like Lyn is. There isn't any blood relationship between us.'

'Maybe not,' Nancy conceded with a fond smile. 'But he always did have a soft spot for you and he was terribly disappointed when you left with Ben and Mary. He's always been one who believes firmly in the family unit and it was very hard for him to make the decision which would actually create such a division within his own,' she explained. 'Even though he may deny it, he was no better than Ryan and Glen were when it came to refusing you anything you had your heart set on.'

Tracey's brows arched expressively, finding that no easier to credit than when Justin had said the same of his grandson. It would appear that with the passing of the years any of those inconvenient breaches in their strong-willed characters had been carefully expunged.

Silence reigned for a time after Nancy's thought-stirring words, then, with a diffident type of movement with one hand, Tracey asked the question that had been niggling at the back of her mind for some weeks now—ever since Mr Gatehead had first read her father's will, in fact.

'If Dad was so keen on us coming back here,' she began

slowly, 'why didn't he bring us himself after my mother died?'

'I'm afraid I can't really say with any certainty,' she was advised rather sadly. 'Perhaps it was because he himself didn't want to return if, as you say, he never experienced the desire to even talk about his own family at all, or perhaps it was just a case of his pride wouldn't let him after what had happened. Soft-hearted he may have been, but even as a child Ben always had that unbending pride which could never accept the thought that others may have been feeling sorry for him, or worse, were pitying him.' She sighed and half smiled. 'Anyway, the main thing is that he intended for you two girls to return to the family, and for that we're grateful.'

With so much to dwell upon and chew over in her mind, it wasn't surprising that Tracey found sleep slow in coming once she had said goodnight to Nancy and wearily made for her bed. It had been an eventful day and even though she was no more reconciled now than she had been when she arrived to remaining on Nindethana for the specified period, she could see it was becoming increasingly difficult to discover a way in which to challenge her guardian's dominance without seeming unbearably petty in view of Nancy's undoubted pleasure in having them there.

CHAPTER FIVE

'CAROL's suggested we might like to go riding this morning. See some of the property, so to speak,' said Lyn at breakfast the next morning after helping herself to bacon and eggs from the various chafing dishes set out on the sideboard in the dining room.

'Mmm, we can watch the musterings in the Old Bore Paddock too, if you like,' added Carol helpfully from her place at the table. 'Ryan was saying last night that they expect to be out there for most of the day.'

On the verge of saying, 'No,' upon hearing that their guardian was likely to be present, Tracey stopped in the act of pouring her coffee and glanced through the open doors to the sun-filled gardens beyond the verandah. It was another of those clear, cloudless days which brought every colour vividly alive and so typified the outback that it was impossible for her to deny the rising fascination to sample the touch of that white-hot sun and feel again the wholly satisfying sensation of being carried swiftly onward by an innately surefooted piece of horseflesh.

'All right,' she acquiesced suddenly, and returned to the table with her coffee. 'How do we get there?'

'Well ...' Carol gave the matter some deep thought. 'I was thinking we could follow the creek for a few miles until we come to the Devil Waterhole, then move on to the old mine workings, and cut across to the mustering yards from there,' she expounded knowledgeably.

'Devil Waterhole?' queried Lyn.

'Wirrabilla,' nodded her informant with a grin. 'That's how the district came by its name—from the waterhole. Native folklore has it inhabited by a devil fish, the literal translation being teeth-water,' she explained. 'There's usually a few eels in the creek, so maybe one of them latched on to somebody many years ago.'

'Sounds delightful,' laughed Tracey while Lyn shuddered expressively. 'Let's pass on to the mine workings. What were they for ... gold?'

'Uh-uh! Opals,' Carol corrected quickly. 'Some time before the turn of the century there was quite a boom around here, but after a few years the finds started to fizzle out and now there's only a couple of derelict stone huts and half-filled mine shafts to show where they were. When we were kids we often used to go noodling—official opal-hunting term,' she grinned, 'over the old mullock heaps, but we never found anything much, and once we decided to dig out one of the shafts, but Uncle Richard—Ryan's father—caught us at it and,' her eyes widened with rememberance, 'didn't he give us what for! My brothers and I were all packed off home in disgrace, but poor Ryan and Glen were sent boundary riding for a couple of months because he said they were older and should have had more sense, seeing as we'd all been warned so often about staying clear of the shafts and their rotting timbers. We never did it again, I can tell you!' she grimaced.

The idea of Ryan being sent on a duty round checking the fences as punishment for his part in the escapade appealed to Tracey's aroused retaliative instincts, and it was left to Lyn to enquire tentatively, 'Uncle Richard—he's dead, isn't he?'

Carol swallowed a mouthful of coffee and nodded. 'That's right, he died about ... oh, five or six years ago now. Isn't that right, Mum?' she sought verification as her mother entered the room.

'What's that, dear?' quizzed Nancy once she had offered her morning's greetings and ladled some fluffy scrambled eggs on to a plate.

'Uncle Richard died about five or six years ago.'

A double crease appeared between Nancy's eyes as she concentrated. 'Yes, I suppose it would be close on six years now,' she endorsed slowly, before detailing for Tracey and Lyn's benefit, 'It was one of those freak accidents that happen at times. We'd had three good seasons in a row followed by a very dry one and, of course, with such favourable conditions the bushfires reaped a grim toll throughout that summer. Anyway, it was late one afternoon when the men had just about managed to bring a particularly bad outbreak under control that the wind suddenly changed directions and set the blaze off even stronger than it had been before—only in the opposite direction this time. Dick and the two men with him didn't have a chance. It came back at them so rapidly that they were trapped down in the gully when the fire jumped from one side to the other and left them no escape route,' she concluded her narration on a sigh.

The disturbing images the story created had them all quietly solemn for some moments until Tracey's murmured, 'I'm sorry,' broke the heavy atmosphere, and in a deliberate attempt at digression Nancy forced a brightening smile to her lips to question lightly, 'And what are you three planning to do today?'

In their desire to keep the conversation alive they all answered at once, with the muster, the mines and the water-hole all receiving a mention as each one unconsciously indicated their prime interest, and by the time the general laughter and explanations which followed had died away their previous gloomy thoughts had temporarily been dispelled.

'You make sure you keep clear of those mine shafts, that's all,' Nancy warned later as they left the dining room together.

'I know, I know!' Carol held up her hands in a gesture of surrender. 'I've already told Lyn and Tracey what happened the last time we tried exploring them,' she grinned.

'As long as you remember that when you're there,' her mother returned dryly, and prompting Tracey to advise, 'Don't worry, Nancy, we'll be careful,' as they prepared to descend upon Mrs Gray in the kitchen in order to obtain packed lunches for later in the day.

This accomplished, it wasn't long before Tom, the native stockman in charge of the station's horses, had saddled up three suitable mounts, and with the earth singing beneath flying hooves they were taking the friskiness out of the animals, only too glad to be on the move and following between the gums and leathery-leaved coolibahs the meandering path of the creek as it flowed from the natural spring within the homestead grounds.

At last, in a rocky depression that sliced across the landscape as if gouged out by some prehistoric force, they came to the waterhole and dismounting, cautiously picked their way down the pebbly incline to where a deep pool of shadowed water nestled shyly under the protection of a giant overhanging boulder.

Lyn was the first to reach the stone ledge beside it, and kneeling down quickly dug her cupped hands beneath the surface and splashed their contents over her face. The immediate surprised exclamation, 'Heavens! That's *cold*!' had Tracey hesitating before following suit and Carol bursting into laughter.

'I know, it's always like that,' she smiled. 'It comes as quite a shock, doesn't it?'

Tracey knelt down beside her sister and experimentally trailed her own fingers within the chilling depths. 'I thought all underground water was warm,' she commented to Carol, who had now joined them on the ledge.

'Most artesian and sub-artesian bores are,' she agreed, 'but this water never is. They do say it's bottomless, so perhaps that accounts for it,' she suggested blithely.

'Perhaps the cold is also the teeth that legend has in here too,' grinned Tracey, while Lyn backed hurriedly away from the edge, grimacing and laughing nervously, 'I'm not very keen on bottomless things—they give me the creeps.'

'You prefer topless, do you?' joked Carol, her eyes sparkling outrageously.

Forgetting her aversion to the pool for a minute, Lyn started to blush self-consciously, then, with a rare attempt at raillery pointed back towards the water and grinned, 'If that's the other alternative, I think I might.'

After scrambling back up the bank they were soon on their way once more, and leaning slightly forward to the tune of creaking leather, Tracey patted her mount's warm, satin-smooth neck approvingly and took in the surrounding country with interest. It was a totally strange environment; these red soil plains with their low-growing vegetation and mostly stunted trees where the fine talcum-like dust that rose to hang nebulously in the heat-laden air as they passed all seemed designed to emphasise the vastness and isolation of a terrain that made one feel so defencelessly insignificant.

Yet, even so, there was a mystical grandeur and alluring beauty to it all that was impossible to ignore and, against her will, Tracey found she was being drawn to its unfathomable awesomeness by the very immensity and remorselessness she had expected to repel her. Incredulous and not a little chagrined with the turn her thoughts were taking, she gave her head an admonishing shake and turned to Carol.

'You mentioned back there artesian and sub-artesian bores. Is there any difference?'

'Artesian's when you sink a bore, or a well, and the water rises to the surface of its own accord,' the younger girl explained. 'Sub-artesian is when it has to be pumped up.'

Lyn shifted in the saddle and broke in interestedly, 'How many bores would they actually have on the property?' to which Carol gave a half laugh and shrugged.

'You've got me there, I don't really know the exact number. Don't forget I don't usually live here. If you asked me what we've got at home I could tell you right off, but here . . .' she halted and frowned, 'well, I guess around nine or ten would be pretty close, although I do know there's at least two permanent springs, a couple of billabongs and about eight ground tanks. But don't quote me,' she cautioned with a laugh, 'my information could quite possibly be out of date.'

For the first time since leaving the homestead that morning they came across a large mob of sheep, heads down, diligently devouring feed, and riding around them Tracey put forth another question.

'Where *do* you live, Carol?' she asked. 'Is it near here?'

'That all depends on whether you travel by road or air,' Carol returned ruefully. 'We're over the border in Queensland. Up on the Darling Downs, to be exact.'

'That's wheat and sheep country, isn't it?' from Tracey.

'Mainly,' Carol only had time to agree before Lyn joined in with,

'Is our other aunt's property up there too?'

Carol grinned and shook her head. 'No, we like to spread ourselves around a bit. Aunt Rita's place is in central western New South Wales. They crop oilseeds—you know, sunflower, safflower, linseed—as well as raising fat lambs and vealers.'

'Well, the family certainly like to diversify, don't they?' remarked Tracey wryly.

'It's the best way,' offered Carol seriously. 'Then if one particular holding suffers a bad year, the others can support it until the following season.'

Tracey's head tilted consideringly to one side. 'Are you saying that *all* those properties are owned by the Alexanders?'

'Sure.' Carol seemed amused they should find it so hard to believe. 'Plus the property that Glen and Pamela will be taking up when they get back, and another couple of smaller ones further north in Queensland,' she went on, obviously enjoying the widening-eyed sensation she was causing among her companions. 'Then, of course, there's real estate on the coast, a very profitable partnership in a sapphire field on the tablelands, stocks, shares, and interests in so many business ventures it would take an age to repeat them all.' She lifted one eyebrow impudently. 'Would you like me to continue?'

'No, you've convinced us the Alexanders have a sizeable stake in the country,' Tracey gasped dryly, but followed with a sardonic, 'What do they do for an encore?' without thinking for a moment that she would take her at her word.

'Oh, for that there's cotton, sugar, peanuts ...' Carol began with a twinkle, but was cut short by Tracey's humorously defeated,

'Okay, okay, I'll take your word for it. I know when I'm fighting a loosing battle!'

'In that case ...' Carol put her heels to the sides of her mare, 'I'll race you to the top of that ridge over there,' pointing ahead to where a leopardwood tree stood in lonely solitude, its tangled branches stretching up into the heat-faded blue of the sky overhead.

'You're on!' came the spirited call from two answering voices as they urged their horses into a ground-eating gallop that carried them swiftly across the intervening space and up on to the rise within a few minutes of Carol's casually issued challenge.

Reining to a halt, Carol brushed an arm across her per-
spiring forehead and nodded across the dry creek below
them to where uneven humps of sand and stone lay swelter-
ing in the shimmering heat.

'There they are—the old mines,' she exclaimed. 'Coming
down?' and on receiving eager affirming nods began to lead
the way in the rather sharp descent to the gully below.
'Watch where you're going, though, won't you?' she called
anxiously over her shoulder as they reached relatively level
ground once more. 'Some of the shafts that have had their
windlasses removed are pretty hard to see these days.'

Tethering the horses in the speckled shade provided by a
white-limbed paperbark on the edge of the dry stream,
they began picking their way slowly among the great
mounds of discarded waste and cautiously exploring the
mouths of some of the hillside tunnels that disappeared
beneath the sandstone outcrop in a bid to come under the
hard band of material which formed beneath the sandstone
when it came into contact with the deeper claystone and
gave cover for the precious opal dirt which lay between the
two.

With their eyes irresistibly drawn to the stony ground
before them they scrambled to the top of one mullock heap
to peer down an abandoned shaft, its head machinery de-
caying gradually with the ravages of time, and a mute reminder of the men and women who had laboured long and
expectantly in the scorching heat and dust in the hope of
discovering a richly coloured reward.

Tracey undid another button at the neck of her checked
shirt and waved a fanning hand in front of her face. 'It
would want to have been extremely profitable to work out
here all day in these temperatures, wouldn't it?' she queried.
'Were they very good stones they found here, Carol?'

'Some of them certainly were, I believe,' the younger
girl replied as they made their way down on to the flat
again and headed for the masterless huts. 'Although not
black opals like they find at Lightning Ridge, mind you.
These were of the milky variety.'

Lyn looked around her sister to her cousin on the other
side. 'And are they worked out completely? Isn't there any

chance there's still more down there?' pointing as they passed another square shaft.

'There could be, I guess,' admitted Carol with a shrug. 'Look at the number of times they've said the Ridge was worked out, but they still keep finding new areas. Somebody else comes along and digs down an extra foot or so, or tunnels in another six inches and, hey presto! you've got it made. It's just the same as it was in the days of the old gold rushes—one digger gives up his claim and another takes it over and finds an even greater bonanza.' She shaded her eyes with one hand and indicated a low amber-coloured rise on the horizon far to the north-west of them. 'They reckon that's a typical opal-bearing formation out there, but it's never been worked because of the lack of water.'

'Couldn't they put down a bore?' Lyn sought a way to surmount the problem.

'Who's going to pay for it on the offchance there's opals present?' enquired Carol plausibly in return. 'A bore isn't cheap to sink and there's no gilt-edged guarantee you'll find water anyway. No, like a great many other things in the outback, I guess it will just have to sit there waiting for another year and another age to unlock its secrets,' she philosophised with a grin, and led them into the first of the crude abodes still standing.

Small and cramped, the blackened hearth just visible through the layers of permeating dust which covered the rammed earth floor and pitted stone walls, there was a touching pathos to the tiny building which immediately brought to mind the rigours and privations endured by those early prospectors in their efforts to wrest the prized gems from their hiding places. The iron roof was torn and rusty now, several sheets missing altogether—ripped off in some long-forgotten storm—while the unimpeded fingers of sunlight filtering through the floating film of dust raised by intruding feet revealed the headlong flight of a startled lizard as it darted for the protection of some termite-invaded timber in one corner.

Observing the thoughtful looks on her companions' faces, Carol nodded understandingly. 'It gets to you, doesn't it?' she smiled. 'Makes you wonder what they were like, the people living here. Whether they were successful, or walked back to where they came from—broke!'

'No records still existing?' asked Tracey with one last backward look as they left the dwelling behind. 'Copies of licences, or anything like that?'

'Oh, they may still have some of the registers for applications,' Carol agreed, 'but I think that only gives you the name of the person who sought the right to mine the area, it doesn't actually record which claim was mined by whom, and as there are so many shafts and tunnels it's only fair to presume that quite a number of claims were staked out, and trying to sort one from the other would be a full-time occupation.'

'I suppose so.' Tracey gathered up the reins of her chestnut mare and swung lightly into the saddle. 'Where do we go from here?' she asked after the others had mounted also and they began moving along the creek bed.

'Now we're on our way to the mustering yards,' Carol informed them cheerfully. 'And if we get a move on, we'll make it in time to have lunch with Ryan and the rest of them.'

Although this seemed to find immediate favour with her sister, Tracey wasn't so sure she wanted to have lunch with Ryan, preferring to have taken a spectator's role only in the proceedings by watching, instead of participating over a meal, but rather than let her true feelings be known she merely nodded in apparent enthusiasm for the suggestion and allowed her mount to keep pace with the other two as they cut out of the creek and headed east at a swift canter.

'Well, at least we haven't missed them—you can see the dust from here,' said Carol some time later after they had passed through into another paddock during the course of their journey and which had made Tracey and Lyn smile to come across a fence and a gate seemingly in the middle of nowhere.

Soon definite figures became discernible, and easing into a walk the girls moved closer to the yards, watching as sleek-coated dogs hurried their charges from one yard to another and into the race leading to the jetter—a high-powered shower—which sprayed them with a solution to prevent fly-strike. On the other side of the steel yards a flowing bore gushed life-giving water into a drain where sheep that had already been treated were drinking.

There were some half dozen men around the yards, moving among the thronging masses—some working gates, others keeping tally—but it was directly to Ryan's arresting features as he stood talking to Doug Horton beside the first yard that Tracey's eyes involuntarily flew. Dressed in leather-belted, dusty drills and sweat-stained shirt, a grazier's ever-present wide-brimmed hat pulled forward to shade his eyes, there was a primitive aura about him that set her senses throbbing uncontrollably and, as a result, had her mouth pulling into a mutinous line of rejection in disgust at her own unprecedented reaction to an attractive male. Watching covertly from the corner of her eye as Ryan swung lightly forward to greet the two younger girls when they came to a halt, Tracey deliberately stayed back, sliding to the ground and leaning on the yard rail, assuming a single-minded interest in the activity therein.

Lyn and Carol's narrative chatter lapsed on the sound of laughter and sensing someone's presence behind her Tracey spun around, annoyed to find herself already on the defensive as challenging green eyes came into conflict with irate blue ones.

Thumbs hooked in the wide belt above lean hips, Ryan looked down on her scathingly. 'I should have known it would be too much to expect you to comply with any precautions concerning self-preservation out here, shouldn't I?' he snapped, and causing Tracey's eyes to lose some of their belligerence as bafflement took its place, until an irritable hand flicked out to indicate her uncovered head and gibed, 'What sort of egotism is it that makes you think you're not susceptible to sunstroke like everyone else? You think the Flying Doctor has nothing better to do than waste his time treating wilfully inflicted ailments?'

'No!' she glared back at him resentfully. It hadn't been self-opinionatedness at all that had made her refuse Carol's offer of a hat that morning, merely a strong aversion to wearing a head covering of any kind, and certainly that girl hadn't made any great demur when the proposal hadn't been accepted and Lyn had taken the shady headgear instead. 'I never wear a hat,' she continued in the same low, scornful tone. 'My hair's thick and,' reaching up to run slim fingers beneath the curls the sun was burnishing into waves of fire, 'my head is quite cool, and the length stops the sun from reaching the back of my neck,' she informed him with what was meant as a quelling glance.

Not that it appeared to have any effect upon her guardian, for he returned her look with one just as repressive. 'But you will wear one in future,' he advised with such cool absoluteness that Tracey's indignation flared in revolt.

'I will not!' she threw back swiftly. 'I don't need one.'

'You will before you take another horse out of the yard,' he threatened inflexibly, 'because I shall leave orders that Tom isn't to saddle up for you unless you're wearing one!'

'So ...?' she goaded with a shrug. 'I can saddle my own.'

'Not without my permission, you can't, and if I put the word out that you're not to have a mount, then believe me, you won't get one, honey!' he gloated unbearably.

'You mean you'd keep me confined to the homestead for the whole time I'm here?' Tracey gasped, appalled at the thought.

Ryan dissociated himself from the suggestion with a shake of his head. 'Not me, Tracey ... you!' he amended forcefully. 'You're the one doing the confining, because you're just too perverse to recognise the sense of what I'm saying and you've made up your mind to oppose every solitary suggestion I make! Well, if that's the way you want it, it's okay with me, but in the meantime while you're out here, you'll wear a damned hat!' as he removed his own in a sweep of controlled violence and clamped it down implacably on to her curls. 'And it had better stay there!' he commanded ominously before turning on his heel and striding grimly back to the others.

Tracey stared impotently at his departing back, her rising desire to wrench the covering from her head and stamp it into the ground surpassed only by her repugnance for the scene such an action would create in front of the men, and setting the subject of their confrontation more comfortably on her head, she thrust one hand morosely into the back pocket of her jeans and began leading the chestnut to the shade provided by a ring of trees about the bore where the rest of the horses were tethered.

Scuffing up the dust with the toes of her boots as she went. Tracey's thoughts were cheerlessly inward. Grudgingly honest, she admitted that maybe he was right and she was determined to fight every decision he made, but wasn't he just as quick to jump on her every time she opened her mouth too? How was she supposed to know he placed so much importance on wearing a hat? Of course she knew most of them did in the outback and when they were continually working in such a burning atmosphere, day after day, she could understand it, but surely it wasn't a matter of life or death as Ryan made it out to be when one only went riding occasionally? She hadn't been lying when she said her scalp felt cool to the touch and, as far as she could see, there had been no call for him to have been so aggressive about it! Leaving her horse with the others, she joined the two girls who were soaking their hankies at the mouth of the not too warm bore and wiping the dust from hot faces.

'That makes you feel better, doesn't it?' smiled Carol a few minutes later, and then continued, taking Tracey and Lyn's agreement for granted. 'Ryan says they'll be stopping for lunch once the mob they've got in the small yard goes through, so we may as well wait and have ours then too ... okay?'

'Suits me,' endorsed Lyn easily with a last wipe of her hanky across her forehead. 'I'm dying to see what they're doing over there anyway,' with an implicit hand indicating the yards. 'You coming too, Tracey?' she asked.

'Might as well,' Tracey hunched her shoulders uncaringly. There was nowhere else to go, but she refrained from saying so, knowing how such a disgruntled remark would put a damper on her sister's enjoyment, and proceeded to follow them across the clearing with the semblance of a pseudo-anticipatory smile curving her lips.

As had happened with the perspective of the country

itself, Tracey soon found her interest being unwillingly captured as she viewed the bustle within the yards; the scurrying of the sheep; the intermittent shouts of those keeping score of the numbers passing through; the shrill whistles guiding the dogs; and by no means last, the swiftness of the dogs themselves as they harried the sheep into position, nimbly running across the backs of the animals to reach the head of the race if one proved unusually uncooperative, then clearing the fence in a single bound to head for the rear again once the culprit had been urged on its way.

Lunch, however, was another matter, and although Doug Horton and two of the junior jackaroos joined them along with Ryan, their easygoing ways and conversation turning the brief stoppage into a kind of picnic, Tracey found it out of the question to relax while she was so turbulently conscious of her guardian's presence and, in self-defence, she took very little part in the congenial talk, allowing Carol and Lyn the pleasure of parrying the banter while she let her eyes wander in a not altogether insincere attention to her unfamiliar surroundings.

Once she turned back to the others abruptly when someone mentioned her name and found Ryan's clear blue eyes fixed on her speculatively, but as the slight wave of colour rose in her cheeks at this silent appraisal, she tilted her head imperceptibly and discovered that the wide brim of the hat she was wearing under sufferance had other uses besides providing protection for the head—it also proved a very efficient screen for the face if used in the appropriate manner.

All too soon, judging by the younger girls' faces, it was time for Doug and his co-workers to return to the yards, but as she prepared to assist in collecting the remains of their meal, Tracey felt a strong hand on her arm as Ryan held her back while Lyn and Carol moved on toward the horses.

'By the way, Tracey,' he began evenly, no sign of his previous exasperation showing, 'I mentioned this to Lyn last night, but until now there hasn't been an opportunity to advise you of the same.' For a brief instant Tracey thought she detected a certain tautness about the eye-catching mouth, but her own inner wariness was too great for further rationalisation as he continued, 'I don't want either of you riding alone on the property unless you've checked with me first. It's too easy for newcomers to become lost once they're out of sight of the homestead. Understood?'

Oh, yes, she understood all right! It might sound very solicitous, but in actual fact wasn't it also a very convenient method of ensuring that she never received the chance to forget who was in charge; who had the final veto over whatever she chose to do while under his guardianship; who could make her stay in the outback pleasant—or unendurable! Slowly her hands clenched at her sides and her chin lifted marginally higher.

'And if I don't always happen to remember?' she had to challenge his overwhelming dominance with innocently wide eyes. 'You see, unfortunately, my memory's not always the best. Sometimes things go in one ear and right out the other,' she strained the truth mock-sorrowfully.

'Then I suggest we make it a standing rule for you to consult with me every morning, whether you plan to go riding or not, and that should avoid any undue stress being placed on your fluctuating retentive powers, shouldn't it?' he returned with insufferable irony.

Tracey's eyes lost their look of artlessness at her first horrified gasp of, 'You're joking!' but the coolly impassive, 'Am I?' she received in reply assured her he wasn't, and she sought frantically for a way to extricate herself from such an insupportable proposal.

'I thought Nancy said you leave the homestead very early in the mornings?' was her first effort.

Ryan's brows crooked sardonically. 'You'll just have to alter your rising habits, won't you?'

This was getting worse, not better! She searched for another obstacle. 'Ideas sometimes occur on the spur of the moment. How am I supposed to know if you ... approve,' she almost choked on the word, 'if you're not there to ask?'

'In a case like that ...' he paused thoughtfully and Tracey held a hopeful breath, 'I suppose you would just have to curb your impetuosity until I returned. Self-discipline is good for the character, they say,' he taunted with a mocking smile.

'How the hell would you know?' The scornful question came tumbling out as Tracey's simmering resentment boiled over and she discarded her attempts at evading the issue for a frontal attack. 'The way you disregard everyone's wishes but your own, it's obvious you've never practised self-control in your life!' she hurled at him disparagingly, a wresting hand hitting out at the arm detaining her, but only succeeding in bruising itself on contact with the bone-hard sinews of a work-strengthened forearm.

On the heels of a muffled exclamation Tracey's straining figure was hauled urgently back into close proximity as the dark head lowered until it was only inches away from her own and the black-lashed eyes locked hostilely with shining green ones.

'Then what do you think I'm exercising right now, honey?' he bit out caustically. 'Believe me, it's only due to a rigid subordination of my own inclinations that's saved you from reaping what you've really deserved for a long time now,' his intensely blue eyes sent out a cool shaft of warning. 'Don't run your luck right out, Tracey, or you might unintentionally discover just how undisciplined I can become if pushed too hard, too often!'

Some of the challenge in Tracey's eyes faded under the bleak caution and she bit doubtfully at a soft underlip. 'Then stop trying to make me account to you for my every move,' she protested truculently, but followed it with an appeasing, 'All right, all right, if you're so set on it, I'll—I'll let you know when I'm planning on—on going riding.' The partial surrender didn't come easily. 'But that's all, Ryan. Nothing else!' she tried to impress on him emphatically.

Half expecting a curt repression as she was, it caught her doubly unawares when a lazy smile began to lift the corners of his mouth. 'You reckon that's the lesser of the two evils, hmm?' he drawled mockingly. 'But what if I said I wasn't prepared to settle for that one restriction now? Knowing what I do, how can I be sure your memory won't fail you in the future at some particularly adverse moment?'

Not quite certain whether he was merely being difficult for the sake of it, or if his actual intentions were indirectly being revealed, Tracey glared at him irritably, annoyed as much with herself for allowing that smile to affect her with such a discomfiting breathlessness, as she was with Ryan for his self-assured capriciousness, and expostulated sharply, 'Because I agreed to see you before I went riding alone, that's why! What more do you want? A pledge signed, sealed and delivered in writing before witnesses?' she gibed.

With a laugh he released her arm and tilted her head back with one long finger. 'Thanks for the offer, I'll keep it in mind,' he proposed obscurely, and left her to stand frowning perplexedly after him as he strode with feline suppleness across the clearing.

For him to laugh at her provocation had been the last thing Tracey anticipated, and even after a long deliberation she was no nearer to discovering the reason than she had been when he appeared to have taken her words seriously and uttered his surprising acceptance of her scornful offer. With one more glare in his direction she spun on her heel and marched angrily back towards Lyn and Carol.

CHAPTER SIX

THE rest of that week Tracey spent in and around the homestead. The outcome of her last frustrating confrontation with Ryan had left her so confused that she wasn't sure whether she was now expected to seek his approval or not before going riding, either in company or otherwise, but rather than confer with him in order to clarify her position she preferred to familiarise herself with the house and outbuildings instead. As far as she was concerned, he would have to wait for ever before she asked his permission to do anything!

If Nancy was aware of the cause for her constant presence she was wise enough not to question the younger girl too deeply, but Justin was another matter, and obviously found her predilection for the homestead unusual and wasn't averse to saying so in his customary forthright fashion.

'What's ailing you? Why aren't you out with the others?' were his first barked demands on Wednesday morning when he came across Tracey idly flicking over the pages of an outdated magazine on the verandah.

Tracey smoothed her hair back behind her ears with a nervous hand and lifted her shoulders defensively. 'I didn't feel like it,' she offered quietly, her fingers busily flattening the creased corners of the pages.

'Rubbish!' Justin lowered himself with a muffled but irritated grunt into the chair beside her. 'Anybody who rides as well as you do,' and in response to her raised eyebrows, 'oh, yes, I saw you ride out of here yesterday with your sister and your cousin, and nobody who rides that well dismisses the chance to ride again, especially when they've just arrived from the city,' he informed her knowledgeably. 'That is, not unless there's something more important than just "not feeling like it" bothering them.'

With those penetrating blue eyes watching her so closely it was hard for Tracey to keep her tone unconcerned, but by keeping her gaze riveted to the magazine in her lap she managed to quip lightly, 'Where's the rush? I'll be here for the next couple of years.'

'Don't make it sound as if you've been banished to limbo, minx!' he rebuked sharply. 'You were happy enough when you lived here before.'

'I was only two years old at the time—my tastes have changed since then,' dryly.

Justin's lips pressed together thinly. 'But not for the better, eh?'

'Oh, please, do we have to go into that again?' she pleaded wearily. 'I apologise if I was rude, but now I think,' easing forward on her chair, 'I'd better see if I can find Nancy in case I can help her with anything.'

'There's ample help in the house already to enable Nancy to do whatever she wants without your adding to the number,' he told her blandly, a dexterously wielded cane being laid across the arms of her chair to effectively prevent her departure. 'You just stay there, young Tracey, and tell me why you didn't ride over to watch the lamb marking with your sister.' Bushy brows drew intently close. 'It wouldn't have anything to do with your returning with Ryan's hat on your head yesterday, would it? Although why that feather-brained Carol didn't insist you wear one before you left, I don't know! She knows how important it is to have one.'

'It wasn't Carol's fault. She offered me one, but I refused,' Tracey explained quickly. 'And that has nothing to do with my not going with them today. I—I just didn't want to go, that's all,' she shrugged, but added a, 'Didn't want to ask permission either,' acidly to herself all the same.

Justin sighed and removed his cane from her chair, standing it between his legs and resting one hand over the other on top of it. 'This man you were seeing in Sydney—you miss him that much?' he asked abruptly with a shrewd glance from beneath his lashes.

'Boyd?' The name was forced from Tracey in surprise as she swivelled round to face him. Is that what he was trying to put her reluctance to go riding down to? She shook her head slowly. 'No, I don't miss him *that* much, and

I'm certainly not pining away because of him, if that's what you mean,' she replied wryly. Actually it was some time now since she had even spared Boyd a thought, let alone regretted leaving him.

'Tell me about him,' he ordered autocratically.

'Who? Boyd?'

'If that's his name.'

'Why?' If she began with another question again Tracey thought she would scream, but she couldn't seem to stop doing it. 'What possible interest could he be to you?'

'Him—none, but I am interested to know what sort of a man attracts *you*.'

Suspicious suddenly of his motives, and irritated by the brief image of her guardian which inexplicably flashed through her mind, she closed her eyes quickly to dislodge the picture and answered flippantly.

'Oh, I'm not fussy—as long as he looks like a movie star, is as wealthy as Croesus, has his own private island in the South Pacific, and doesn't expect me to be at his continual beck and call!'

'In other words ...' a slight glimmer of a smile appeared in the depths of his sharp blue eyes, 'it's none of my business.'

For the first time Tracey felt a stirring of rapport towards her sister's grandfather and, in consequence, some of her tautness left her and she gave a half rueful smile in return.

'I didn't mean it that way exactly, it's just that I find it difficult to categorise. For instance, how can you utter the old cliché and say you only like all, dark and handsome men, when you know very well it's impossible to find as much enjoyment in the company of someone who's the complete opposite? I—I thought I'd found what I wanted in Boyd, but ...' she faltered, wishing she'd left the matter well alone, then pressed on determinedly, 'but then it turned out he wasn't quite the paragon I'd imagined him to be,' she shrugged.

'Thanks to Ryan?'

'Thanks to Ryan!' she agreed sardonically.

Strangely enough Justin changed the subject after that, going on to talk about the property instead and the days when their renowned stud was still in its infancy under the astute guidance of his grandfather, who had immediately recognised the worth of the then new Peppin breed of Merino with its larger frame and heavier, long-stapled fleece able to endure the sun and dust of the outback which the fine wool Merinos could not.

For all he must have been well into his seventies, Justin still had an acute mind and an able memory, and it made enthralling listening for Tracey as he recalled the good years and the bad; the droughts, the floods and the bush-fires; the depressed markets and the unbelievably buoyant ones; and in the end she was sorry when Nancy came to tell them lunch was ready and his graphic reminiscences ceased.

His accounts had at times thrilled, and at others appalled, but through a combination of the two she could in some measure grasp the dedication and fortitude needed to work this relentlessly unpredictable land, for while bounteously bestowing munificence in one season, it would just as will-ingly sow the seeds for heartbreak and disaster in the next.

On Thursday Lyn and Carol again disappeared soon after breakfast, but having been advised that they were planning to meet with Ryan during the morning, Tracey declined the offer to go with them and spent a quiet few hours bringing Nancy up to date with her brother's activities over the years he was away from his family.

After lunch she wandered out into the beautifully kept gardens and after exploring those areas being prepared for Saturday night's party, kept moving along the flagstoned path which led around the back of the homestead until it reached a gate in the cyclone wire fence on the far side. From there it was only a short walk beneath shady pepper trees to the first of the outbuildings, and finding the door open she stepped interestedly inside.

Obviously this was the stores shed, for it resembled noth-ing so much as a giant warehouse, with shelves stacked high with such an assortment of articles which varied from food-stuffs, wearing apparel, household replacements and riding tack to machinery spare parts; and that was only just what she could see from the door!

'Hello there!' Marty Bradshaw's unexpected voice made her jump as he came out of a small office she now noticed on the right of her. 'Have you come to look, or to buy?' he smiled.

'I was only planning to look, but as I've been instructed to wear a hat when riding,' she wrinkled her nose and grimaced, 'perhaps I'd better buy as well.' She looked enquiringly towards a pile of felt hats on one of the middle shelves. 'Would you have one to fit me, Marty?'

'I should think so, we have a fair range. What size do you take?'

'I wouldn't have a clue,' she laughed, following him down the aisle between tinned food on one side and jeans and shirts on the other. 'Just the one that fits best, I guess.'

Sorting through the pile to the smaller sizes on the bottom, Marty handed her two. 'Try these,' he suggested. 'I reckon one or the other should do.'

The first one she tried was inclined to perch precariously on top of her curls instead of her head and she had them both laughing as her eyes swung expressively from side to side waiting for it to slip lopsidedly over one ear, but the second felt far more secure and Tracey nodded happily. 'Yes, I'll take this one, thanks, Marty,' twirling it slowly round on one finger, her eyes lifting to his questioningly. 'Do I pay you cash for it here . . . or what?' she asked.

Marty shook his head negatively. 'Uh-uh, there's no need. I'll just open a new sheet for you and whatever you want from the store is then ticked up on your account and you can square it off at the end of each month.'

'I see,' Tracey nodded solemnly. It seemed as if another round had gone to the Alexanders after all. She had sworn to herself that she would never touch any of their money, but without a working income she wasn't going to have much choice. Her meagre savings certainly wouldn't last for the length of time she would be on Nindethana and, of course, there would be many such necessary purchases as the hat she was holding to be made during the next two and a quarter years. But one promise she would keep—and that was that when she finally left, she would be taking none of it with her!

In the meantime, though, she suddenly found herself wondering just how much it was costing the Alexanders for their chafing right of guardianship, and who better to ask than their accountant.

'How much are our shares worth in the estate anyway, Marty?' she enquired with such an indifferent curiosity that he peered at her with an incredulous grin.

'For crying out loud! What a funny girl you are!' He shook his head in disbelief. 'Don't tell me you've never even bothered to find out before now!' And in reply to her unconcerned affirmation, 'Well, at the moment I'm not too sure how much it entails altogether because, of course, I'm only in charge of the books for this station—the accountants in the holding company's offices in Sydney deal with the business assets as a whole—but we did receive advice from them last week saying that they would be forwarding initial drafts through shortly for each of you which would be in the vicinity of ...'

Tracey's mind blanked out, stupified, when he mentioned the amount and for the next few minutes she only registered what he was telling her in spasmodic snatches: '... lump sum ... Ben's share ... gathering interest all these years ... yearly intervals from now on ... never be any need for you to work again ...' until she realised he had finished and a heavy silence fallen, broken only by her own somewhat jerky breathing. In a daze she looked up at him wide-eyed. 'But that's a ... *fortune*!' she gasped, still bemused. 'In all my wildest imaginings I never expected it to be *that* much!'

'Sure is,' he concurred with an understanding smile at her expression. 'But then, right from the beginning, the family appear to have been extremely fortunate in that those who have controlled the estate have had good sound heads for business management and I suppose you could only call it an uncanny sixth sense at times as to when to buy and when to sell. I don't know whether that's a trait they've managed to acquire over the years, or whether it's just plain inbred ... I just wish I had it too!' he laughed ruefully.

Tracey's answering smile was vague, her thoughts elsewhere. My God, what a responsibility, she mused distractedly. She wasn't used to dealing with such large

amounts and, if the truth be told, she found the idea of pos-
sessing such wealth, even temporarily, more than a little
daunting. Oh, sure, it was only natural that among her
first thoughts should have been a flare of emotion knowing
that it would enable her to purchase anything she had ever
desired, but that had been immediately suppressed beneath
a weight of less eager feelings, and by no means the least
of these was the fact that although she had always considered herself as Ben Alexander's daughter in everything
but birth, she still didn't feel as if she had any right to this
unexpected inheritance. The unfair guardianship she appeared to have no choice but to accept—the fruits of Alexander labours were something else!

Deliberately pushing the disturbing thoughts aside,
Tracey moved down the aisle towards the brilliant sun-
shine that splashed through the doorway. 'And is this where
you spend your working hours?' she asked Marty over her
shoulder as she drew abreast of the glass-partitioned office
occupied by a paper-littered desk and a variety of cupboards
and filing cabinets.

'Yes, that's home from home, all right,' he laughed, stopping beside her and extending one hand invitingly towards
the opening. 'Care to come in and join me for a cup of
coffee?'

'Thank you, I'd like that,' she replied quickly, glad of
some company where she didn't need to be constantly on
her guard, and preceding him into the cluttered room where
a whirring fan overhead brought relief from the pressing
heat which had produced beads of perspiration to dampen
her hairline while they had been among the stores.

'I'm sorry it's only instant,' Marty apologised as he rum-
maged for an unchipped mug in a cupboard beside the small
sink tucked away in one corner, smiling triumphantly when
he found one and scooping a spoonful of dark brown beads
into it from a screw-top jar on the bench once he had
plugged in the refilled electric kettle.

Dropping her hat on top of an unused filing tray, Tracey
shook her head and smiled wryly. 'That doesn't matter, it's
what I'm used to,' she owned, taking the seat in front of the
desk and looking about her with interest.

At the framed photographs—some slightly askew—of magnificent-looking rams, their great horns symmetrically curved, their fleeces thick and deep, and their broad backs covered with a multitude of various coloured ribbons; a pair of deadly-looking rifles mounted the wall behind his chair, their barrels appearing blue in the light from the window; and a couple of long, coiled stockwhips hanging on a peg near the door.

Marty poured boiling water into the mugs and brought them over to the desk along with a container of sugar. 'Sorry there's no milk either,' he grinned. 'I've accustomed myself to drinking it black because I found the milk goes sour too quickly in here, even with the fan.' He looked at her enquiringly. 'I can send back to the house for some if you want it, though.'

'No, thanks, Marty, I'm fine,' Tracey waved away his offer lightly, stirring sugar into the dark liquid and then watching while he did the same with the shared spoon.

From a short inspection of the revolving bubbles in his mug, Marty's head came up and he grinned reflectively. 'From your remark about having to buy a hat, I gather Ryan hasn't given any indication yet that he's ready to abdicate his position as the boss around here,' he teased. 'Still, not even you could expect him to change overnight— it could take some time, I suppose,' with a judicious look of amusement which immediately had Tracey pulling a face at him.

'I wasn't planning on spending an aeon here,' she countered sarcastically. 'That is how long it takes to erode granite, isn't it?'

Marty threw back his head and laughed aloud, completely unperturbed by her dour gaze. 'Don't be such a sore loser, Tracey,' he commended with a chuckle. 'Didn't I warn you that Ryan would be too hard a nut to crack?'

'Who said anything about cracking him? I'd just like to lower him a peg or two, that's all.' She crossed her arms on the desk and glanced across at him with a delightfully beseeching twinkle in her eyes. 'You wouldn't have any suggestions as to how I might go about it, would you?'

He shook one finger at her vigorously. 'Stop trying to

confuse my loyalties, you little rebel,' she was ordered in mock admonishment. 'The best suggestion I can offer is that you stop trying to rock the boat, because if you don't, you're very likely to come an awful thud in the not too distant future.'

Tracey leant back in her chair, arms folded over her midriff, eyes searching the ceiling. 'Now where have I heard recommendations like that before?' she pondered mockingly before her gaze returned to his and she let out a heavily despondent sigh. 'I should've known you'd support him ... you're all the same!'

His lips twisted wryly. 'Oh, no, you don't, you're not going to con me into feeling sorry for you either!' He refused to be taken in by her air of helplessness and smiled widely at her crestfallen look of pretended reproach.

'*Marty!*' The door to the building was suddenly thrust further open with a crash as Ryan strode urgently past it. '*You* don't happen to have seen Tracey, do you? So help me, if she's gone riding without letting anyone know, I'll ...'

Whatever vehement threat he had been about to make was never uttered as he caught sight of her when he swung into the office, but there was enough savage fury in his face for Tracey to experience an inward quake at the thought of it being directed against herself. If she had ever been tempted to disregard his orders she now knew better than to contemplate such a reckless action. But as she hadn't ignored them, she felt safe to hold his smouldering gaze defiantly.

'Mmm, you'll ... what?' she prompted, one eyebrow arching insolently. 'Send me to bed without any supper?'

'No, I had something far more physical in mind,' he advised levelly, apparently not the slightest discomfited by having been proved wrong in his assumptions regarding her whereabouts. 'And you'd do well to remember that for future reference.'

Would she? Tracey's aggravation at his high-handedness grew until she could hardly contain it, but by gritting her teeth in the form of a submissive smile, she managed to put the palms of her hands together and bend her head deferentially low.

'Yes, sir! Whatever you say, sir!' she mocked impertinently. 'Would you like me to self-destruct now, sir?'

Ryan pushed his hands deep into the pockets of close-fitting denims—Tracey wondered if that was to avoid using them on her—and shook his head in a rueful gesture to Marty, who was openly smiling.

'Got any suggestions?' he drawled.

The question was so similar to that which had been put to him only shortly before that Marty's smile broadened uncontrollably, and the more so when Tracey complained, 'That's my line!' in a disappointedly proprietorial voice.

At least there was one point Tracey could find in her guardian's favour—he didn't have to have things spelt out for him, for he was quick to realise the implication in their behaviour and an acknowledging smile shaped the well-cut curve of his mouth.

'Then seeing that we appear to be so in tune today, why let our sharing stop there?' he suggested enigmatically.

Initially, Tracey had thought he was referring to the mug of coffee she had just picked up, but he merely replaced that on the desk and it wasn't until he had effortlessly bent and swung her off the chair, exchanged places, and deposited her in his lap with an inescapable arm clamped about her waist that she caught his meaning. Her chair! Apart from Marty's it was the only other in the office, and he intended they should occupy it together!

Tracey turned to glare indignantly down at him, but on finding his head so near and his eyes filled with a lazy amusement at her evident dislike for the situation, she swallowed hastily and swung her head away to begin squirming sulkily within his grasp. But not for long, because his tightening grip brought her into even closer contact with his solid physique, and rather than make what she was certain would turn out to be an undignified effort to slip free of his hold, she held herself stiffly and attempted to display just the right amount of interest in what they were saying.

Only that wasn't terribly successful either, for as their discussion lengthened Tracey became feverishly aware of Ryan's fingers moving against her side in a negligently caressing motion—just as one would absently fondle the

ears of a dog, she mused dryly, and spared a thought to
wonder if he realised what he was doing.

When it didn't cease within the next few minutes she de-
duced it must have been an unconscious action on his part,
but that judgment unfortunately in no way alleviated her
own heightened feelings at his touch which she thought
would stifle her breathing altogether if she didn't move away
soon. In desperation she leant forward to retrieve her coffee,
annoyed to find her hand unsteady when she grasped it,
but willed herself to drink it nonchalantly as if it was the
most natural thing in the world for her to be sitting where
she was.

Inwardly she berated herself roundly. What on earth was
the matter with her to allow Ryan to affect her to such an
extent? So he was attractive—that she wouldn't deny—but
surely she wasn't so adolescent as to be swayed by good
looks alone? And just because she could feel his hand on
her skin through the thin cotton of her shirt, did she have to
become all breathless and weak-kneed about it? Get a hold
of yourself, Tracey, she commanded exasperatedly, you're
letting the heat get to you! If you're not careful you'll find
yourself pleased to have been made his ward!

That did it! With that thought uppermost in her mind
it was comparatively simple to almost—though not quite—
disregard the arm still imprisoning her as she tried to fathom
ways in which to exact retribution for his uncaring dismissal
of her wishes. Outright defiance clearly wouldn't do—if this
afternoon's example was anything to judge by, Ryan Alexander would be a remorseless opponent if he was ever provoked into completely losing control of his temper. Sarcasm
usually brought forth intimidation, or else no result at all,
which at times was worse—so she couldn't see that as being
a line to pursue to any great length. Using her wide-spaced
eyes to advantage had worked when she was younger—
according to Justin—but she doubted she could be as
fortunate now. And that left ... what? Submission? Never
that, she told herself fiercely. There had to be *some* way.
It was just going to take her a little more time to discover
it, that was all, she decided indomitably.

But now that she was returning from her reverie there

was still the problem of Ryan's disconcerting touch to overcome, and as time progressed and neither of them seemed in any hurry to conclude their conversation, Tracey knew she couldn't stay within the circle of his arms any longer—not if her shallow and quickened breathing wasn't to betray her altogether, that was!

She began moving restively again, but was proud of the casualness in her tone as she murmured considerately, 'I can see you two have a lot to talk over, so if you'll excuse me, I might wander back to the house and leave you to it,' and made a tentative movement to rise to her feet.

'Sorry to have left you out of it, honey, but as I was here I thought I'd get these matters settled with Marty,' came Ryan's bland reply, without his relinquishing his grip one iota. 'Stay around a bit longer and I'll walk back with you.'

'There's no need—I won't get lost,' she half laughed shakily, addressing her remarks to the doorway rather than look at him, and beginning to panic in case he wouldn't release her. 'And—and—oh, there's Nancy now!' on a shuddering sigh of relief as she saw the older woman pass the window. 'I—I want to have a word with her about something before I forget,' she rushed on inventively, scrambling to her feet immediately she felt Ryan's hold slackening, hastily returning her mug to the table, and bidding farewell to Marty all at the same time.

'Here!' Ryan's voice reached out to her just as she reached the door. 'Don't forget your hat,' he called as she turned back enquiringly—she could afford to act more naturally now that she was free—but when he tossed it accurately across to her outstretched hand their eyes met briefly and Tracey bit at her lip in anguish as the heat of embarrassment washed over her.

He knew! Never had she been so certain of anything in her life. He knew all too well what he'd been doing, and more humiliating still, he knew the effect it had had on her! She could read it in the provocative depths of those blue eyes and the indolent tilt of that disturbing mouth.

It took a little while for her to regain some control of her rioting emotions, but when she did it was to breathe in deeply and acknowledge his action with a carefully in-

souciant, 'Thanks,' before contriving to saunter jauntily
from the room in an effort to prove to him how wrong his
premises had been.

The homestead was really beginning to come alive by
Saturday afternoon, for during the preceding twenty-four
hours there had been a steady stream of guests arriving—
many of those with the furthest distances to travel having
elected to fly in the day before in order to be refreshed and
relaxed when it came time for the party to get under way.

Most of these were relatives, and included among their
number were Nancy's husband and Carol's father, Clive,
as well as his two sons, Ross and Lance, both as yet un-
married, and at twenty-five and twenty-two respectively,
were an easygoing pair who greeted their reunited cousins
with every evidence of pleasure and promptly joined their
sister as unofficial guides and companions.

With the advent of such an influx of strangers, Tracey
had been worried that Lyn might revert to her old shy and
painfully timid self, but it seemed that a week spent in the
gregarious Carol's company had, if not completely brought
her out of her shell, at least made her more willing to attempt to participate in any conversation rather than remain
an apprehensive observer only.

Although it had been a particularly warm day the five of
them had decided upon the tennis courts as the perfect way
to escape the general hustle and bustle in the homestead
after lunch as more friends and acquaintances of long standing began arriving; some braving the dust-strewn roads but
more preferring to make use of the convenient airstrip,
until it resembled a miniature airfield with the many and
varied planes positioned around it.

The now familiar whine as yet another aircraft circled
the homestead had them all involuntarily staring skywards
when they were taking a breather after a hard-fought game
of mixed doubles wherein Tracey and Lance had challenged
Ross and Carol and only scraped to a win by the skin of their
teeth, and it was Carol who excitedly broke the silence when
the registration signs became discernible.

'That's Aunty Rita and Uncle Owen!' she exclaimed,

squinting upwards against the glare. 'Frank'll be with them and that evens up the numbers. Come on, Lyn, we'll go and get him.'

'Don't you think it would be better if you waited for them to land, and drive over to the house first?' Ross quizzed dryly, stretching long, tanned legs before him and helping himself to an icy can of beer from the cooler chest they had brought down to the courts with them. 'I hardly think you'll get him here any faster, even if you run all the way to the strip.'

Carol pulled a face at him, but subsided into a wicker chair gratefully anyway. 'I suppose so. At least it gives me more time to get my breath back after that game.' She eased her short pleated white dress away from her back and pushed perspiration damp hair away from her forehead. 'Do you know if anyone mentioned if Noeleen and Dennis were coming?' she now asked, with an informative, 'That's Frank's older sister and her husband—they've got three of the most gorgeous little girls you've ever seen,' to Tracey and Lyn.

Ross turned enquiring eyes to where Lance stood beside the cooler, but only received a non-committal shrug by way of reply, and then lifted his own shoulders indifferently. 'How on earth would we know? You're the one who's been here all week with Mum. Why didn't you ask her?' Dark brown eyes twinkled incorrigibly. 'Why? Still feel in need of Noeleen's protection from the merry widow, do you?' he teased.

'Huh!' Carol wrinkled her nose disparagingly. 'Merry's right! Poor Philip was hardly cold in his grave before she was back here drooling over Ryan!'

'Oh, come on, Caro,' he censured lightly. 'Just because Lana inadvertently hurt your tender feelings once, there's no reason to malign the woman for the rest of her life.'

'Malign her? I'd like to murder her!' Carol retorted heatedly, and Tracey's eyes widened in astonishment at her intensity. It wasn't like Carol to get so worked up about anything. 'And it wasn't inadvertent either! Just because she smiles sweetly and butters up your ego, it doesn't mean she's the same to everyone else, Ross!' she informed him tartly.

Tracey's eyes swung worriedly to Ross, waiting for him to retaliate with a sharp criticism, but it was like beating your head against a brick wall trying to quarrel with Carol's good-natured brother, and he merely took another mouthful from his can and grinned unconcernedly.

'You're just cut up because she's showing an interest in your beloved Ryan. You've idolised him ever since you were knee-high to a grasshopper and now it's reached the stage where you'd find fault with any female who happened to look sideways at him. Face facts, Caro,' he urged tolerantly. 'Ryan's not about to seek your approval for whom he sees, so you may as well get used to it. As for Lana—well, don't you think you might be building mountains out of mole-hills over one thoughtless remark made years ago?'

Carol swung her racquet in an imaginary serve and then ran her fingers lightly over the strings, sighing. 'Stop reading me homespun little homilies, brother dear,' she demurred ruefully. 'And don't try and make it sound as if I've got the biggest crush of all time on Ryan either, because I haven't! Sure, I like him a lot—who doesn't?' and it was only due to the strongest self-discipline that Tracey refrained from raising her arm to register one dissenting vote. 'But to my mind, Lana Renfrew is an A1, world-beating bitch and no matter what you say you'll never manage to convince me otherwise!'

'Hell's bells, kiddo, watch your language!' a grinning Lance suddenly entered the conversation. 'Them's awful strong words for a little thing like you, and Mum'll have your hide if she ever hears you!' he warned.

'Nothing surer,' corroborated Ross smiling. 'So I suggest we have a change of subject. How about you go and round up Frank—he should be at the house by now—and we'll have a few more sets of tennis, eh?'

Her temper subsiding as fast as it had risen, Carol dropped her racquet on to a chair and nodded agreeably. 'Okay. Coming, Lyn?'

As the two of them left the courts and headed across the green lawns, Ross leant his head further over the back of the chair to call, 'And see if you can find Ryan while you're there too. He owes me a re-match after the thrashing he gave me last time. I feel as if this afternoon might be *the* time for me to turn the tables for once.'

'That'll be the day!' Carol's laughing taunt floated back to them before she and Lyn ducked beneath the drooping branches of a bauhinia and disappeared from view.

Ross shook his head cheerfully and smiled across to where Tracey was pouring herself a glass of chilled fruit juice. 'Don't pay too much mind to Caro,' he recommended indulgently. 'She's had this thing about Lana ever since she was in her early teens—I can't even remember now what originally caused it—but for the last few years, every time the family's had a get-together down here, I rather think she's been loading the rifle and letting Noeleen fire the bullets at Lana because she's well aware they didn't hit it off that well when they were at school together. With any luck, now that you and Lyn have arrived, and being closer to her age group, it will give her something else to think about and, at the same time, make her realise how misplaced her dislike has been. I've always found Lana to be okay, but if she and Ryan do get together permanently then I wouldn't like to see young Caro hurt, because Ryan's not the sort to stand any outside interference in his personal affairs—and that includes well-intentioned kindred meddling as well,' he concluded succinctly.

'I see,' Tracey relayed her comprehension thoughtfully.

Although she found Ross's brotherly concern rather endearing, on the matter of Lana Renfrew she decided to reserve judgment. Admittedly, it was hard to imagine the virile Ryan Alexander being interested in any female who dared to be anything but a model of perfection, she mused sarcastically, but conversely it did strike her a little strange that neither Carol nor the unknown Noeleen could take to her. Ross could perhaps have been right when he said that after having hero-worshipped her cousin for so long, his sister now felt antagonistic towards anyone who might alter their camaraderie—situations like that did occur —but what of Noeleen? With a husband and three children, surely the same couldn't be said to apply to her? No, Tracey

pondered, she would wait until she had met this—what had
Ross called her, the merry widow?—for herself. At best,
in view of Carol's outburst, it was an intriguing description!

Once the two girl's returned with the twenty-four-year-
old, laughing-eyed, devil-may-care Frank in tow, however,
there was no time left for Tracey to dwell on the absent
Lana's virtues or vices, for it quickly became a matter of
returning either verbal or sporting volleys and smashes—
and sometimes both together—until they had to cry quits
earlier than anticipated because no one visualised being able
to see the night out otherwise, so energetic had been the
games. Of Ryan there was no sign as Carol and Lyn hadn't
been able to locate him in the house when they went to find
Frank, and although they had left a message for him to
join them when he returned, no such appearance eventuated,
and Tracey couldn't make up her mind whether she felt
reprieved or deprived by his absence.

CHAPTER SEVEN

THE blinding fiery flare of the sun was so low on the horizon that its last crimson rays were encroaching far on to the verandah outside her bedroom by the time Tracey had finished dressing in a pair of lime green flared slacks with a matching lime, black and white broad-striped top; applied a silver-green shadow to her eyelids, thickened her already long lashes with mascara, and covered her soft lips with a bronze lipstick. Seeing the lightly tanned skin beneath the auburn hair, not for the first time in her life she thanked her lucky stars for a creamy skin instead of the less fortunate milky white one of a normal redhead.

A knock on her door had her swinging to face it wonderingly, but after only a moment's hesitation it was pushed open and Lyn and Carol slipped inside one after the other. Carol immediately pulled a mock grimace of disappointment as her eyes flickered over her own crisp pink and white checked pit-suit and then over Lyn's trim navy and green outfit.

'And we thought we looked good!' she complained with a grin. 'Will you take a look at her?'

Lyn's face assumed a lugubrious expression. 'What are you grousing about?' she asked jokingly of the girl beside her. 'This is only your first time—you wait until she's been doing it to you for a few years, then you'll really have something to worry over.'

Shades of Ryan! Tracey could feel the dismay growing within her. Was it really so hard for Lyn to follow in the footsteps of a prettier elder sister? Tracey wasn't vain by any means, but she wasn't blind either, and there had been plenty of the opposite sex only too willing to comment favourably upon her features throughout the years for her not to be aware of the fact, but until now it had never occurred to her that Lyn might feel disadvantaged because of it. She opened her mouth to speak, but Lyn beat her to it.

'At least there's always a supply of good-looking men around the house, so I suppose that's some consolation,' she laughed teasingly up at her sister.

'Oh, good!' exclaimed Carol with exaggerated elation, her eyes flashing cheekily. 'Does that mean we get to share the leftovers?'

Some of Tracey's dismay began to dissipate. If Lyn could joke about it then maybe the situation wasn't quite as bad as she had imagined, and a wry smile crooked her lips.

'Cut it out, you two,' she ordered amiably. 'Or you'll have me as self-conscious as I don't know what before the evening's even begun.'

'Okay, we'll take pity on you,' Carol acceded, but promptly followed it with an unrepentant, 'We wouldn't want to put you off balance—that might be to our detriment in the long run.'

Tracey pointed dramatically to the door. 'One more word and out you go,' she threatened the pair of them with a grin. 'At this rate I'll never be finished.'

'I thought you already were,' commented Carol in surprise as she and Lyn made themselves comfortable in matching upholstered chairs and prepared to wait.

Lifting one leg of her slacks, Tracey waved a slim unshod foot in the air. 'I still have to dig out a pair of sandals yet,' she said, padding over to the wardrobe and delving into its capacious insides, 'and I was also considering putting my hair up instead of leaving it loose,' as she withdrew a pair of wedge heels, their dainty straps of black patent leather shining, and slid her feet into them.

'Oh, no, Tracey, leave it like it is,' Lyn exhorted earnestly. 'It's far too pretty to be pulled into such a severe style as you usually use when you put it up. Leave it loose,' she advised again with a round-eyed look as if amazed at her own temerity in counselling her sister on any subject.

'Yes, I agree, it looks nice that way,' Carol added her weight to the deliberation.

'Two to one against,' laughed Tracey. 'All right, this is the way it stays,' and she ran a final comb through the shining curls.

The sound of footsteps and men's voices could be heard

as a group passed down the hall and Lyn nodded her head towards the door. 'It's like Pitt Street on a Friday afternoon out there,' she smiled nervously. 'I've never seen so many people in one house before!'

'Oh, that's nothing,' Carol grinned. 'You should have seen it when Glen and Pam were married—that weekend it *was* crowded! We had to split everyone up—the women had the bedrooms and the men were relegated to sleeping on the verandahs—it was the only way to fit them all in.'

'Heavens!' Just to think of it had Lyn becoming more apprehensive by the minute and without giving her more time to enlarge it within her mind, Tracey winked encouragingly and suggested, 'Come on then, let's take the plunge and get it over and done with. The intros are always the worst.'

Eventually, once they had made their way along the verandah and down on to the gently sloping lawn where coloured lights and lanterns outlined tall figures and cast subtle shadows over the colourful array of clothing being worn, it was Justin who imperiously claimed their attention and took the honours upon himself to make Tracey and Lyn known to the multitude of guests who had only arrived that day and they didn't as yet know.

Of these it was mainly the closer relations, such as Frank's parents, Rita and Owen; his elder brother Kent, and fiancée Sheryl; and, of course, the interesting Noeleen and her husband, Dennis, who caught Tracey's undivided attention—it was an impossible task to attempt to remember the names of more than a handful of the others present— while overall there was a general feeling of conviviality, the muted sounds of conversation and laughter, the clinking of glasses, and the mouthwatering aroma of roasting pork and charcoal grilled steaks permeating the warm air.

During the social round of introductions, Tracey's gaze had kept wandering—involuntarily most times—searching for one particularly outstanding figure among the crowd— her guardian! When he did finally appear her eyes linked with his for only a few seconds before passing compulsively on to his companion. This then must be Lana Renfrew! As if on cue, Carol's sharply indrawn breath as she too caught sight of them was enough to confirm the supposition.

Tracey's mind rapidly stored information like a computer. About thirty, maybe a little more; perfection in the shape all right, and the expensive form-moulding red lace outfit seeing that every curve was shown to advantage; not very tall, a good two or three inches less than Tracey's five foot five; long, blue-black hair piled high into a complicated coronet of curls and whirls; a beautifully preserved white skin which obviously wasn't allowed into the sunlight unprotected; and a model face which would have sent any professional photographer into raptures at a single glance. Unaccountably Tracey's heart sank. She should have known nothing but a flawless beauty would meet Ryan Alexander's exacting standards! Not that she cared one way or the other, mind you! It was just the principle involved that was causing her so much aggravation!

'Ah, there he is.' Justin's steps quickened, not needing his cane now that he had been dissuaded from riding for the past five days, and he headed unswervingly towards his grandson.

'If she has another dig at me tonight, I swear I'll ... I'll punch her right in the eye!' muttered Carol direfully out of the corner of her mouth as they lagged a little behind her grandfather.

Tracey grinned, imagining the furore. 'Is that what she does? Pick on you?' she whispered back.

Carol grunted disgustedly. 'That's a nice way of putting it—ridicule would be more accurate!' she grated through clenched teeth. 'But she always does it, oh, so sweetly, as if she's really trying to be helpful in letting you know that you're a trifle overweight, or that your hair doesn't really suit you the way you're wearing it, or the colour of the dress you're wearing just isn't you! It mightn't be so bad if she made her spiteful little comments in private—but she doesn't—it's always in front of everyone so you end up feeling about this big!' holding up a thumb and forefinger half an inch apart. She let out her breath heavily. 'I hate her, Tracey, I really do! She's the fly in the ointment for every party we come to down here and, just for once, I wish I could find some way to put *her* nose out of joint instead

of it always being the other way around,' she sighed despondently.

'Then why is she invited? Surely others can see what's
going on?'

'Well, she's invited—or invites herself, I'm never sure
which it is—because she's Philip Renfrew's widow. He and
Ryan were always the best of mates until Philip was killed
last year in a polo accident. I have heard talk that she only
married him in a fit of pique because she couldn't get Ryan
to come up to scratch in the first place. Looks as if she's
having more success this time, though,' she interposed
acidly. 'As for the others—well, you heard Ross this afternoon. She's as sweet as pie to the men—it's the members of
her own sex she doesn't like—although, now I come to think
of it . . .' she paused and looked to where Justin was some
three or four feet ahead of them, 'I sometimes wonder if
Grandfather isn't awake to her. Of course, with him being
too old to catch her interest, she doesn't particularly bother
to go out of her way to be overly nice to him, and on a few
occasions I've caught him watching her with a certain look
in his eye that, if he looked at one of the family in the same
way, would mean decided *t*-trouble!' she accentuated the
first letter expressively. 'Whether he's holding his silence in
case Ryan has any definite intentions in that direction, I
don't know. The only thing I am sure of is that up until
now, there's only been Noeleen and myself to do battle with
the very . . . merry . . . widow!'

Arched brows lifted high in interrogation. 'By that, am I
to assume you're proposing I join your forces too?' Tracey
queried dryly.

Suddenly the younger girl grinned. 'You won't be given
any choice,' she gurgled. 'One look at you and dear Lana
will consider she has an arch-rival and immediately throw
the first of her poisonous darts.' She chuckled again. 'Welcome to the firing line, comrade!'

There was no time for Tracey to reply to this descriptive
piece of banter, or even to dismiss as absolutely ludicrous
the idea of her constituting a rival for Lana Renfrew, for
as they joined Justin and the couple by the steps he began
to speak and immediately names and expected responses had

been exchanged, continued loquaciously, 'Although I don't imagine she would remember you, but seeing that you're so much older I expect you can still recall when Tracey lived here before, Lana, eh?'

Which Tracey had to admit wasn't the most tactful way to put it, and she could have sworn she heard a delighted noise escape Carol's lips somewhere to the left of her. Apparantly Lana didn't consider it sensitive either, for her dark eyes positively glared at him before she managed to veil them and put a tone of amazement in her voice.

'Of course! The little redhead who was always under our feet and Ryan had to take with him so we could get on with our games.'

You're being told you were a nuisance, Tracey, she thought amusedly to herself, and waited for the next instalment as Lana sent her a penetrating stare before smiling possessively up at the man beside her. 'That's one of the things I've always admired about you, darling ... your tolerance in accepting surplus responsibility.'

For the first time Ryan spoke, although his eyes were fixed lazily on Tracey and not the woman beside him. 'A family should always support its members, Lana,' he replied blandly, reminding Tracey of the instance when he had said the same to her and she had disrupted such a family connection so vigorously.

'Exactly, darling,' Lana almost purred with satisfaction. 'A *family* should—I couldn't agree with you more.'

With very little effort Tracey decided it would become extremely easy to dislike Lana Renfrew intensely, and could sympathise with Carol if this was a sample of the irritating, pin-pricking treatment she had been subjected to over the years, but in her own case she wasn't about to accept it lying down and she passed back a look as guileless as the older woman's had been malicious.

'Oh, goodness, you've echoed my very words,' she exclaimed ingenuously. 'Do you find it annoying too when outsiders can't mind their own business?' with innocently wide eyes.

Lana's eyes narrowed grimly and then her lashes fluttered becomingly as she gazed archly at Ryan and deliberately misconstrued, 'I think your—er—ward, is trying to tell you —not very skilfully, I must admit,' with a vinegary smile of condescension, 'that she wants out, darling. I expect she's missing all those swinging parties which seem vital to her generation,' her mouth drooped with admirable commiseration.

'But naturally,' Tracey wasn't averse to swiftly agreeing, her taunting eyes challenging her guardian rather than his girl-friend. 'I mean to say, how could one possibly be expected to get through life if there isn't at least one sex orgy a week, bucketfuls of beer to wallow in, and an unlimited supply of Mary Jane to drag on every few hours?' she mocked. 'It's true—you've guessed!' she confessed sensationally. 'I'm hooked!'

'You will be ... by a good, hard left ... if you're not careful,' Ryan threatened lazily. 'I doubt if you'd know a reefer of marijuana if you saw it, and the only person you might be fooling with your play-acting is your grandfather,' whose countenance was wearing a decidedly horrified expression. 'So just cool it, honey, before you really put a match to the fireworks, hmm?' he goaded infuriatingly, and began moving slowly across the lawn to the barbecue area with a gloating Lana clinging monopolistically to his arm.

Tracey turned her back on them nonchalantly, but inwardly fuming. Oh, yes, it was all right for his girl-friend to call her a nuisance, an outsider, and imply that her morals might be somewhat tarnished, but any attempts by her to retaliate—even mildly—were obviously to be frowned upon! At least there was some consolation. Lana Renfrew certainly wasn't the acme of perfection she appeared on the surface—she had a malevolent tongue and evidently wouldn't hesitate to use it on anyone who displeased her.

Suddenly an unexpected thought flashed across Tracey's mind, a germ of an idea which she hugged to herself delightedly, spinning around again to watch consideringly as Ryan and Lana stopped to talk to a couple standing beside the barbecue. *Was* that the way to defeat her guardian? She wondered pensively. Unfortunately, it wasn't to be until a few more hours had passed before she could return to that

tantalising question, because Justin was now fragmenting
her thoughts with demands to be assured that she had indeed only been joking with regard to her previous mocking
confession, and it eventually took all of Lyn's persuasive
powers as well to convince him of the fact.

'Then why say it?' he queried heavily as they too retraced
their steps towards long, covered tables which were now
groaning under the weight of an unbelievable array and
assortment of food. 'Is that the type of person you wanted us
to think you were?'

'No, not really,' Tracey shrugged defensively. 'It was just
a spur-of-the-moment reaction to Lana's comments, I
guess.'

Justin raised his hand to acknowledge some friendly greetings and then, 'You didn't care for Lana Renfrew?' he
probed.

That was putting it mildly! A sideways glance from beneath long, curling lashes followed and Tracey wrinkled her
nose with distaste. 'You could say that,' she acceded.

'Hear, hear!' muttered Carol expressively from Tracey's
other side.

'What about you, Lynette?' Justin now enquired of the
youngest member of the foursome. 'Did you take exception
to Lana's remarks too?'

Never one to readily comment upon friends or acquaintances, Lyn sort of hunched away from the question for a
time and only offered, 'Well, she did—um—seem to be a
little ... caustic, didn't she?' in a conciliatory tone after
some deliberation.

'In that case, it would appear as though we're all in agreement, wouldn't it?' Justin's blue eyes twinkled surprisingly
and incorrigibly. 'Personally, I can't stand the woman—
never could,' he revealed gruffly.

'Then why didn't you say so before?' Carol immediately
demanded to know. 'All these years Noeleen and I have been
putting up with her snide little hints and you've never said
a word to indicate how you felt!'

Justin chuckled shamelessly. 'Mainly because I considered the pair of you weren't doing too badly by yourselves with your own brand of retribution and there didn't

seem to be any need for me to interfere. Besides,' he flexed his shoulders with a sigh, 'I'm getting too old to be embroiled in such matters—you youngsters can fight it out between yourselves. But just remember,' he gave them all a long, level look, 'I'm backing the Alexanders for a win!'

The three young voices raised in merriment drew considerable attention from the other guests—including a watchful glance from Ryan and a decidedly contemptuous sneer from Lana, noted Tracey—but it wasn't long before they were engulfed by a confidence-building crowd of males and were being ushered to seats at one of the many tables arranged beneath the spreading branches of a trio of trees.

'Tucker's ready,' beamed Frank as he retrieved two large plates from the table and Ross prepared to pour the wine. 'What will you have, Tracey? A sample of everything to begin with?'

'Good heavens, no!' she protested with a laugh. Having already seen the amount and variety of the food being cooked she knew that even a small portion of each would probably be enough to feed her for a week, and as well as that there were bowls piled high with salads, dishes of cold meats and platters of cheese, together with a mouth-watering display of desserts already amassed on the table in front of her. 'No, just a steak with pineapple, banana, and a side salad will do, thanks, Frank,' she smiled.

'You're sure?' He frowned his disbelief at such a small appetite and went off shaking his head in wonderment after she had again laughingly confirmed her wants.

Soon the table was filled to capacity as the men returned with brimming plates and everyone prepared to do justice to the deliciously cooked victuals. It was, in the main, a collection of Alexander cousins and partners who occupied their particular table—excluding Ryan, of course, Tracey noticed—and with so many present it wasn't surprising that the meal progressed with a great deal of talking and laughter.

As they had never been accustomed to large family gatherings, it was a new experience for Tracey and Lyn to witness the easy familiarity with which their relatives all treated each other, and after a time they found themselves

unconsciously accepting similar roles when they were included in conversations with such lighthearted fraternis-
ation.

As soon as everyone had eaten their fill, Mrs Gray and her
reinforced army of bright-eyed house girls began clearing
away the debris and, at Nancy's request, Ross and Lance
set up the stereo on the verandah in order that any couples
who wished to dance could do so, and as the suggestion was
greeted with great acclaim it wasn't long before a vast
number of youthful figures could be seen gyrating to the
sounds of the current Top Ten.

In the interval which followed half a dozen energetic
sessions of the Bump, Nancy herself renewed the selection
of records on the spindle and immediately the first had
dropped on to the turntable and the dreamy music issued
forth, there was a chorus of, 'That's more like it,' and, 'Now
that you can dance to,' from some of the older guests as
they too rose to their feet to join in.

Sitting back, relaxed, Tracey raised her rounded glass
to her lips and surveyed the dreamlike setting over its rim.
With no need to be restricted to the confines of an handker-
chief-sized dance floor, the couples were taking advantage of
the occasion and moving wherever they wished. Some,
loverlike, beneath the concealing fronds of the willows by
the creek; others seeming to float ethereally over the close-
clipped lawns; older guests preferring the stability of the
wide flagstoned paths; and still more making use of the
darkened verandahs surrounding the homestead.

As her eyes ranged again over the dancers on the lawn,
Ryan and Lana suddenly whirled into her line of vision—the
engaging smile curving his mouth causing Tracey to in-
comprehensibly experience a moment of pure cattiness
against the red-garbed girl in his arms—and her thoughts
abruptly returned to their earlier glimmerings.

Being only human, she wasn't above wanting to give Lana
a set-down in retaliation for her corrosive hints, and if Ryan
had considered it commendable to disillusion her in respect
to Boyd's fallibility, then why shouldn't she reciprocate by
doing the same for him with regard to Lana? A mischievous
sparkle had her eyes shining greenly. In the meantime, of

course, it was to be hoped that, even if she wasn't completely victorious, Ryan would have felt the sharp edge of Lana's poisonous tongue enough times to recompense Tracey in some small degree for his obstructiveness in her life!

During the next change of record Tracey watched absently as the two persons foremost in her thoughts returned to the table they were sharing with Justin and some family friends, silently agreeing with Carol's passionately uttered, 'Good lord, doesn't it make you sick? She looks just like a cat with a bowl of cream!' as there was absolutely no need to ask to whom she was referring.

Noeleen slid quickly on to the chair at Tracey's right hand when Frank vacated it in order to dance with Lyn and while Dennis, her husband, refilled their glasses from the bottle in the freshly replenished ice bucket.

'Why don't you split them up?' she grinned, her dark brown eyes twinkling.

'Split who up?' Tracey frowned.

'Ryan and Lana, of course, who else? Go and ask him to dance,' Noeleen prompted.

As much as the first idea fitted in with her plans, Tracey couldn't go along with the second. 'I can't do that!' she half laughed.

'Of course you can—he's your guardian, isn't he? Who has a better right?'

'That's not the point,' Tracey protested with a smile. 'It's not up to me to ask him to dance—it's supposed to be the other way round.'

'Oh, rot!' Noeleen dismissed the suggestion carelessly. 'Women have now got equal pay, equal rights and equal opportunities. So make the most of yours and go and ask Ryan to dance with you,' she urged. 'I'm dying to see the look on Lana's face when you do.'

'*You* go and ask him, then,' Tracey laughed outright. 'That way you'll have a better view.'

'I would if I thought it would have any effect, but you could hardly classify me as competition ... not only am I a cousin, but I'm married as well. No, it's got to be you— you're the only one of us who's not related to him,' she

pointed out logically. 'Isn't that right, Carol?' she sought
confirmation from the girl who had moved up to take the
seat on Tracey's other side and was avidly listening to
everything being said.

'That's right,' Carol nodded knowledgeably, and added
her own plea, 'Go on, Tracey, go and ask him.'

'No.' Tracey shook her head in humorous exasperation.
'Think what a feather in Lana's cap it would be and, more
important from my point of view, how humiliating if he
should refuse.'

Noeleen's certain, 'He wouldn't do that!' and Carol's
just as positive, 'Of course he wouldn't!' came instan-
taneously, but for all their assertions Tracey wasn't satisfied.
If either of them asked him, maybe not ... but if she asked
him, it was more than probable!

'Surely there must be someone else here you can ask—
not all the single girls can be related to him,' she tried to
shift their focus away from herself.

'But they don't happen to have your looks,' Carol vetoed
her tactics dryly. 'Besides, with your colour hair we figure
you're not the type to passively forgive and forget dear
Lana's cutting comments. You would like to see her discomfited for a change, wouldn't you?' she grinned disarmingly.

Tracey sighed defeatedly. Yes, that she would very much
like to behold, but by inviting Ryan to dance she would be
placing herself in an extremely vulnerable position where
it would be all too easy to have the tables turned against her,
and although Carol and Noeleen's prime object was the
besting of Lana, that consideration occupied only a small
part in Tracey's overall scheme—the main element being
the amount of annoyance she could inflict upon their own
cousin. But if she didn't take this opportunity, when was she
going to start her campaign?

'All right, I'll do it!' she threw up her hands in surrender. 'But if he refuses, I'll ... well, I don't know quite
what I'll do,' her lips twisted wryly. 'Probably crawl into
some dark corner and die of embarrassment, I expect!'

'He won't refuse—you'll see,' promised Noeleen
bracingly, while Carol chuckled her delight and immediately

pressured, 'Go on then, ask him now before they change the records again. It won't have nearly the same effect on Lana if you're dancing three feet away from him.'

'I can't at the moment,' Tracey grinned in a rather relieved manner and took a long swallow from her glass. 'He's dancing with your mother.'

Carol and Noeleen had been too intent on persuading Tracey to take up their suggestion to be bothered watching the dancers, but now both their heads swung to investigate the couples moving in the subdued lamplight.

'And I suppose my mother will be next,' forecast Noeleen disappointedly. 'Oh, well, it can't be helped, I suppose. We'll just have to make sure you're there in time to claim the one after, Tracey,' she proposed complacently.

'Thanks!' Tracey's eyes opened wide in mock gratitude. 'I'm beginning to feel like the fatted calf being prepared for slaughter.' And wasn't that the truth! 'You don't happen to have any other schemes in mind which call for me to put my head in a noose, do you?'

'Not yet ... but we'll certainly give it some thought if you'd like us to,' teased Carol, and received a threatening look from Tracey in return.

'Don't you dare!' she ordered, not altogether jokingly. 'I think I'm getting cold feet as it is.'

This statement promptly had the other girls murmuring words of encouragement which Tracey really only listened to with half an ear because she was too preoccupied with the sensation of quaking apprehension that had taken hold of her stomach to pay them much attention. Unfortunately, the feeling didn't diminish during the remainder of Ryan's dance with Nancy, and although with Dennis's return to the seat beside his wife the conversation reverted to general topics, it couldn't relieve Tracey's tension, and by the time Noeleen's mother's accurately predicted dance with Ryan was concluded, she was anything but calm and composed.

On the receiving end of surreptitious digs in the ribs from Carol, and enthusiastic eye signals from Noeleen, Tracey took one last mouthful from her glass, placed it firmly on the table, and with a resigned sigh pushed back her chair and rose gracefully to her feet. Knowing it would be her

undoing if she looked down into the two expectant faces
watching her, she determinedly kept her eyes to the front,
ran suddenly damp hands over slender hips, and walked
purposely around the side of the table.

That, she was to discover ruefully, had been the easy
part! The homestead grounds had never seemed so huge,
and before she was even halfway across she was wishing
herself anywhere but where she was, for Ryan had begun to
watch her approach with all the dedication a scientist might
apply to his microscope. To Tracey it seemed as if she was
moving in slow motion; giving her ample time to see Lana
lean across the arm of her chair to say something to Ryan
and then, on finding his interest elsewhere, following the
direction of his gaze, eyes narrowing and lips thinning
hostilely when they encountered the nearing figure; and
Ryan's electrifying blue surveillance which never wavered
for one nerve-racking footstep.

The nearer she came the more her stomach churned, but
in a valiant effort to ignore it she forced a breezy smile to her
lips and a lighthearted swing to her walk. Halting some few
feet from where Ryan was seated at the head of the table, she
swallowed convulsively and linked her fingers tightly together.

'May I please have this dance?' she requested huskily,
striving to keep her smile in place, and totally unaware of
the winsome supplication contained in her wide eyes.

Ryan eased back in his chair leisurely. 'Is that a request
for my permission ... or a personal invitation?' he drawled.

If it hadn't been for Lana's mocking derisive snigger—a
humiliating sound she purposely didn't bother to disguise—
Tracey might have let fly with the condemnatory, 'Oh, go
to hell!' which rose within her and promptly fled ignomi-
niously. Instead she steeled herself to stand her ground, the
flickering movement of her tongue creating an enticing
sheen on soft lips which she curved into a tantalising
smile.

'An invitation, of course,' she gave voice to her reply in a
sensuously warm tone. 'Do you accept?'

His dark head dipped in a wry salute. 'How could I refuse?' he quizzed laconically, turning to excuse himself to

a clearly peeved Lana who said something sharply in return, but what it was Tracey had no idea, for she was too conscious of the deeply relieved breath sighing between her own lips. At least he hadn't refused—that was something!

The feel of his hand on the skin of her back through the thin material of her top sent shivers down Tracey's spine when Ryan took her in his arms, and for a time she found it necessary to concentrate undividedly upon matching her steps to his in order to give her emotional balance an opportunity to regain its perspective, although she still couldn't quite refrain from giving Lana a triumphantly challenging glance just before they waltzed away from the vicinity of the table.

'Am I allowed to enquire just what all this is in aid of?'

The sardonically spoken words brought Tracey back to her surroundings with a jolt, a rosy colour of dismay climbing creamy cheeks as she momentarily thought he might have witnessed that last smug look, then shaking the idea away and staring upwards innocuously.

'As you're my guardian I didn't think you would object to my exercising the prerogative of a ladies' choice,' she dimpled outrageously before assuming a downcast expression and enquiring mournfully, 'Would you rather I hadn't?'

If anything his arm tightened, pulling her closer against the warm, hard length of him. 'Now why would you think that?' he mocked lightly. 'That smile of yours is quite devastating when you care to use it—as you probably already know—and I'm as susceptible as the next man.'

Strong reservations prevented Tracey from believing that remark, but she slanted him a gleaming look from the cover of dusky lashes anyway. 'Promise ...?' she quipped audaciously, and found herself on the receiving end of a laughing smile that sent wild incoherent signals throughout her nervous system and nearly had her legs buckling under her when Ryan stopped moving to cup his hands about her face, his disturbing lips so near to her own.

'I don't know what you're up to, honey, but one thing I will give you ... you sure know how to go about it,' he relayed ironically.

'I—why should you think I was—was up to something?'

Tracey faltered jerkily, cursing herself mutely for allowing him to gain an advantage through an overwhelming but intrinsic masculinity, which continually rendered her powerless to rationally control her own responses.

'Aren't you?'

'Of course not!' She tried to put some conviction into her denial, but owing to the dryness of her throat only succeeded in sounding slightly doubtful. 'You just like to think the worst of me, that's all!' turning defence into attack.

The magnetic blue eyes above her filled with a lazy kind of challenge. 'And now you're trying to correct that impression, hmm?' as one thumb smoothed its way over softly provocative lips.

'Something like that,' she shrugged, willing to clutch at any face-saving straw at such a time of vulnerability.

'How like?'

Tracey's eyes suddenly lost the grey they had been sheltering behind and sparkled greenly again. 'That's for me to know, and you to find out,' she taunted with a half laugh, determined to recover her previous nonchalance.

Strong white teeth showed in a rueful grin, one hand encircling her back firmly as they resumed their dancing. 'Don't worry, honey, I will,' he assured her confidently. 'But in the meantime, I'd suggest you keep a close eye on your brew, little witch, in case it spills over and catches you in its toils instead.'

Which was quite a possibility, Tracey had to concur, because it appeared that Carol and Noeleen's part of the scheme was working admirably. Lana evidently wasn't pleased with the situation and her eyes were reaching out like a pair of dark laser beams bent on destruction. If looks could kill ...! Tracey gulped and hoped not all of Lana's frustrations were to be vented in her direction—surely she would manage to save some for Ryan! If she didn't? Tracey refused to consider the consequences, for it would mean the reason for her participation in the plan was doomed and she would be back where she started, having to rely on defiant unco-operativeness against a seemingly unbeatable opponent!

On the fading notes of stringed instruments the music

came to a finish and catching at Tracey's hand, Ryan began pulling her along beside him. 'As we're the closest, it looks as if we've been elected to change the records,' he said, opening the screen door and allowing her to precede him on to the for once deserted verandah. 'Any suggestions as to what we should play now?'

Tracey hunched her shoulders lightly. 'More of the same, I guess, then everyone's happy.'

'You sort through those, then,' he indicated a pile of extended and long-playing discs on a stand, 'while I put these away,' deftly removing some from the stereo and returning them to their appropriate covers.

Following his suggestion, Tracey chose a couple of longplays at random and handed them across for Ryan to set on the turntable, moving backwards a few steps afterwards, closer to the door, and suddenly anxious to rejoin the rest of the guests.

'Are you coming?' she enquired shakily as the opening bars of the first track floated into the air.

'Why the rush?' his brows interrogated satirically. 'This surface is better for dancing.'

Tracey looked about her nervously. 'Um—the others—someone might want you for something,' she put forward hopefully.

'I doubt it.' His eyes slid over her consideringly. 'What's the matter, Tracey?' he taunted mockingly. 'Isn't your little plan working out as you wanted?'

'I don't know what you mean—I don't have a plan,' she prevaricated uneasily. While they had been in the general view it was relatively simple to be flippant, but in the shadowed, intimate confines of the verandah it was something else again! Now, desperately attempting to appear indifferent, she shook her head and essayed a casual, 'I was only trying to bury the hatchet,' in a suitably reproachful tone.

Ryan's expression was openly disbelieving. 'In my back, I don't doubt!' he drawled.

Glad of a legitimate excuse to escape, Tracey shrugged in defeat. 'Oh, well, if that's the way you feel . . .' reaching out thankfully for the door, but gasping in surprise when

Ryan's long legs covered the ground between them so unexpectedly and a long fingered hand gripped her wrist
relentlessly.

'No, you don't, my mischief-making little ward,' he de-
rided softly, swinging her away from the door and back into
the imprisonment of his arms, one hand spanning her jaw
and tilting her head upwards. 'I have a few words of warning for you first, honey,' he imparted sadonically. 'In future,
before you start playing games I'd consider it advisable, if
I were you, to make certain that both sides are planning to
abide by the same set of rules,' and without giving Tracey
a chance to reply his mouth lowered to hers in a kiss that
was both a chastisement and an undeniable possession.

In a daze, thoughts skipped through Tracey's mind with
all the capriciousness of thistle seeds carried on the wind.
That she hoped no one outside could see them; that Ryan
Alexander's lips didn't persuade—they demanded; and most
important of all, that she should have been making some sort
of physical protest against his overpowering action instead
of compulsively responding!

In a belated effort to offer resistance she abruptly
wrenched her chin out of his grasp—catching him off guard
and breaking the stunning contact, her breath coming
ragged and heavy—but freedom was to be a shortlived
thing as Ryan smoothly slid his hand across her back to the
nape of her slender neck, stilling any further liberty seeking
movements and renewing his assault on her already raw
emotions with lips which provoked rather than ordered
this time. How Tracey wished they didn't! If she had experienced trouble in resisting before, it was nothing as to
now!

This new challenge was designed to arouse and, with
growing dismay, Tracey realised it was proving extremely
successful. The futile opposition of her fingers ceasing their
struggles and clinging instead to the wide leather belt about
his waist, the thoroughly male frame disturbing in its nearness, and her own desires rising as a result of his stimulating
virile mastery.

'Ryan darling, you were gone so long I thought you might
be having trouble.'

Tracey stiffened at the seductive lilt in Lana's voice and the sound of footfalls on the verandah steps. Not so Ryan, merely releasing Tracey's lips unhurriedly, his arms only gradually—reluctantly almost—falling away from her pliant form, thickly lashed eyes watching intently the drowsy green gaze turned towards him.

His mouth curved hauntingly and he called back softly, 'Nothing I couldn't handle, thanks.'

It seemed to Tracey there was a vein of sardonic amusement in the tone, and the idea mortified to such an extent that her first reaction was a violent one, her right arm circling towards his head, palm outstretched—only to have it caught in mid-air when Ryan's fingers closed tightly around it. In the dim light his teeth gleamed tauntingly as he moved his head slowly from side to side in a negating gesture which goaded unbearably and had Tracey dragging her arm painfully out of his grasp and twisting away resentfully.

She was still breathing heavily when she passed Lana at the doorway and in no mood to tolerate the pseudo-surprised, 'Oh, Tracey, I didn't know you were here,' which she was greeted with and her eyes flashed an ironic, 'I'll bet you didn't,' before the older woman continued with a simper, 'I thought u must have gone into hiding after making a spectacle o. yourself and placing poor Ryan in such an awkward position by inviting him to dance with you.' She laid a hand on Tracey's arm in a supposedly considerate motion. 'I know you won't mind my saying this because it's for your own good, and I do realise of course that all kinds of permissiveness are accepted in the city these days, but really ... we're not used to such forward behaviour at our parties, and we wouldn't want anyone to get the wrong ideas about you, would we?' she smiled astringently.

It had been all Tracey could do not to shake that insincere little hand away in disgust when Lana was talking, but suddenly a tinkling bell in the depths of her subconscious sounded a reminder. This was too good an opportunity to miss! She was not sure just who compromised the 'we' that Lana had seen fit to mention, but at the moment Tracey was only too willing to agree.

'Oh, no, *we* wouldn't want *that*!' she exaggerated in her most horrified voice. 'But luckily I have a very ...' she halted and her eyes half closed suggestively, 'co-operative guardian, and he's just been demonstrating some of your basic customs for me.' She gave a fair imitation of an empty-headed giggle. 'I'll have to watch my step in future, though, as it doesn't bear thinking about what an initiation into the finer points might entail,' with a gibing look in Ryan's direction before continuing on her way down the steps, but her pace slowing when she heard Lana's voice behind her.

'Co-operative guardian ...? Demonstrating basic customs ...? An initiation into the finer points ...? What on earth is she talking about, Ryan? What's been going on between you two?' Tracey could hear her demanding peremptorily, and a wide grin split her face. Let's see him get out of that one unscathed, she thought happily, her steps increasing jauntily as she hurried down the path and across the lawns. Ryan Alexander was about to be served up some of his own medicine!

CHAPTER EIGHT

TRACEY flung back the single covering sheet and scrambled quickly out of bed the following Monday morning, checking the time with her watch and sighing with relief. She wasn't late. Today was the day when act two was to go into operation, and in less than fifteen minutes she had showered, dressed in casual riding gear and, parting her hair in the middle, tied it into two shoulder-length bunches and secured them with twisted rubber bands—a procedure which immediately reduced her age by five years—if one concentrated solely on the make-up free face and not on the fully mature, curving figure beneath it.

Without forgetting her hat—she didn't intend to spoil her chances by being caught on the wrong foot at an inopportune moment—she slipped quietly out of her room, crossed the verandah, and headed singlemindedly for the horse yards, climbing on to the top rail and giving Glory—the mare she had ridden the week before—the two lumps of sugar she had secreted away from the dining room the night before. Stroking the playful head as it nuzzled into her, seeking more of the sweet confection, Tracey's air of expectation diminished slightly as her period of waiting lengthened and her thoughts wandered back over the preceding days.

The two cousins had been anxiously awaiting her return to the table after her dance with Ryan on Saturday night and were bursting with curiosity to hear what had occurred—especially in view of the fact that they had also seen Lana entering the homestead only minutes before Tracey reappeared on her own. It hadn't taken her long to give them the gist of the happenings—she'd had absolutely no intention of disclosing everything that had taken place—and feeling that one victory deserved another to keep it company, it had only been a matter of time before they came up with today's plan after hearing Lana's suggestion the previous evening that Ryan accompany her on an early morning ride.

Glory suddenly began pushing more determinedly at the bulge in the pocket of Tracey's jeans, and with a smile she extracted a small apple she had been intending to eat herself. 'Okay, okay, I'll share it with you,' she laughed, taking one bite and holding out the remainder, thus earning for herself the mare's obvious gratification as she munched contentedly and Tracey's thoughts returned to their original theme.

Apart from members of the family, Lana had been the only guests to extend her visit past Sunday and it had become Carol and Noeleen's single objective to see how quickly they could shorten her stay. But as their only slightly veiled innuendoes that it was time she returned home had been contemptuously ignored, they were pleasurably anticipating the outcome of Tracey's assiduity in convincing Lana she would find it far more enjoyable elsewhere.

For the hundreth time Tracey's eyes flickered suspensefully back to the homestead, but this time steadied as the two expected figures came into view; Ryan wearing his customary drills and matching bush shirt; Lana fastidiously outfitted in buff coloured jodhpurs, highly polished boots, and a classic white silk blouse which would have done any show-ring proud. Tracey cleared her throat and twirled her hat between nervous fingers. To permit the plan any chance of success she firstly had to receive Ryan's permission to join them, and after Saturday's little contretemps she wasn't sure what her reception was likely to be because she had studiously avoided him ever since.

Lana was the first to notice her—and not pleased with the extra presence as evidenced by the thinning lips—but Ryan's eyes ranged over her indolently, taking in the schoolgirl scrubbed face and bunches, no doubt making his own assessment, decided Tracey apprehensively, for absolutely no sign of what he might have been thinking registered on those compelling male features.

'Are you going riding somewhere too, Tracey?' enquired Lana with false brightness, clearly attempting to preclude any efforts at association with Ryan and herself.

Unluckily for Lana it was the type of opening Tracey

had been hoping for and she fiddled diffidently with the band of her hat. 'Well, I would have liked to,' she began, lifting her gaze to the level of Ryan's chest but not quite daring to reach his face. 'But it doesn't seem as if the others are going this morning,' keeping her fingers crossed that Ryan didn't already know that they were going riding after lunch today instead, 'and as I'm not allowed to go on my own ...' she let her voice sigh away despondently, eyes wistful as they turned to survey the horses in the paddock beside her.

'Then I suppose you'd better come with us, hadn't you?' Ryan's voice broke the significant silence dryly.

'Oh, *really* ...!' Lana immediately protested angrily, then hastily disciplined her mouth into a beguiling smile for Ryan's benefit. 'I'm sure Tracey would find us dull company, darling. Perhaps some other time ...' she proposed dulcetly.

'Oh, no, I wouldn't find it dull,' Tracey interposed swiftly, worried lest the offer was about to be withdrawn. 'And I promise not to get in the way,' she assured the older woman innocently. 'You go ahead with whatever you were planning to do and I'll just tag along behind,' she proffered magnanimously.

Still averse to the idea, Lana turned to Ryan for support, Tracey holding her breath until his wry, 'I know it sounds too good to be true, but I don't really think we have any choice in the matter, Lana,' gave her the outcome of his decision, whereupon her eyes twinkled delightedly while Lana flounced irritably away and waited coldly for her mount to be saddled. Tracey gladly saddled Glory herself without waiting for assistance.

Breaking into a relaxing canter as soon as they were through the gate, Ryan and Lana led the way in a northerly direction, following sandy tracks across the treeless plain, Tracey demurely keeping pace for the moment—her plan wasn't to go into action until they were too far from the homestead for her to be sent back on her own. A solid gallop conveniently took them completely out of sight of that oasis of green before they slowed to a walk, and glancing back, Tracey almost chuckled to see the clouds of .dust they were churning up.

From then on Glory was edged a little into the lead whenever Tracey could do so without it seeming too obvious, pretending to be not quite in control of the little horse beneath her and trusting that Ryan wasn't aware of how experienced a rider she really was. With Glory she could find no fault. It seemed the mare was easily bought; a couple of lumps of sugar, an apple, and she was a devoted friend for life. She pranced when urged, propped obediently with only the slightest amount of pressure, and being trained for stock work, she would pivot sharply when called upon to do so.

And while all this was taking place Lana was finding it harder and harder to control her temper. The continuous complaints of, 'Tracey! For heaven's sake, stop kicking dust all over us!' and, 'Tracey! Can't you stop that horse from swinging into Dandy?' were becoming more shrill each time she repeated them, and although Tracey apologised profusely on every occasion, Lana showed no indication of being mollified.

'Oh, I am sorry, but my, she's full of beans today,' excused Tracey leaning forward to pat encouragement into the silky neck after yet another, 'Tracey! Will you get that horse out of my way!' as Glory crossed the path of Lana's grey gelding and on command docilely jibbed once more.

'Isn't she?' concurred Ryan softly from Lana's other side, but there was no sound of tolerance in the tone—it was dangerously cool in fact—and it was only the knowledge that he wasn't likely to exact retribution while anyone else was around that enabled Tracey to continue her campaign with any sort of equanimity.

What she hadn't bargained for, however, was that by the time they returned to the homestead Lana would be past caring whether she retained her studied amiability in Ryan's presence or not, and directly they halted beside the feed shed she had climbed down out of the saddle, thrown the reins over Dandy's head, and snapped, 'Well, thank you, Tracey, for making that the most abominable ride I have ever had to suffer! I don't believe I've felt quite so dirty and gritty in all my life!' and gone storming towards the house, brushing handfuls of red dust from her clothes as she went.

Tracey bit hard at her lip to stop from grinning at the sight of such disarray as the small figure receded into the

distance, but her period of amusement wasn't destined to
last long as a harsh, implacable order curtly reminded her
of her own predicament.

'Get down off that bloody horse, Tracey, before I drag
you off!' Ryan grated furiously, closing the gap between
them with long determined strides.

Wide green eyes tried to look guiltlessly astonished. 'Wh-
why? What have I done?' she played for time and heeled
Glory closer to the shed doorway and what she hoped
was an avenue to freedom.

His gaze held hers relentlessly. 'My ... she's full of
beans today,' he mimicked, then inexorably, 'That mare
is one of the quietest and most obedient on this property.
She does not, I repeat—*does not*—balk, pivot, or dance
without reason!'

'Well, maybe today she did have a reason,' Tracey offered
helpfully with a placatory half smile which faded almost as
soon as it was born.

'And we both know what it was, don't we? Your hands
and heels!'

'Oh, and why would I do a thing like that?' she queried
fearfully. Now that she had reached the doorway there
didn't appear to be anyone inside to come to her rescue as
she had hoped there might be, and Ryan was still advancing
intimidatingly.

'Quite frankly, I'm past giving a damn as to why!' he
reached Glory's side and dragged the reins from Tracey's
unresisting fingers. 'Now, are you going to dismount under
your own steam, or am I going to do it for you?' his free
hand reaching up for her arm.

Tracey jerked it rapidly out of his reach and kicked one
foot free of its stirrup. 'All right, all right,' she acceded
nervously, and promptly took him unawares by dismounting
on Glory's offside—equestrian etiquette was the least of her
worries right at the moment! With the mare's bulk acting as
a solid barrier between them, she eyed him aggravatingly
across the saddle. 'So, I'm down ... now what?' she dared
to ask.

'Round here!' he stabbed a finger at the ground beside
him.

Her hair bounced against her neck as she moved her head

from side to side. 'I can hear whatever you have to say perfectly well from where I am,' she said.

'I wasn't planning to *say* anything!' he advised incisively.

Tracey frowned. Then what did he have in mind? No, he wouldn't dare! The frown disappeared and she glared at him belligerently. 'You lay a hand on me, Ryan, and I'll—I'll scratch your eyes out!' she threatened frantically when he ducked under Glory's neck and, in defence, she raced in the other direction around the hindquarters. Adding a breathless, 'I'll sue you for assault too!' as they again reversed their positions, 'And for—for physical cruelty! You can't ...'

The desperate defiance was abruptly curtailed by Ryan diving beneath Glory's girth and bringing Tracey to the ground with an outcry that was half surprise and half trepidation.

'You let go of me, Ryan!' she panted feverishly, struggling to find her feet and extricate herself from his grip at the same time. 'Being my guardian doesn't give you any right to ... oh, you *fink*!' she choked wrathfully as he imperturbably hauled her over one bent knee and proceeded to dust the seat of her jeans with an increasingly hard, punishing hand.

'I hate you!' she continued her tirade the minute he swung her back on to her feet, hands clenched at her sides with the force of her feelings. 'You're a monster and a brute! You're unfeeling and—and ...'

'And you're a little witch who deserved exactly what she got!' he cut in with a mocking tilt to his mouth. 'I warned you, didn't I, not to play games unless you were sure of the rules?'

'Rules! What rules?' Tracey demanded sarcastically. 'The only ones you know are Rafferty's! You make them up as you go along!'

Ryan's smile broadened. 'Which should be just one more reason for you to beware, honey,' he drawled lazily.

Fighting wildly against the uncontrollable wave of attraction which swept over her as a result of that wide smile, Tracey looked down her nose at him scornfully. 'Huh! Of you?' she jeered with all the disparagement she could inject.

If anything his smile became even more pronounced, so that it was completely unexpected when his hand sliced through the air and wrapped itself in one of Tracey's bunches, immobilising her head while his lips closed over hers roughly, shatteringly.

'Of me,' he confirmed softly a few brief seconds later, releasing her dismissively as he turned on his heel and strode lithely back to the big black stallion he had been riding.

Tracey lifted tentative fingers to her mouth and stared after him shakenly. Damn him. Why couldn't he have been elderly and white-haired like she had always pictured guardians to be? Why did hers have to be a young, disturbingly attractive, intensely vibrant male with a devastating ability to set her pulses racing insanely when she least wanted them to? She had been fiercely indignant and resentful at being so summarily spanked—even though she had to admit that a niggling suspicion she might have overplayed her part that morning was there too—until that fleeting but vitally stirring kiss had effortlessly despatched all coherent thought to the nether regions of her mind and left her feeling provokingly tantalised rather than scandalised.

'You want me to unsaddle Glory for you, Miss Tracey?'

'What?' Tracey spun out of her daydream, her brow furrowed, to see Tom's dark lined face watching her enquiringly. 'Oh, no—no, thanks, Tom. I can do it,' she smiled gratefully, her own hand going out instinctively to the saddle flap. Her eyes slanted towards the grey picking delicately at a tuft of grass surrounding the nearest fence post. 'Dandy looks as if he could use some help, though,' she suggested wryly.

Tom's liquid black eyes shone a little brighter. 'Mrs Renfrew did seem in a hurry to reach the homestead this morning, didn't she?' he remarked blandly, and ambled over to the gelding.

While her hands worked automatically, Tracey's thoughts were free to wander. If Tom had been close enough to see Lana storm off irately, then was it not also possible that he had witnessed the subsequent incidents as well? A burning fire of humiliation trailed along her veins and she dragged the saddle angrily from Glory's back. If word of

what happened went round this station, she would hate
Ryan Alexander till the day she died!

The subject of her violent thoughts suddenly spoke beside her. 'Here, I'll take that.' Ryan made a move to relieve
her of the heavy gear.

'No, thanks!' She wrenched the leather petulantly away
from him. 'You've lent me a hand quite enough for one
day!' with a gibing grimace as she pushed around him.

A muscle flickered faintly at the side of his mouth as he
looked down at the stiffly held figure. 'Suit yourself,' he
finally shrugged indifferently and, thrusting his hands into
the back pockets of his pants, strode away from the yard
without a backward glance.

Tracey kept her face averted and continued on into the
shed, heaved the saddle up on to its customary bracket, and
rubbed the palms of her hands irresolutely down the sides
of her jeans. If she attempted to rub Glory down or clean
any of the tack she knew that Tom would only go over it
all again once she had left. He took great pride in keeping
his charges and their equipment in excellent condition and
didn't quite trust anyone else to give them the care and attention he would himself. But if she followed Ryan
directly to the house it would probably mean having to face
him and Lana over the breakfast table—and that was a
circumstance she didn't relish!

In the end she decided it might be more prudent to forgo breakfast altogether that morning—and especially so
when it was more than likely that Carol and Noeleen would
also be at the table and wouldn't be averse to making some
facetious remarks concerning Lana's appearance if they had
happened to see her dishevelled return—and with this in
mind Tracey headed for the verandah and the seclusion of
her own room.

Even this was denied her, however, for as she turned
the corner she came across Justin idly surveying the
grounds from one of the wicker chairs, and although she
would have continued past him with only a casual greeting, a commanding nod of his head indicating the lounger
beside him had her pulling a wry face and lowering herself gently on to its comfortable length.

'You're the second one I've seen stalk up from the yards with a scowl,' he came straight to the point as usual. 'What's been going on out there?' a demanding finger pointed to the silent paddocks beyond the homestead boundary. 'You all get thrown this morning?'

Tracey gave a short rueful laugh. 'No, not really. Did you think Lana looked as if she had been?'

'Lana? What's she got to do with it?' he frowned. 'I was referring to my grandson. His face was as black as thunder when he marched into the house a short time ago.'

'Was it?' she asked naïvely, finding it extremely difficult to keep her pleasure from showing. Good! Why should Ryan have it all his own way? And with any luck at all he would be feeling even less happy by the time Lana had finished venting her rage on him when he attempted to placate her. A delighted chuckle rose in her throat and was quickly suppressed, but not before the vigilant Justin had seen its birth.

'Just what was that for, young lady?' he questioned peremptorily, the bright eyes unwavering in their intent regard. 'Was it you who put that look on Ryan's face?'

'Probably,' Tracey admitted dryly, busying herself with removing the rubber bands from her hair and finger-combing it back into its natural curly fall. 'Haven't you noticed that we're like the proverbial oil and water and don't mix very successfully?'

'Oil and water, my foot!' he snorted disparagingly. 'The only reason you two don't mix is because you're determined not to! You had no qualms about mixing with Ryan when you were younger.'

Tracey unexpectedly found herself on the defensive and gave a condescending smile. 'Which only goes to show that like most two-year-olds, I wasn't very selective about the company I kept. I'm older and wiser now,' she reminded him airily.

'But not by much, apparently, if you think continual defiance is going to achieve anything where Ryan's concerned,' he returned her smile with a chastening one of his own before a furrow of remembrance channelled across his forehead. 'Anyway, where does Lana Renfrew fit in all this? Why should she look as though she'd taken a fall? Was she hurt, or something?' the questions came rapidly.

'Oh, no, nothing like that,' she rejected his assumptions with a shake of her head. 'Only—um—a little dusty,' and she couldn't stop a small grin from appearing.

'May I ask how that came about?' ironically.

Shining white teeth chewed at a soft bottom lip. 'I think I'd rather you didn't,' she replied candidly.

'Ryan took exception to it, though?' he quizzed surprisingly instead of pursuing the matter directly as Tracey had expected.

Unconsciously a hand briefly found its way to the seat of her jeans. 'Naturally,' she agreed sardonically. 'Doesn't he always take exception to everything I say or do?'

'He never used to.'

'Oh, Justin!' She sighed and raised her hands in a gesture of defeat. 'That was a long time ago ... we're different people now,' she tried to convince him earnestly. 'Besides, your grandson seems happily occupied elsewhere these days and I doubt he's all that anxious to have me tagging along like I've been told I did before,' wryly.

'He took you with them this morning, didn't he?'

Tracey looked at him askance and then burst out laughing. 'You're incorrigible!' she grinned at him in nonplussed exasperation. 'I don't know what you're trying to prove, but believe me, Ryan only allowed me to accompany them because I,' she lifted one shoulder detractingly, 'sort of made it hard for him to do otherwise. Somehow, I get the impression I won't be invited again,' she laughed unrepentantly.

The faded blue eyes slanted shrewdly. 'Who did you set out to aggravate, Tracey? Lana ... or Ryan?'

A wary glance from beneath silky lashes and, sensing there would be no recriminations forthcoming, Tracey chuckled animatedly and confessed, 'Both, I hope.'

At so much frankness Justin's lips twisted into a grudging smile, but his head moved in warning. 'For your own protection, don't ride him too hard, Tracey,' he advised soberly. 'He'll make an implacable enemy if you go too far, and he does hold all the aces at the moment.'

Implacable! How apt, Tracey scowled. With that cleft in such a strong, determined jaw it was the most suitable description of all. But as for her guardian having the winning hand—well, as far as she was concerned that hadn't yet been decided. She swung her feet to the floor and rose leisurely, hands resting lightly on slender hips in a challenging stance, a mettlesome smile on her lips.

'Ah, but you're forgetting that in some games the ace isn't the highest trump in the pack. If it's going to be euchre then he can keep all those aces—I'll be content with the right and left bowers,' she winked irrepressibly.

'And if it's poker?' he proposed with dry contrariness.

Tracey shrugged blithely. 'At least I'll have a pair of openers,' he grinned as she turned to leave and promptly collided with a tall, solid figure only inches behind her.

There was no need for her eyes to travel past the bronzed throat to the disquieting features above it for Tracey to discover whom she had made contact with so precipitately —her clamouring senses had already done that quite adequately—and her first reaction was to round on Justin with a reproachful glare for not having made her aware that his grandson had joined them. Unbearably conscious of his nearness, she waited tensely for him to divulge how much he had overheard.

Thumbs hooked lightly into the belt about his waist Ryan scanned the proud profile beside him alertly. 'A pair of openers for what?' he asked.

'We were discussing—er—card games. Poker, to be exact,' put in Justin hastily, noting the less than relaxed expression, but on recalling her previous humiliating treatment Tracey suddenly wasn't prepared to be so conciliatory and faced her questioner rebelliously.

'No, we weren't,' she refuted Justin's excuse carelessly 'We were discussing the chances of my winning our next altercation! Perhaps you'd like to add your comments on the matter too!' she swept one arm wide with sarcastic invitation.

Justin's desperately adjuring, 'For God's sake, Tracey!' she barely heard. She was too occupied in steadfastly battling to hold an inscrutable gaze. And, for once, she was positive she would have succeeded, if Ryan's shapely mouth hadn't suddenly curled provocatively to apprise in a slow drawl, 'Your chances, honey, are precisely nil ... the same as they've always been. I'm surprised the outcome of our last skirmish didn't finally convince you of that,' with a taut grin at her discomfiture when a bright glow of colour stained her cheeks and her hands clenched furiously at her sides. 'Or is that the reason you're now enlisting Justin's help?'

'I wasn't asking for his help—I don't need anyone's help!' she boasted with a well simulated confidence. 'You're not so omnipotent that you can't be cut down to size! In fact, you remind me of the saying Dad was always quoting when he was teaching us to ride ... "There's never a horse that can't be rode, and never a rider that can't be throw'd",' her chin lifted in mockery.

'I was wondering how long it would take you to come back to your pet theme,' he laughed—a rich sound that sent wayward feelings down Tracey's spine and made it increasingly difficult for her to retain a scornful look when confronted with such undisputed amusement. His eyes sought Justin's with a smile. 'Romeo Wilcox was of the opinion that the squatters have been a law unto themselves for too long and it's time somebody took us to task. Tracey's burning desire at the moment is to be that somebody!' he explained sardonically.

'Not necessarily all of them, Ryan. Just one will suffice,' she smiled bitter-sweetly, pointedly.

'Specifically ... me!'

Fine brows peaked impudently. 'You guessed! How very perceptive of you.'

'But not very discerning of you! As another saying goes ... "Forewarned is forearmed", my pet,' he retorted coolly.

The casual endearment had Tracey taking a deep, controlling breath. 'Your ward I may be, but your pet ... oh, no,' she jeered. 'You can keep that sort of expression for those who I'm sure would be only too elated to revel in the term.'

'Such as?' he queried softly, too softly.

'How should I know?' she returned nonchalantly, for

once heeding Justin's cautioning gestures in the background and refusing to allow the most obvious name to tumble from her lips, although she couldn't help adding in a disdainful tone, 'There might be dozens vying for the doubtful honour. Out here I suppose it's a case of the poor females having no choice but to tolerate what's available.'

'Quite possibly,' his eyes narrowed in grim acknowledgment, turning an icy, forbidding blue, 'but at least they're not peevish little termagants with a narcissistic preoccupation for inflicting trouble and embarrassment on everyone who has the misfortune to come in contact with them!' he informed her derogatorily, and added succinctly over his shoulder as he headed for the screen door, 'I might suggest you try following their example ... you could only improve!'

'Who said I wanted to?' she flung defiantly after him, but the only response was the sound of the door swinging closed and she dropped moodily down on to the lounger again.

Peevish ... narcissistic ... termagant! Tracey flashed indignantly through the descriptions. If she was, it was nobody's fault but his own! What else had he expected in return for an unwanted guardianship—undying gratitude? She shifted restlessly in her seat and visibly jumped when Justin laid a hand on her arm. She had completely forgotten he was there.

'You're attempting the impossible, Tracey,' he advised gruffly. 'Believe me, I know my grandson very well, and when he gets that particular look about him you can rest assured he isn't about to tamely surrender.'

Tracey chewed at her lip pensively and expelled a long sigh. 'But neither am I, Justin. So where do I go from here?' she asked ruefully, without really expecting him to be able to supply an encouraging answer.

CHAPTER NINE

By the following weekend all the visitors had left the homestead with the exception of Carol who had cheerfully stayed on to keep the two girls company. Tracey had been sorry to see Nancy and the rest of her family leave because, not only had she felt comfortable with them, but their presence had also to some extent provided a buffer between herself and Ryan. Lana's departure, accompanied as it was by arch looks and coy reminders for Ryan not to forget he was dining with her and her in-laws the next Friday, brought a feeling of disgust for the blatantly enticing performance and one of relief at being freed from her irritating and stifling residency.

Gradually the property settled back into its efficient routine, and as the days lengthened into weeks Tracey discovered she was spending more and more of her time with Justin, or with Marty in the office, rather than with the two younger girls, for they invariably made arrangements to either go with, or meet, Ryan at some time during their peregrinations, and for the present she preferred to keep a bulwark of distance between them.

It wasn't that she had abandoned any of her previous ideas, but those unanticipated kisses had set in motion a chain of disturbing thoughts which she was at a loss to fully understand, or even completely categorise. That her guardian was a magnetic specimen of rugged individualism she had never attempted to deny, but she hadn't expected to find herself fighting an increasing attraction as well as a threatening domination and so, for the time being, at least until she developed a stronger defence against that demolishing maleness, she wasn't anxious to provoke ripples on uneasily calm waters.

Today Justin had reverted to his most irascible again because no one had been able to prevail against his intention of going riding with Tracey the previous afternoon and when evening arrived he was paying painfully for his obstinacy and, guessing that there would be no exceptions to receiving a good dose of his bellicosity the next morning, Tracey had absented herself from the homestead with Marty immediately after breakfast—noticing with a grin how Carol and Lyn promptly did likewise—and had been helping to take stock of the stores for the last couple of hours.

'Hey, come back to earth!' Marty snapped his fingers in the air with a laugh. 'I'm still waiting to hear how many shirts you've got up there.'

Tracey shook her head and grinned down at him from her superior position at the top of a step-ladder. 'I'm sorry,' she apologised, 'but I thought I heard the sound of a plane and wondered who it might be. Didn't you hear anything?' she enquired with a slight frown.

'Can't hear a thing these days with the noise that fan's making in the office,' he replied cheerfully. 'Remind me when we've finished here to get Eddy to have a look at it, will you?'

'Okay,' Tracey acquiesced easily, dismissing her previous thoughts and turning back to the job in hand. 'Do you want these as a total amount, or split up into sizes?' she asked.

It was almost an hour later before Tracey had relayed all the relevant details from that particular row of wares for Marty to mark off on his appropriate supply sheets and, returning to the office, he immediately set about telephoning across to the station hand's cottage while Tracey began making them both a welcome mug of coffee. In the middle of spooning the sugar into the first beaker, her hand stilled and her head came up sharply. There it was again. It *was* a plane she had heard earlier, she was certain of it now, even with the clangorous rattling of the fan overhead, and she stared interestedly through the window, watching for its appearance above the pepper trees and the homestead roof.

Seconds later the sun glared brightly over a rising aircraft and on seeing the distinctive markings along the fuselage Tracey drew in her breath and flashed an interrogating glance in Marty's direction.

'It's the Flying Doctor,' she told him swiftly. 'What's he doing here? Is someone sick?'

Patiently holding a persistently ringing receiver to his ear, Marty shrugged lightly. 'Search me! No need to look so worried, though, it's probably only Doc Nesbitt dropping in on his way back from a call,' he replied incuriously.

A strange foreboding settled heavily about Tracey and she moved her head slowly in a dissenting movement. 'I think I'd like to check anyway, just to make sure,' she said, hastily pouring the now boiling water into his mug, stirring, and placing it on his desk. 'Do you mind?'

'Good lord, no! Go right ahead,' he exclaimed, replacing the unanswered phone with a rueful smile. 'As much as I appreciate your help, I'm still not your boss. As you're a member of the Alexander trusteeship, strictly speaking, I'm *your* employee, not you mine,' he reminded her good-naturedly.

'Mmm, I suppose you are at that,' chuckled Tracey, momentarily diverted. 'I'd never thought of it like that before.' A pause. 'Maybe you'd better be extra nice to me from now on or I might be tempted to throw some of my new-found weight around,' she suggested with a teasing glint.

'Heaven help me!' Marty's eyes rose skywards expressively. 'I've seen the effect you have on Ryan when you start on those little tricks of yours, my girl. What are you aiming for, Tracey? Emancipation ... or capitulation?'

Mobile lips moved evocatively. 'The thought had crossed my mind,' she admitted pertly, but his unwitting mention of Ryan brought with it a return of her puzzling disquiet and her smile faded rapidly as she headed for the door.

Marty's called, 'If you see Eddy, tell him we need him down here, will you? I can't raise him on the phone,' she acknowledged with an impassive, 'Will do,' and then she was hurrying along the path, unmindful of the tiny droplets of perspiration breaking out at her temples as the full force of the midday sun beat down on her unprotected head.

Pushing in through the screen door on to the verandah the first people she encountered were Lyn, with unmistakable tears in her eyes; Carol, looking white and distressed;

and Justin who was flailing the air furiously with his cane.

'I—I saw the plane . . .' Tracey fumbled, her eyes searching all three of them worriedly.

'Oh, Tracey, it was terrible!' Lyn started crying again and left her cousin to take up the story.

'It was one of Glen's Brahmans—they had them in the yards and—and it turned on him unexpectedly,' Carol whispered throatily.

Tracey's nails dug into the palms of her hands frustratedly. 'Turned on *who*?' she almost shouted, discarding grammar impatiently.

'Ryan, of course!' Justin roared just as fractiously. 'The damned beast swung back and caught him off guard! Those *bos indicus* breeds are always unpredictable! I've a good mind to . . .'

But Tracey didn't wait to hear what Justin had on his mind; she was already racing down the hallway to Ryan's room, her heart thumping agonisingly beneath her ribs. One perfunctory knock on the panelled door and she rushed inside in the same headlong fashion, coming to an abrupt, jolted and breathless halt, nerveless fingers released their hold on the handle and the door swung closed gently.

After anticipating him to be almost at death's door, Tracey's shocked and bewildered eyes couldn't assimilate the scene of Ryan in the process of calmly extracting a fresh shirt from within his wardrobe. Dark blue denims were already belted about the lithe waist and the smooth skin covering the muscular bare back turned to her gleamed like oiled copper. Feverishly relief and anger intermingled within her bloodstream, but the most devastating emotion of all was the one of desire to reach out and trail her fingers uninhibitedly over the warm brown skin.

Swallowing convulsively, she held herself stiffly and pushed the traitorous thoughts away. 'I heard you—you were hurt,' she began falteringly.

'Did you now?' The ebony-framed eyes that swung to intercept her gaze were discouragingly cool. 'Well, I'm sorry to disappoint you, Red, but it looked worse than it actually was, so I'm afraid you're just going to have to put up with my guardianship for a while longer. Better luck next time.'

his mouth crooked caustically as he slid long arms into the sleeves of his shirt.

Not even indignation at the hated nickname could overcome the unendurable hurt Tracey experienced with the utterance of such callous sentiments and she about-faced frantically lest he should see the scalding tears that flooded her eyes, bowing her head so that it almost rested against the door for support.

'I'm sorry too! I should have realised my concern would be unwelcome,' she choked huskily.

As her hand touched the door knob another hand simultaneously settled on the nape of her neck. 'My turn to apologise,' she heard him murmur heavily. 'That remark was unwarranted.'

Hardly able to speak because of the lump in her throat, Tracey shook her head restlessly and stammered, 'I know we're always fighting, and that I—I've said I wanted you cut down to size, and—and all that, but I never really wished you any physical harm, Ryan,' with a brief, tear-drenched look over her shoulder. 'I saw the plane leaving and then they all said that—that ...'

She was spun around to face him and a gentle finger laid across her trembling lips. 'Sssh!' she was commanded softly. 'It's all over now,' but still the words kept flowing persistently.

'You see, I didn't know how badly you were hurt, but—but the way everyone was talking, I thought—I thought ...' She broke off, unable to voice the worst fears which had consumed her, and comforting arms encircled her lightly, pulling her closer.

'I know, I know.' His forehead lowered to rest on hers. 'There was a lot of blood—there always is in an accident of that sort—but Andy Nesbitt had it cleaned and patched in no time.' He tapped at an uncustomary bulge at the side of his thigh. 'I'll survive,' he teased wryly.

'You could have been killed!' Tracey accused, shocked eyes turned upwards, her fingers hesitantly tracing the various red weals and grazes that were now visible on the bronzed torso within the opening of the unbuttoned shirt.

'A refresher course for a lesson I thought I'd learnt years

ago. Don't let your mind wander when you're dealing with cattle.'

'Don't joke about it—it's not funny!' she censured heatedly.

Her wrists were gripped tightly and her touch removed from his bare skin. 'Nobody knows that better than I do, honey,' he retorted sardonically, releasing his hold on her once her hands were safely at her sides once more.

Tracey burnt with humiliation at his action and took one step backwards stiffly. 'I'm sorry,' she flushed warmly, deprecatorily. 'I'm not usually so—so ...'

'For God's sake, Tracey!' he interrupted with a groan, arms reaching out and compulsively dragging her roughly back to him, cradling the bright head against his chest. 'I took your hands away for your own protection, not because I didn't want you touching me. Reaction causes people to do things they would never consider under normal circumstances and, right at the moment, my own stability is suffering much the same backlash as yours ... and that makes for a pretty explosive combination, honey,' he counselled tautly. 'There's only two things on my mind at present—you, and that bed over there—and if you stay with me much longer I won't be able to vouch for the pair of you never meeting.' Suddenly it was Ryan who took a step away this time, and then ran a hand wearily round the back of his neck. 'Get going, Tracey,' he prompted brusquely, 'because if you don't ...'

His head moved expressively and he allowed the sentence to trail away with implicit meaning, but Tracey couldn't accept the well-intentioned advice. Those tormenting minutes being held within his arms had unleashed an overwhelming hunger to savour more of their tempting stimulation and she moved shyly towards him.

'And if I don't ...?' she enquired throatily, not quite able to meet his deep blue gaze, her hands sliding beneath the open shirt and lingering bewitchingly on the warm flesh of his waist.

'God, Tracey, I'm not made of wood!' he implored hoarsely, his fingers digging painfully into her shoulders. 'What are you trying to do to me?'

A half diffident smile lit her features transiently. 'I would have thought that was obvious,' she ventured softly.

Without another word Ryan relinquished his grip to swing her high in his arms and carry her to the large bed where he lowered her on to the blue and black striped cover, a hand on either side of her head as he leant over her.

'You're an illogical, idiotic ... gloriously enticing little redheaded witch,' he breathed huskily and tantalisingly against the corner of her mouth, and then his lips closed possessively over hers.

Tracey had been kissed many times before, but never quite like this. This was both subjugating and inviting, and as all repressions fled she responded freely; her lips parting willingly beneath such a subtle pressure; her body relishing the rousing weight pinning her to the soft comfort of his bed; and her hands gliding pleasurably over the tensed muscles to sink deeply into the dark hair of his head.

An aching desire exploded in every nerve as his mouth moved slowly, intensely down the side of her neck to the sensitive hollow at the base of her throat, and she was only half aware of the fingers deftly unbuttoning her blouse until, with a startled gasp which was stifled by the return of compelling lips, she felt the freedom of swelling breasts being released from their covering and spilling into skilfully caressing hands which stirred her to a pitch of sensual delight she had never before experienced and had her moving provocatively under the hardening frame pressing against her.

Neither of them heard the knock on the door, if there was one, nor the sound of the latch being released; the first intimation that they weren't alone was received in the form of Justin's half affronted, half blustering ejaculation, 'What the hell is going on here, Ryan? I came to see how you were feeling.'

Ryan indolently levered himself into a sitting position on the side of the bed and raked a hand through his tousled hair, his body partially shielding the hot embarrassed Tracey as she fumbled furiously with the fastenings of her clothes.

'As you've probably already gathered, I'm feeling better, thanks,' he gave his grandparent a wry but direct look.

Justin snorted disparagingly, but his eyes wavered uncertainly from one to the other before his lips thinned and he shook his head in despair. 'I only hope to God you both know what you're doing,' he grunted heavily, and took himself back out of the room with a firm slamming of the door.

Tracey scrambled from the bed with alacrity. Having been brought back to her senses so suddenly by a third person, she felt cheap and shameless, and Ryan's apologetic, 'I'm sorry about that Tracey. I should have thought to lock the door,' had her flinching away from his compassion.

'It doesn't matter,' she tried to shrug it away indifferently, but only succeeded in sounding stiff and unnatural. 'Like you said, reaction makes people do strange things. It was probably fortunate that Justin did interrupt us, otherwise we—we might have—we both might have ...' She knew she was starting to lose track of what she had intended to say, but with Ryan rising to his feet and moving closer, she had to keep talking so that he didn't get a chance to speak before she had edged her way to the door. If he apologised for touching her, she would die from humiliation! 'I—I hope your leg mends soon and that it doesn't cause you too much inconvenience ...'

'Stop it, Tracey!' Ryan erupted savagely. 'You're ...'

'Not, I'm not,' she desperately denied whatever he was going to say, dodging away from his outstretched arm and continuing with the same impetuous haste, 'I just think I'd better be leaving now. There's a f-fan that needs attention and I have to find Eddy. Marty couldn't raise him on the phone,' she explained superfluously, her fingers twining together nervously.

'Tracey!'

There was a pleading tone in the voice which tore her apart, but when he began, 'I'm ...' she clamped her hands over her ears and shouted back, 'Don't say it! I don't want to hear it!' as she flung open the door and whirled into the passageway.

Safely inside her own bedroom, Tracey shakenly slid the lock across the door and wrapped her arms about her midriff to ease the searing pain as she stumbled to the dressing table and lit a much-needed cigarette. The eyes that stared back at her from the tilted mirror were dark and haunted, every vestige of green erased. What a devastating way to discover you're in love, her lips twisted with mockery, and she groaned disconsolately. Although Ryan's desire might have been generated by a reaction to the circumstances, hers had been brought about by something much deeper and stronger!

She drew deeply on a cigarette and expelled the smoke slowly, stretching exhaustedly out on her bed, her eyes blindly staring at the ceiling. And to think she still had another two years or more to go! She groaned again and closed her eyes, but that only brought back the memory of Ryan's intoxicating lips and dynamic masculinity, and her lashes flew apart swiftly to dismiss the picture. Oh, God, why hadn't the realisation come sooner? Why had it taken tormenting minutes of intimacy in his arms before her heart finally told her head the reason for those inexplicable surges of breathless vulnerability?

For a few moments she lay still, then with purposeful resolution she turned and stubbed out her cigarette. One thing she was certain of—Ryan was never going to be given the opportunity to find out how she felt. Just to think of the domination he could exert should she inadvertently give him cause to suspect how deeply her emotions were in-volved was enough to have her inwardly cringing. No, she didn't intend to ever give him that much power over her, it was far preferable that he continue to believe her willing participation had been due to an involuntary repercussion over which she had no control, the same as his own had been.

Besides, there was always Lana to consider. One woman hanging on his arm and making avid advances was surely sufficient for any man! With any sort of luck Lana would see to it that his thoughts were engaged elsewhere rather than on dissecting Tracey's inner feelings.

After cold reviving water had been sluiced over her face, her hair neatly combed, and a confidence-giving splash of colour smoothed over her lips, Tracey felt reasonably convinced she would be able to return to the office and explain her prolonged absence to Marty with a fair degree of equanimity. Her thoughts she had carefully tucked away into rigid compartments, but as she hurried down the steps she was still hoping for at least a few hours' grace before having to confront her guardian again.

'Tracey!'

Please, not now! her nerves screamed tortuously in response to the imperative call, but as there seemed no dignified way to prevent his overhauling her, she waited leadenly beneath the shady branches of a purple bauhinia for Ryan to catch up to her, but without once turning her head in the direction of his summons.

Two warm hands came down on her shoulders and spun her around impatiently. 'I think you and I have got some talking to do,' he dictated watchfully.

Tracey withdrew imperceptibly from his touch and forced an unconcerned expression into her eyes. 'There's nothing to discuss,' she told him as steadily as possible. 'I'm not looking for any apologies, excuses ... or repeats! I would rather just try to forget it ever happened and thereby make life a whole lot easier for both of us,' she concluded reasonably.

'You really believe that?' Ryan's eyes registered his patent disbelief and his lips softened lazily. 'You really think you can pretend it didn't happen ... that it's never likely to happen again?'

The disarming curve to his mouth was nearly Tracey's undoing, but his logical premise thankfully helped to harden her resolve. Oh, yes, if she didn't incontrovertibly convince him otherwise, it was likely to happen again! Even now it was an exquisite torment to stand so close and not slide her arms around his rugged proportions—and that was partly the trouble. Though she might be able to dredge up adequate reserves of willpower to resist her own longings, she certainly didn't have enough to repulse him as well. Swallowing hard, she set about destroying any preconceived notions he may have been harbouring.

'I don't see why not ... I have before,' she eventually

answered his query with a carefully insolent appraisal. 'It wasn't too difficult to forget Boyd's lovemaking, and I can't for the life of me see why the same shouldn't apply to you,' she shrugged insouciantly. 'Maybe I'm more like my mother than any of you realise,' she went on deliberately. 'She apparently liked variety too. Why tie yourself down to one, when the world's full of ardent and obliging males, I always say,' piquantly.

'So now it's on to the next conquest, is it?' His regard was coolly enquiring. 'How do you plan it, Tracey? A new month—a new lover?'

She pretended to give his suggestion due consideration. 'Well, I wouldn't have exactly called you a conquest, but yes, I do usually prefer to keep most of my affairs reasonably short,' she advised offhandedly.

'You've never come across one in all their number that you felt could satisfy your sexual desires for any length of time?'

'Obviously not!' she retorted as a steady flush crept up her cheeks as a result of his implication. He wasn't behaving in the least like she'd expected.

'But in the meantime, I was one of your conveniently ardent and obliging males?'

'Why not? You seemed co-operative enough,' she goaded pertly in an effort to obtain the required reaction, but that didn't appear very effective either, for his mouth merely quirked enigmatically and he drawled,

'Who were you planning to try out next? Marty?'

'Maybe,' her chin angled upwards defiantly.

For the first time Ryan looked really angry. 'Cut it out, honey,' he ordered inflexibly. 'You're no more interested in Marty than I am.'

This was more like it. 'And what makes you such an authority?' she taunted sarcastically.

'Because you're nothing but a highly imaginative little romancer, that's what!' he countered sardonically, and then smiled, 'Just how green and inexperienced do you think I am?' so wryly that Tracey could hardly breathe. 'Do you honestly believe that a man can't tell when he's making love to a girl who doesn't know the score? Your response this morning may have been freely given, but that was because it took you by surprise and you couldn't control it ... definitely not because of a calculated expertise!'

'Some men like the innocent approach,' she pointed out indomitably.

'Maybe so, but you've overlooked the most important factor,' he grinned down at her complacently. 'If there's one thing that experience can instantly recognise, it's that very same quality when it's present in others!'

'You still can't be certain,' valiantly holding out to the last.

'I'll tell you how certain I am,' he drawled indolently. 'I'm willing to hand over this property—lock, stock and barrel—to the first person who asks me for it if you've ever been to bed with a man in your life!'

There had to be some way to put doubts in his mind, hadn't there? A stray thought lingered longer than the others and Tracey's eyes widened smugly. 'If I said I had, you couldn't prove otherwise,' she gloated.

Ryan's ensuing roar of laughter had her expression turning doubtful and she bit at her lip in consternation when he cupped her face within two hands to tease. 'There's one hell of a way to refute it, honey. You want me to show you?'

'No!' Tracey dragged out of his hold and turned her back on him, her mind a chaotic jumble of contradictions. 'I don't want you to show me anything, Ryan, except the rooftops of Sydney when you fly me back there! Oh, why do you keep insisting I have to stay on Nindethana?' she threw back at him despairingly. 'Why don't you admit that I don't fit in here?'

'Why won't you admit that you do?' he counter-questioned levelly.

'Yes, that's right, be facetious about it,' she stormed. 'For one stupid moment I forgot—you always have to have the last word, don't you?'

'With you around I've found it advisable,' dryly. 'That is, if I want to retain any of my sanity at all.'

Tracey swung back to face him, her eyes large and pleading as she returned to her original theme and urged, 'Then don't keep me around! Make it more pleasurable for both of us by letting me go!'

'Forget it, Tracey!' Ryan's voice cut harshly through the air between them, apparently more riled by her entreaty than her previous efforts to annoy. 'You're staying here until the period of my guardianship runs out, and that's the last I want to hear about it!'

'Damn you, Ryan Alexander!' Unbidden tears welled into green eyes at the thought of all the days ahead that would each seem like a year with a secret such as hers to hide. 'What harm did I ever do you that you're so determined to make me pay so heavily for it?'

'Let's just say it's because you're such soothing company to have around,' he mocked.

It was obvious her ploys to change his mind were having little effect, and Tracey could feel the weight of defeat decending inexorably. One last hope remained and she sought its refuge desperately.

'Before she left, Nancy invited us to spend some time on their property. I'd like to take up her offer, if—if you agree, of course,' she forced out the request resentfully.

'For how long?'

Tracey caught her breath hopefully. 'A month?' she ventured in a whisper.

'With your sister and Carol?'

'If they want to come.' She didn't care who else was there as long as it wasn't himself!

Magnetic blue eyes surveyed the taut waiting figure and unknowingly beseeching features in consideration. 'Okay, honey, you've got your month,' he finally let her know his decision. 'When do you want to leave?'

Having achieved a small victory, she could afford to be generous. 'Whenever it's convenient.'

Ryan's lips twisted wryly as if he read her thoughts. 'Let's see now ... Wednesday, that suit you?'

She nodded happily, eyes shining, and even stood compliantly when his fingertips trailed evocatively along the side of her jaw and he queried at his most provoking, 'You reckon it will solve anything?'

Thick dark lashes fanned down to shut out the achingly

attractive image. 'I don't know what you're talking about,' she denied huskily.

'You don't believe that "absence makes the heart grow fonder", then?' he taunted aggravatingly.

Never having had reason to put it to the test before, Tracey didn't know whether she did or not, but she had no intention of even allowing him a glimpse of the doubts his words had created and lifted her head in a challenge.

'Sorry, I was planning to make "out of sight, out of mind" my motto,' she quipped derisively.

'But not too far out, I hope,' he counselled repressively. 'As long as you remember, honey, it's only for a month— not a couple of years.'

'And then you'll be taking up the reins again, so to speak?' Her lips pouted in a sarcastic moue. 'How thoughtful of you to remind me!' She paused and then added a bitter, 'As if I could ever be *that* lucky to forget!' as a parting shot before spinning irritably away and continuing down the path, surmising that if she didn't want him retracting his permission altogether then discretion demanded that she watch her increasingly gibing words and remove herself post-haste from his exasperating vicinity.

Lyn and Carol had received the news of Tracey's proposed visit to the older girl's home with united approval and it hadn't taken them very long in deciding to accompany her, for as Carol put it, 'It's harvest time and we always have a beaut party afterwards,' which, of course, was the most relevant influence as far as she was concerned.

Tracey's diffident, 'Do all the family attend?' had momentarily brought a frown to Carol's forehead, but then it cleared as she cross-questioned, 'Oh, you mean from here, and Aunt Rita, and Noeleen, and everyone?' to which Tracey had given an acknowledging nod, 'Some years they do, sometimes they don't. It all depends how busy they are themselves, but mostly it's friends and neighbours from around home,' she had gone on to explain, while Tracey sighed with relief.

Justin had merely muttered a concise, 'Sounds like a good idea,' when told of the intention, and although Tracey had fully expected him to make some forthright comments regarding her conduct of the morning, surprisingly he made absolutely no reference at all to the scene he had unwittingly disrupted, but she had noticed some extremely complex looks being tossed to and fro between himself and his grandson at dinner that evening which neither of them seemed particularly anxious to make the reasons therefor public, and which in the end Tracey gave up trying to decipher. If they wanted to keep their own secrets, then let them—she had more than enough to contend with in keeping her own hidden!

They reached Satinwood—Carol's picturesque, bougainvillaea-covered home on the fertile Darling Downs—in time for lunch on Wednesday, and as Ross drove them from the airstrip to the homestead Tracey and Lyn couldn't help but gaze in awe at the acres upon acres of waist-high wheat stretching away into the distance and which the breeze rustled playfully as it soughed between the ripe golden heads.

The landscape here was totally different from that which they had left only hours before; the earth a deep rich black; the trees a brighter, softer green; the sun not quite so ferocious in its intensity; the sky more colourful, cooler to the eyes. But strangely enough, to Tracey at least, it didn't compel the same kind of affinity that the magnificently stark and inimitable red soil plains of the outback did. Not that she would have openly admitted as much, but she found herself missing those washed-out skies, the overly-generous warmth of the sun, and the dusty, timeless look of undersized trees and defiantly tenacious undergrowth.

After a relaxing meal in the large, high-ceilinged dining room, with Ross and Lance blatantly trying to outdo each other with their speculations as to which of them was the star attraction to have prompted the visit, the family adjourned to the tiled and partially enclosed verandah for coffee at a lacy white wrought iron table, the matching chairs spaced conveniently about it.

'You're sure you won't stay the night?' Nancy's softly spoken husband asked of Ryan once everyone was comfortably settled.

'No, thanks, Clive, not this time,' came the reply so quietly that Tracey's eyes flew from their contemplation of the brilliantly flowered borders surrounding the building to Ryan's face wonderingly. If it was his normal practice to stay overnight on these trips, was it because of *her* presence that he was refusing on this occasion?

'But you will be returning for the harvest dance?' Nancy pressed earnestly, while Carol added her own confident, 'Of course he will! Won't you, Ryan?'

Tracey suddenly found her watchful gaze being returned by a wry blue one, then it was just as abruptly transferred to Nancy and Ryan shook his head apologetically.

'Sorry, Nancy, not this year, I'm afraid. Not unless it coincides with the date fixed for the girls' return, anyway,' he smiled ruefully and Tracey immediately knew her prior assumption had been correct and, contrarily, the knowledge hurt that he was as reluctant to remain in her company as she was in his.

The disappointed comments which followed his decision didn't make Tracey feel any more comfortable, either, so that by the time Ryan was ready to leave on his return flight she was feeling distinctly remorseful knowing that she was the inadvertent cause, and she surreptitiously edged closer as he and Ross headed for the steps to criticise awkwardly under her breath, 'You didn't have to deliberately miss their party on my account.'

When Ryan stopped to reply, Ross continued onwards to the waiting station wagon with an easy, 'I'll wait for you outside, mate,' and Tracey shifted restively from one foot to the other under a considering cobalt gaze.

'You said you wanted a month, and that's what you're getting. Why complain?' he questioned evenly, his whole attitude one of indifference.

'But I didn't know about the party then. How was I to know you usually come up here at harvest time?' she muttered reproachfully.

Broad shoulders rose negligently. 'There'll be other years.'

'But that's not the point!' Tracey's voice rose and she lowered it again self-consciously. 'They all sounded so let down when you said you wouldn't be coming and—and it's making me feel like the prize heel of the year,' she complained morosely.

'So now you're suggesting I reconsider in order to make you feel better? That's a change for the books, isn't it, honey?' His scepticism was almost tangible. 'I was under the impression it was my company you were trying to avoid.'

'For myself, I couldn't care less if I never saw you again!' she lied brazenly. 'It was them I was thinking of—*your* family,' with a covert but angry movement to indicate the group around the coffee table. 'If you weren't so busy being sarcastic you might have managed to recognise that fact,' she snapped.

'Oh, I realise all right!' his glance slashed at her savagely. 'What you're trying to say is, that I should now considerately reverse my decision just so you can salve your ruffled conscience. Well, nothing doing, honey!' he jeered. 'You see, I happen to be pleasantly anticipating these next four glorious weeks of respite from juvenile irritations and querulous tantrums. Believe me, a return to our previous peace and quiet, as well as more compliant feminine company, will be most welcome!'

Tracey paled at the calculated disparagement and drew in her breath sharply. Anger should have been her paramount emotion, but to her despair she discovered it wasn't—jealousy was! A green-eyed, devouring pain that clawed its way through her insides and, in defence, had a brittle smile of indifference being coerced on to trembling lips.

'Well, good for you!' she gibed insolently. 'As long as you don't forget to advise your so admirable feminine company that I was altruistic enough to keep her place in your bed warm during her absence! That little piece of information should make her *real* compliant!' she choked bitterly, and nearly cried aloud when his fingers gripped her arm with such force that she was sure it would break in two.

'You ever make a crack like that again and I'll slaughter you, Tracey!' he rasped furiously, releasing her arm as if he couldn't bear to touch it any longer, and striding down the steps to the waiting vehicle without another word.

Rubbing a soothing hand over the scarlet imprints his fingers had left, Tracey watched Ryan's departure with sombre eyes. 'You already have,' she whispered her confession defeatedly.

CHAPTER TEN

UNTIL her weeks at Satinwood, Tracey would never have believed that days could seem so short, nor nights so long. The daylight hours had been easily filled watching the voracious headers as they methodically stripped each paddock of its bountiful produce; riding in the hopper trucks to the silos to watch the grain being lifted into the storage bins; and then seeing the wheat trains being bulk loaded and setting off for the coastal port terminals. Other days were spent helping to muster and cull the sheep; the greater percentage of the young male lambs being despatched for butchering and sale as prime lamb; the females being retained for wool production, breeding, and in later years, mutton. Visits to neighbouring properties occupied a lot of time too, as did leisurely rides across country, games of tennis, picnics, and afternoons spent swimming in the near-by lagoon.

But it was the nights which haunted Tracey—long periods of fitful dozing and self-analysis which even the fatigue brought about by a full and energetic day couldn't overcome. Ryan's facetiously quoted proverb often came back to bait her in the darkest of all hours just before sun-up, her own retorted adage being completely submerged, for, although he might have been out of sight, he was certainly never out of mind!

Anything and everything seemed to serve the purpose and defeat her. The angle at which Lance wore his hat; a particular nuance in Ross's voice; the sound of stockboots on the verandah; the whine of a light aircraft overhead; a casual reference at the dining table. The list was endless, and so were the disturbing hours that Tracey spent recalling him in daydreams.

She had hoped, and even partially believed, that a month away from Nindethana would allow her to bring him into some sort of biddable perspective, but he still loomed dominantly in the forefront of her thoughts, swamping reason and defying all her attempts to rationalise him into a minor category. The mere thought of Ryan being with Lana, or worse, making love to her, was capable of generating a most demoralising desperation and, even though her head kept insisting that time would be her salvation, her heart wasn't about to be so philosophically persuaded, with the result that she would promptly throw herself into another day's activities with every semblance of not having a care in the world—and then lay awake for most of the night wishing herself back on Nindethana and indulging in one of their verbal brawls. In spite of the fact that she never seemed able to triumph in any of their continual harangues, she was swiftly coming to look upon them as expedient if only for the fact that Ryan was *there* when they took place.

The harvest party—held in the informality of the woolshed—had been a huge success in everyone else's opinion. Although, after his parting remarks, Tracey hadn't really expected Ryan to change his mind and put in an appearance, subconsciously she had been trusting he would do exactly that, so by the time the dancing was well under way and she finally had to accept that her unadmitted hopes were forlorn ones, she had had to force herself to appear happy and untroubled while internally craving the solace of some secluded corner where she could nurse her sorrows in private.

On the day of their arranged return it was, understandably in the circumstances, Tracey who was packed and waiting for Ryan's arrival first. All morning her eyes had been drifting skyward at five-minute intervals, ears straining, but when the plane eventually landed and Ross drove him back to the house she was the last to offer any form of greeting. From the rear of the family group she feasted her eyes tormentingly on the broad, virile frame, noting miserably that though she had been cursorily included in his initial polite salutation, the remainder of his attention and questions were being directed to the others.

The flight home in the afternoon was no more satisfying either. With Lyn's confidence growing daily since teaming with Carol, she was rapidly becoming almost as talkative as her cousin was, with the effect that if one of them wasn't enthusiastically engaged in regaling Ryan with a thorough summary of events that had taken place, then the other one was, and leaving Tracey very little choice but to sink once more into her own dejected thoughts. The only time she brightened being when the painted roof of the homestead came into view and she sighed contentedly. She was home! It had taken a month's absence to make her realise just how firmly the station had dug itself an unassailable niche in her system, and in acknowledgment she breathed fervently of the warm air immediately she set foot on the dusty red earth.

Happily, at least Justin appeared genuinely pleased to have her back again, for without his uncomplicated presence during the following week Tracey didn't know what she would have done. Ever since their reunion at Satinwood, Ryan's whole attitude towards her had been one of cool detachment. His words—and only then when they were absolutely necessary—impersonal to a degree bordering on discourtesy, and in consequence Tracey became more and more dispirited as each day passed. Her eyes reflected an inner apathy with a grey lacklustre gaze, her movements became increasingly listless, and when a smile was required her mouth could only dredge up a pale ghost of its former curving allure.

'There you are!' exclaimed Carol brightly one morning some ten days after their return as Tracey was just finishing her breakfast. She always made a point of being last to the table these days in order to avoid Ryan's cutting disinterest as much as possible. 'I just saw Grandfather in the study. He said he'd like to see you if I could find you,' the younger girl continued cheerfully.

Tracey dabbed at pale lips with a napkin and rose to her feet. 'Thanks, Carol. I'll go and see him now,' she replied softly, wondering why a specific summons had been thought necessary. 'Do you know what it's about?' she suddenly frowned.

'No idea,' Carol grinned, and shrugged nonchalantly, then, 'Lyn and I thought we might go back to the old opal

mines today and try our luck with a bit of noodling. Want
to come?' she enquired lightly.

'I—er—I don't think so—not today, thanks. I'd better
see what Justin wants first,' Tracey refused yet another
offer to accompany them on an outing. 'I also have some—
some letter writing to do,' she fabricated uncomfortably
lest Carol should feel offended by her continuous rejections,
and sighed with relief when that girl only smiled again and
said equably, 'Okay then, we'll see you later,' and continued
on her way with a quick step while Tracey headed in the
opposite direction.

'Come in and shut the door, Tracey,' she was bidden a
few minutes later on reaching the study. 'I wanted to have
a talk to you and we're less likely to be disturbed in here
than elsewhere,' Justin informed her gently.

Apprehensively obeying, Tracey took a softly upholstered
seat parallel to the black hide couch Justin was occupying
and smoothed her hands over the fabric of her navy slacks.
'Yes?' she prompted nervously.

If possible, it seemed that Justin was almost as uneasy
as Tracey was, because it took some considerable time for
him to settle himself more comfortably, scratch at the side
of his neck, and clear his throat before starting to speak.

'I—um—I had a discussion with Ryan about you last
night,' were his first hesitant words which had Tracey
gripping her hands together tautly. 'And he—we—decided
that, all things considered, it might be more satisfactory
after all if we allowed you to—er—have your own way.'

All things considered? Have her own way? Tracey stared
at him blankly. 'I'm sorry, I don't understand,' she chewed
at her lip in confusion.

Justin made a furious motion in the air with his hands.
'You can leave here! Go back to living in Sydney!' he
snapped irritatedly. 'That's what you've always wanted,
isn't it?'

Up until six weeks ago she would have agreed un-
reservedly, but now the positions were reversed—she
wanted to remain, but Ryan wanted her to go. However,
her pride began to reassert itself as she contemplated Ryan's
sardonic amusement if he ever discovered her defenceless-

ness where he was concerned and she gave Justin an unwavering look.

'Yes, that's what I've always wanted,' she corroborated
staunchly.

'This doesn't mean that Ryan will be any the less your
guardian, young lady,' he was swift to impress on her
decisively. 'You'll still be accountable to him for your
actions and I shall expect you to keep in regular contact. I
don't intend letting any of my son's family disappear again,'
he advised heavily.

'Oh, Justin, I'm sorry,' she whispered contritely, a tentative hand reaching out and being briefly clasped by two
gnarled, work-roughened ones, knowing that under his often
testy exterior there beat a very sentimental heart. 'I promise
I'll write every week if you want me to,' she vowed
sincerely.

'No need to be *that* diligent,' his mouth pulled down at
the corners ironically. 'But maybe one a month wouldn't go
amiss,' he eyed her humorously from under iron-grey brows.

'I won't forget,' Tracey assured him with something like
her normal smile, but the newly cheerful light in her eyes
was extinguished instantly when Ryan unexpectedly entered
the room, closed the door and leant back against it with his
arms folded across his chest, a long-suffering expression on
his face.

'All set?' his eyes ranged interrogatingly towards his
grandparent.

'Not quite,' Justin replied with a hand indicating that his
grandson should take a seat, but which was studiously
ignored. 'There's still a few things I'd like to get settled.'

'Well, you won't need me for that.' Ryan pushed himself
off the door and thrust his hands into the back pockets of
his pants, his gaze transferring to Tracey. 'We leave at eight
tomorrow morning—right?'

Tracey was stunned. So soon! How anxious he must be
to see the last of her! 'But—but I haven't made any arrangements regarding accommodation,' she directed her appeal to
Justin rather than her guardian. 'Without the house to go
back to,' now she couldn't resist a pointed look at Ryan,
'I'll have to find somewhere reasonable to stay while I hunt
for a flat,' she explained defensively.

'There's no need for that, arrangements have already been made,' Ryan answered curtly. 'You'll be a resident at the Goodman Hotel for the remainder of my guardianship.'

'But I can't afford to stay *there*!' Tracey's voice thinned in horror at the thought of the expense involved in such a proposal. The Goodman was way out of her league!

Ryan's mouth levelled with exasperation. 'You *can* afford it,' he bit out coldly, reminding Tracey of her still untouched inheritance. 'But you don't have to anyway. The estate will be covering all expenses incurred at the hotel.'

'But—but I don't want ...'

'It was my idea, Tracey,' Justin broke in hurriedly. 'I wanted to make sure you were being looked after properly and that we could get in touch with you at any time if we had to. Flats are always so nebulous—you move into one, then change for another, and before you know it you've lost track of someone.'

Which one member of the family wouldn't regret in the slightest, she mused despondently. Her eyes sought Justin's apologetically. 'It's very thoughtful of you, but really I would prefer ...'

'Please, Tracey, for my sake,' he interrupted her again. 'I'm old-fashioned—I don't like hearing of young girls living on their own with no one to protect them. I'll feel happier knowing there's someone responsible there to look out for your welfare.'

How could she refuse? His concern was touching, especially so after ten days of Ryan's slights, and nodded slowly in agreement. 'All right,' she murmured throatily. 'I'll stay at the Goodman if that's what you really want.'

'I do,' he concurred emphatically, leaning back and giving a contented sigh as Ryan opened the door and, taking her cue, Tracey preceded him from the room.

When she would have continued on to her bedroom, Ryan put out a hand to detain her, but removing it as soon as she halted and turned to look at him warily. For a moment she wondered if she wasn't inventing things, instead of the cool appraisal she had lately come to expect there seemed to be a compassionate softening in the blue depths of his eyes, but a disbelieving shake of her head confirmed that it was indeed a figment of her imagination, for when he spoke they held all the warmth of a glacier in a snowstorm.

'I have an important engagement in town tomorrow, Tracey, so kindly make sure you're on time. I don't want to be late arriving,' he ordered brusquely.

Some of her old defiance must have still been buried deep within her, for now it came rushing to the surface and she mocked, 'I wouldn't do that for the world, Ryan! You can take my word for it, your anxiety to see me gone is nowhere near as strong as my desire to leave! I'm sure I shall be here waiting long before *you're* ready,' before turning on her heel and making for her room with her head held rebelliously high.

Someone, whether Ryan or Justin she didn't know, had already informed Lyn and Carol of her imminent departure by the time Tracey next saw them, and although her sister was obviously disappointed to see her leave, she didn't appear unduly upset by the fact. Another point to you, Ryan, Tracey scowled to herself. Lyn was finally standing on her own two feet and accepting life as it came! All the same, she had to admit that Lyn's almost casual acceptance had hurt her more than a little, but she forbore to say anything for fear of prejudicing her sister's newly discovered independence.

Tracey was also as good as her word the next morning and succeeded in her determined effort to be waiting before Ryan was ready to leave, but when her bags had been stowed in the car and it was time for farewells, astonishingly it was Justin she realised she was going to miss the most— discounting Ryan, of course—and his last-minute adjuration, 'You're sure you won't stay?' had tears filling her eyes as she went up on tiptoe to kiss the lined cheek, whispering brokenly, 'I can't, Justin! You know I can't!' before breaking free and rushing down the steps and into the vehicle to preclude him saying anything further.

As she had expected, conversation on the trip down was minimal, Ryan's contributions being so few and far between that after they had passed the halfway point Tracey lapsed into complete silence and didn't speak another word until they reached the airfield and were making for Ryan's hired car. With her nerves strained to the utmost by the trying flight she put in an aspiring bid for deliverance.

'If you're in a hurry to keep your appointment, I can catch a taxi from here,' she offered helpfully.

By way of an answer Ryan tossed first one and then the other of her cases into the boot, slammed the lid shut and stalked to the passenger's door. 'Get in!' he ordered tersely, pulling the door wide. 'I'll let you know if I'm running late.'

'You do that,' she muttered sarcastically, giving him a baleful glare and flouncing into the vehicle. 'You do just that and see how much I care!' she continued in the same disgruntled tone, while he strode around to the driver's side and slid in beside her.

'Did you say something?' he asked as the car began moving, and making Tracey jump guiltily until she concluded he must only have seen her lips moving and not been able to hear what she said.

Concentrating her gaze on the road in front of them, she hunched her shoulders dismissively. 'Nothing you'd be interested to hear, I'm sure!' she sniped.

A slanted glance raked briefly over the defiantly angled profile and from the corner of her eye Tracey could see the knuckles whiten as his hands tightened around the steering wheel. 'All this,' a nod of his head indicated the sprawling western suburbs they were travelling through, '*must* agree with you. That shrewish hostility of yours is rampaging to the fore again!' he gibed hatefully.

Tracey's hands clenched convulsively on the strap of the bag in her lap, all desire to answer in kind draining away with the recalled knowledge that their permanent parting was so close at hand. Tears burnt at the back of her eyes and she murmured, 'I'm sorry,' in a subdued voice.

'Because it agrees with you, or because you allowed your animosity to show again?' came the relentless taunting.

Resentful and unbearably goaded, Tracey rounded on him furiously. 'Who cares? Why don't you just shut up, Ryan, and concentrate on driving faster? The quicker we get there the better, to my mind!' she perjured herself bravely.

A muscle flickered steadily in the side of his jaw. 'For

the first time ever it seems we're in accord,' he returned sardonically. 'You echo my feelings exactly.'

Tracey had only ever walked past the marble façade of the Goodman Hotel previously, not having had any reason to pass through the automatic doors and feel her feet sinking in the deep pile of the amethyst carpet as she took in the meticulously co-ordinated silver and charcoal décor like she was doing at the moment.

The Alexanders must be regular and valued guests if the manager's personal attentions were anything to judge by, Tracey guessed wryly, because he not only greeted Ryan with a great deal of deference but he also accompanied them to the suite of rooms set aside for Tracey's use to confirm that they were acceptable.

Tracey wouldn't have believed it possible that anything in such a luxurious establishment could have been otherwise. Whenever she had stayed at an hotel before—and there hadn't been many occasions—the accommodation had been positive rabbit hutches in comparison with the spacious elegance of the rooms she was about to occupy and, somehow, she found the prospect just a little intimidating. It seemed ridiculous that after a hard day in an office somewhere—she fully intended getting another job and not touching a cent of her inheritance—she would return to these sumptious surroundings to sleep. If Ryan and herself had been on better terms she could imagine laughing with him about it, but as things were she merely stood and stared ruefully at the expensive fittings while Ryan assured Gordon Thomas, the manager, that the suite was satisfactory and that Miss Alexander would let him know should there be anything else she required.

Miss Alexander wasn't too sure she would dare do anything of the kind, but she gave the departing Mr Thomas an acknowledging smile as if in confirmation and wandered over to the wide windows of her sitting room to gaze at the panorama spread below. The deep blue waters of the harbour, sprinkled with the white sails of yachting enthusiasts even on a weekday, sparkled invitingly back at her, while to the left there was an interrupted view of the bold arch of the Harbour Bridge as it overlooked the soaring shells

of the Opera House, the crenellated walls of Government
House set amid green lawns and cool leafy trees, and immediately below, the crowded streets and voluminous traffic
which appeared Lilliputian from her extravagant vantage
point.

Sensing rather than hearing someone behind her, Tracey
drew a deep breath and turned slowly. 'I suppose you'll be
wanting to get going now,' she remarked in a low tone, her
glance holding an uncertain point over Ryan's shoulder and
not his face.

'Shortly,' he agreed, and held out a printed brochure
which she took with cold nerveless fingers. 'Gordon gave me
that for you. It lists all the facilities the hotel has to offer
and gives times for meals in the main dining room, the
Bistro, and the Charcoal Grill, etcetera. If there's anything
else you want to know, just ask him, he's very obliging.'

'Yes, I noticed.' She had to say something, no matter how
mundane.

'You realise of course that as your guardian I'll still have
to make periodic checks as to what you're doing?'

'I know,' Tracey's head nodded swiftly, her responses
becoming more stilted with each passing minute.

'And you'll remember to write? Justin will be disappointed if you don't.'

But not you! her heart cried miserably. 'I'll write,' she
promised, head downbent.

'Well, I think that just about wraps it up.' She heard him
sigh—in relief, she supposed. A firm hand surprisingly
grasped her chin and tilted her head upwards. 'If you must
have admirers, try and make sure they're not married this
time, hmm? It would be as well for you to remember that
Nindethana will still be waiting should you ever be tempted
to step too far out of line,' he advised with a glittering gaze
of blue steel.

Because she was so devastingly aware of the feel of his
hand against her skin, Tracey unthinkingly rushed into
speech. 'Like a sword held over my head? You do it an in-
justice!' she censured, and received an intent scrutiny for
her spontaneous frankness.

'So-o,' Ryan drew the word out with nerve-racking tautness. 'It wasn't the outback you objected to so strongly after all—it was solely my presence, my guardianship, eh?' His head lowered disturbingly near. 'Well, let me tell you something, Red,' he taunted with the use of that maddening name, '*your* presence didn't exactly set my world on fire either! And you seem to have forgotten, it was my idea to send you down here—you're not what I would call endearing company to have around, you know!'

Tracey valiantly swallowed the hurt his words inflicted and broke contact with him savagely. 'Yeah, yeah, you've told me all that before,' she drawled impudently. 'But now, if you don't mind, I'd like to do some unpacking, so ...' she threw out an arm expressively towards the door and, wheeling around, marched away from him into the adjoining bedroom.

The decided slam of a door a few seconds later had Tracey throwing herself abjectly on the bed and dissolving into a storm of long-suppressed sobbing. Although she kept telling herself she should have been pleased to have had the final say for a change, there was no pleasure attached to the knowledge when the only thing her brain would keep remembering was that Ryan hadn't even said goodbye!

CHAPTER ELEVEN

TRACEY pushed back the breakfast trolley glumly and lit a cigarette. She had taken to having most of her meals in her rooms during her two-month residency at the Goodman. In the beginning she had felt a little lost sitting at a table for one in the massive dining room, but in the smaller, more cosy Bistro or Charcoal Grill, there usually seemed to be at least one off-the-leash husband looking for a good time, and the speculative and inviting glances which appeared at the sight of her unaccompanied always managed to erase any enjoyment she might have found in her meal.

It was still only eight o'clock and she drew restlessly on the cigarette. With the office where she had found employment so close to the hotel there was never any need for her to leave until almost nine, but this morning, of all days, she thought should have felt different in some way. It was her twenty-first birthday! Normally a time for celebration; a general acceptance of having come of age; the key to the door, and all that! But here she was alone, with absolutely nothing to distinguish it from any other working day and not even any mail, or one small card from Lyn to signify its importance. That had occasioned the worst soreness of all, that her own sister should have forgotten!

She heaved a sigh and stubbed out her cigarette, moving disconsolately to the window and looking out over the city. Already the streets were beginning to fill as tiny figures scurried to and fro along the pavements, across roadways, disappearing into buildings like industrious little ants rushing for the safety of gigantic steel and concrete ant hills. How could she ever have believed she wanted to return to all this? Many were the times she had found herself involuntarily stopping work in the office and just dreaming of the silence of the outback, the distant horizons filled with nothing more strident than a bleating sheep, while around her numerous voices, adding machines, ledger machines, typewriters and telephones all intermingled in a cacophony that offended the eardrums.

She didn't bother to turn away from her introverted contemplation when there was a knock on her door, merely calling, 'Come in,' and expecting to see young Daryl, the waiter, enter and collect her trolley. But when the door still hadn't opened after a couple of minutes she frowned and walked over to it, wondering who on earth could be calling on her at that time of the morning. If Gordon Thomas ever wanted to see her about something he usually waited to have a word with her when she came in from work in the afternoons.

As she pulled the door wide her eyes stared disbelievingly and her legs grew weak. 'What—what are you doing here?' she queried breathlessly of a stunningly attractive Ryan as he leant negligently against the door jamb. Casually dressed in white flared denims with a navy short sleeve knit top, he was irresistibly male!

His mouth curved lazily. 'Don't you know what day it is?' Easing himself into an upright position, he followed her as she walked dazedly backwards into the room, an accurate hand closing the door as his gaze stayed locked with hers.

Tracey licked at suddenly dry lips and moved a hand vaguely. 'It—it's Friday, of course,' she returned faintly, her thoughts and emotions still not functioning correctly. Since his appearance they had been in a condition of shocked numbness.

'Fancy that,' his eyebrows lifted ironically as he crossed to the trolley and felt the coffee pot. 'Be a good girl and ring down for some more, I could do with a coffee. You look as if you could too,' his lips quirked as he made himself at home in one of the chairs and proceeded to disconcert her yet again by abruptly reverting to his original subject. 'Don't tell me you've forgotten your own twenty-first?' He looked at her enquiringly.

Tracey rapidly finished telephoning her order through to room service and replaced the receiver with a thud. 'Oh, that,' she managed to make it sound of little importance.

'No, I hadn't forgotten, I just wasn't planning to do anything about it, that's all.'

'No favoured escort to help you celebrate?'

'No,' derisively.

'The family thought there should be.'

She blinked in puzzlement. 'I beg your pardon?'

'The family considered you shouldn't spend such an occasion on your own,' he explained patiently.

'And is that why—why you're here?' she asked hesitantly, fearful of a disparaging denial.

There was no contradiction, however, only a lazily concurring, 'Hence my being here.'

'But what if I had made other arrangements? It was a long way to come on the offchance,' Tracey had to ask.

A gleam appeared in his eyes which instantly made her wary. 'We didn't think it probable,' he informed her blandly. 'On both nights when Justin phoned you, he spoke to Gordon first, by whom he was advised that as far as he was aware, you rarely went out at night, and even more rarely entertained anyone at the hotel. It was a fair bet that you wouldn't be making arrangements for today either.'

'You mean Justin's been using the manager to spy on me? That my every movement has been watched ever since I came here?' in horrified anger.

'Of course you haven't been spied on,' he denied casually. 'Justin was worried about you.'

'Then why didn't he ask *me* if there was something he wanted to know?'

'He couldn't be certain you'd tell him the truth,' dryly.

The arrival of the waiter with another pot of coffee and more cups prevented Tracey from replying, but immediately he left she sprang to her feet and rounded on Ryan sarcastically.

'So the family decided I was to be pitied and that you should be the bunny with the unenviable task of keeping me company, is that it?' she exclaimed heatedly. 'Well, thanks for nothing! It seems you've had a wasted journey, because I don't need anyone to help me observe my birthday—nor any other anniversary, if it comes to that!' as she paced agitatedly about the room.

When the cutting reprisal she had been anticipating didn't eventuate, Tracey stopped her pacing and stared at him confusedly. She certainly hadn't expected to find him helping himself calmly to the coffee she should by rights have poured for him, and leaning back comfortably with a tolerant smile curving his lips. Her hands came to rest on her hips and she eyed him challengingly.

'Well?' she demanded impatiently.

Ryan took his time stirring his coffee and rested one ankle across the knee of his other leg. 'I refuse to argue with you on your birthday,' he grinned.

'Oh!' Tracey's eyes mirrored her uncertainty and she dropped down moodily on to the sofa opposite his chair. 'I meant what I said, there was no need for you to have made the journey down,' she repeated with a decided pout.

'But I did, so why don't you stop trying to find fault for all the wrong reasons and go and get changed, hmm?' he suggested with a quick glance at the watch strapped to his wrist. 'The minutes are slipping by and you're the one who's wasting time, now, honey.'

Just the thought of spending a whole day in Ryan's company—whether he kept his word and refused to argue or not—was sheer heaven to Tracey. The only worrying doubt being whether she could conceal her feelings well enough for such a period. To him it constituted a suddenly indulgent whim towards his ward—to her it meant much, much more to share a few hours with the man she loved.

As she made up her mind her lips lost their discontented droop and she rose to her feet again, eagerly this time, and then her face fell. 'But I can't!' she lamented dolefully. 'It's Friday and I've got to go to work. I can't just take a day off whenever I feel like it!'

'Then you must be the only one on the payroll who doesn't,' he commented wryly. 'But there's no need for you to worry about it—everything's been arranged.'

Two deep creases formed between Tracey's eyes. 'What's that supposed to mean? What's been arranged?' she queried perplexedly.

His eyes rose skywards. 'Do me a favour, honey, and for once just take things as said, will you?'

It was the first time Tracey could ever remember Ryan looking uneasy and she immediately became suspicious. 'No!' she refused emphatically. 'I want to know exactly what's been going on behind my back. Just *what* has been arranged, and with whom, Ryan?'

'It was arranged with your employers that you have to-day off,' he divulged with a resigned sigh.

'With Mr Whitehouse?' Tracey found it hard to accept and still more difficult to understand.

'He's only your immediate boss—R. J. McCarthy and Associates are your employers,' he returned knowledgeably.

Oh God, had Gordon Thomas ferreted that out for them too? 'And ...?' she prompted mutinously.

Ryan replaced his cup on the tray and agilely gained his feet, hands being thrust into his pockets as he leant wide shoulders against the mantel over the fireplace. 'R. J. McCarthy happens to be my maternal grandfather—Justin, Glen and I are three of the Associates,' he admitted rue-fully.

So that was why the advertisement for the position she now held had suited her qualifications as if made for them. This was exactly what it had been intended to do! Tracey could have screamed with resentment and mortification.

But she didn't. Instead her shoulders slumped dejectedly and she suggested in a lifeless voice, 'It was all a farce letting me come back to Sydney, wasn't it? I suppose you own the hotel too?' The last with a depressing type of sarcasm.

His wry, 'Not entirely—only half,' brought green eyes upward in bewilderment.

'But *why*?' she cried poignantly. 'I agreed to stay here when Justin asked me to. I promised to write regularly, and I did. What more did you want of me, Ryan? Why was it so necessary to make a fool of me as well?' she trembled despairingly, tears beginning to spill on to her lashes.

The distance between them was soon closed as Ryan stepped forward to wrap comforting arms around her, and Tracey was too distressed to pull away. 'I'm sorry, Tracey, but he thought he was doing it for the best,' he murmured softly, his chin resting on the top of her head, his hand soothing as it stroked over her hair. 'You know how frightened to death Justin was at the idea of you vanishing again.' One hand found her chin and tipped her head away from his chest. 'It wasn't his intention to make you unhappy, honey. Believe me, that was the last thing in the world he wanted.'

An unhappy swallow removed part of the lump in her throat. 'But I'll never be able to show my face in that office again,' she protested.

'Except for old R.J. himself, no one else in the office knows,' his lips descended sensuously to kiss away the tears staining her cheeks, 'and he's as likely to tell anyone as the birds are not to fly.'

With his mouth burning a line across her face it was impossible for Tracey to think straight. All she wanted was to feel those lips covering her own, and it was only due to a rigid self-discipline that she managed to reproach sorrowfully, 'But it was all so unfair! So damned unfair and underhanded! I—I...'

She couldn't continue. Ryan's lips were caressing the corner of her mouth and the next moment, with a moan of surrender, her own were clinging passionately to his, inviting an ardent exploration as she melted weakly against him, her hands sliding around the supple waist to the broadening muscles of his back.

All thoughts of further recriminations were buried as Tracey willingly responded to the hungry dominance of Ryan's exciting mouth until, like a cloudburst pouring reviving rain on to those below, the realisation that she was unresevedly placing her innermost emotions on display materialised from nowhere and she rapidly dragged herself out of his embrace, breathing heavily and brushing the back of one hand over still tear-wet eyes. How could she have allowed herself to become so intoxicated that she forgot his actions had only been dictated by sympathy, and not by any warmer feeling as hers were?

'I'm sorry ... I was upset,' she hunched away from him embarrassedly, trying desperately to make her excuse sound plausible. 'But I'm a big girl now and kissing away hurts doesn't make them better any more,' she informed him tautly in an endeavour to appear calm and unperturbed.

White teeth showed in a slow, lazy smile. 'Kissing always makes it better,' he drawled, making Tracey flush hotly under the amused regard as he continued, 'So now will you go and get ready, birthday girl?' with a teasing inflection that sent her heart pounding uncontrollably.

'I don't think I should after having those shabby tricks played on me.' She felt she had to make some sort of stand.

'But you will!'

Apparently Ryan had already decided for her—as always —but today Tracey had no desire to gainsay him. Halfway to her bedroom she turned back interestedly. 'Where are we going?' she asked.

'It's your birthday,' he shrugged easily. 'You choose.'

Tracey considered deeply for a time, and then, 'Well, the forecast on the radio this morning did say the temperature was expected to reach the high thirties today,' she sent him a gauging look. 'Would the beach be okay? There won't be the crowds that you usually get over the weekend,' helpfully.

'Suits me—I said it was your choice.' He lit a cigarette and grinned at her through the smoke as it spiralled upwards. 'You forget, where I come from we don't get to see that much water unless there's a flood. It makes a pleasant change to spend a few hours at the beach,' he set her doubts aside evenly.

Dressed in pre-faded, flared jeans with a plaited belt of the same material hugging her slender waist, and a pale mauve crocheted top with a deeply scooped neckline, Tracey sat contentedly beside Ryan as they headed eastwards across the city and prepared to make the most of this one day when she had him all to herself, and determined not to consider the aching loneliness she would again experience when he left. For today it was enough that he was with her and in such a captivating mood!

A mood, nevertheless, that threatened to raze her defences to the ground, she was to find as the day wore on. Although she was on her guard against letting her feelings show too much, there were instances when they were im-

pervious to any sort of control and she regretfully knew her
heart was in her eyes when she looked at Ryan. She felt as
if she was being pulled in opposite directions at the same
time, sometimes wanting to respond wholeheartedly to his
vibrant fascination, but then at others wishing she could
withdraw into herself completely.

It was a glorious morning; the sun brilliant in the clear
blue sky overhead; the sand too hot for walking on so that
it was a mad laughing scramble to reach the water's edge
before the feet blistered; and the surf running co-opera-
tively high as it thundered on to the shore with spray
thrown diamond-like into the sky to disturb the ever-
present gulls when they came in low, looking for food.

Afterwards it was back to the city for lunch at a rest-
aurant in one of the converted Bond Stores down at The
Rocks—Sydney's birthplace on the harbour foreshore
which nestled beneath the southern approaches to the Harbour Bridge.

Seated at a comfortable table for two with the suffused
light of a coachman's lamp casting soft shadows over them,
Tracey looked about her attentively. Though much of the
building had, of necessity, had to be replaced, as much of
the original as possible—or cleverly simulated original, it
was difficult to tell them apart—had been retained so that
the overall effect was indeed one of another day and age and
Tracey warmed to its colonial charm immediately.

A morning's vigorous surfing had given them both
ravenous appetites and their conversation was only spasmodic until they had each devoured a large plate filled with
incomparable Sydney rock oysters, but while they were
waiting for the steaks which were to follow, Tracey's fingers
slipped up and down the stem or her wine glass absently,
her thoughts elsewhere.

The day was disappearing so quickly! Already it was half
over and she wanted to find out how much time together
they had left, but wasn't quite sure how best to go about it.
Clearing her throat nervously, she looked up and found
Ryan's gaze surveying her features thoroughly, and that
didn't help in any way.

Actually he was the one to speak first. 'Your nose is sun-
burnt,' he relayed with a grin.

'What?' Tracey blinked at him vaguely, so far had his comment been from her own anxious thoughts. But recovering swiftly, she put a finger self-consciously to its dainty proportions. 'I thought I might catch it when we were in the surf for so long,' she admitted ruefully. 'But as long as it has the pink glow of sunrise and not the crimson glory of sunset I won't mind too much.'

His head tilted judiciously to one side. 'On you, I daresay either of them would look equally good,' he commented lazily. 'Now what was it you were going to say when I caught you off guard?'

The unexpected compliment, together with his counter-question, disrupted Tracey's carefully planned words entirely and she started to stammer annoyingly. 'I—er—oh, nothing much,' was her confused beginning, and she shrugged as offhandedly as possible. 'I was just—er—wondering when you were—um—going back home.' Finally she succeeded in getting a savage grip on herself and concluded her probing with, 'I suppose you'll be flying out later this afternoon, won't you?' in a creditably unconcerned tone.

'I had no plans along those lines. Are you suggesting that I should have?' his brows quirked ironically.

'No!' The answer was too vehement and she amended it rapidly to a more moderate, 'No, of course not. As I said, I was only wondering, that's all.'

He leant his elbows on the table and rested his chin on his clasped hands. 'Why?'

'I—well . . .' she shook her head evasively. 'You promised you wouldn't argue with me today,' seeking refuge in the reproachful reminder.

His lips curved wryly as his eyes held hers intently. 'And nor have I . . . as you very well know! But, just this once, I would have been interested to hear the truth of what was behind that enquiry of yours, honey.'

Partly as a result of their congenial morning, and partly in response to his candour, Tracey suddenly found her gaze dropping to the table top as she confessed huskily, 'It's been such a nice day so far that I wanted to know how long there was left before it ended.'

The silence which followed had her clenching her hands regretfully in her lap, not daring to look up until she heard

Ryan's voice suggesting, 'Such honesty deserves a reward, wouldn't you say?' when she at last hazarded a glance from beneath shadowed lashes to find a velvet-covered oblong box lying on the table in front of her. 'Happy birthday,' he smiled lazily across at her.

'For me?' she sought verification in a throaty whisper, smoothing her fingers tentatively over the lid.

'For you,' he agreed. 'I don't think it would suit anyone else.'

Nervously Tracey fumbled with the clasp and lifted the lid suspensefully. A stunned gasp and her eyes returned to his dazedly. 'Oh, Ryan, thank you ... it's beautiful,' she breathed devoutly. 'It's the most beautiful thing I've ever seen,' with her gaze dropping unbelievably to his gift once more.

It was a bracelet, no more than three-quarters of an inch wide, but the workmanship was exquisite. It spelt her name in the most delicate threads of gleaming gold, each letter outlined in diamonds which reflected every colour of the rainbow back into her glistening eyes.

'Aren't you going to wear it?' he asked as she closed the case reluctantly on its beauty.

Tracey looked down at her outfit disparagingly. 'Not with these,' she half smiled. 'But you can see it tonight—I have just the dress to wear it with.' She stopped and a rosy glow covered her face which had nothing whatever to do with her slight case of sunburn. 'That is, if you—if I ...' her voice faded in embarrassment.

'Don't stop—you were right the first time,' he smiled devastatingly, the electrifying blue of his eyes overpowering her unerringly. 'I envisaged being around this evening too. Your birthday doesn't finish until twelve, you know.'

To Tracey's great relief the arrival of the waiter at that moment with their succulent steaks obviated any need for her to return that look of Ryan's, because she was certain that if she had, the animated glow in her eyes caused by his announcement would have indisputedly told him what she least wanted him to know.

Fortunately the remainder of the meal saw a return of their earlier affability and the afternoon was spent exploring

The Rocks area itself; walking along cobbled streets where convicts had tramped many years before, their fingerprints still visible in some of the hand-formed bricks; visiting Cadman's cottage, built early in the eighteen hundreds and now the oldest surviving dwelling in the city, which contained a waterfront museum; browsing through other restored warehouses where modern hand-made goods were on display—pottery, leatherwork, native art, and many more—as well as craftsmen demonstrating the traditional skills of the glassblower and candlemaker; following the winding streets arm in arm seeing who could be the first to espy the unusual—an old-fashioned letterbox, a gas street lamp, and more evidence of the convicts' helpless lot with the marks of picks gouged into the sandstone blocks that were used so often in the colony's early buildings.

Tracey almost waltzed into her suite when they returned to the hotel later that day. She wasn't particularly interested in why Ryan's attitude towards her should have altered so dramatically since their last meeting, because she didn't particularly care! He was absolutely irresistible when he chose to be, and today had been so *right*! A knock on her door only minutes after his departure for his own room had her whirling around and rushing towards it enthusiastically.

'Lana!'

To say Tracey's happy expression fell was an understatement, because it collapsed as she saw the Alexanders' neighbour standing in the hallway.

Precision pencilled brows rose affectedly in the flawless face in accompaniment to her sweet derisive, 'Aren't you going to invite me in?' and it was only good manners that stopped Tracey retorting with the bald, 'No!' which was on her lips and changing it to a grudging, 'Of course,' as she waved an arm in the direction of the brocade-covered sofa, adding, 'Take a seat, won't you?' while she closed the door with a disgruntled thud.

Seeing her visitor dressed so fastidiously in pale lemon silk, a double strand of pearls encircling her throat, her make-up immaculate and with not one hair out of place made Tracey feel like some unkempt, overly-voluptuous schoolgirl, and as standing beside the sofa while Lana took the seat offered and meticulously arranged the folds of her dress over crossed knees only seemed to emphasise the unfavourable comparison, Tracey lowered herself irritably into the chair opposite and eyed the older woman askance.

'Well, dear,' the word grated annoyingly because it was obvious it had only been used so attention could be drawn denigratingly to Tracey's youthful fashions. 'First of all, I understand that congratulations are in order for your birthday,' Lana smiled, but it was merely the stretching of lips, there was no warmth behind it at all. 'I do hope you liked Ryan's present—I had a dreadful time trying to decide what would be just right for him to give you. But then men are always so helpless when it comes to choosing gifts, aren't they?' she simpered confidentially.

In spite of the air-conditioning Tracey felt frozen. She couldn't bear to think of that beautiful bracelet having been selected by Lana, but at the same time she couldn't totally ignore the grain of truth in her comment either. At birthdays and Christmas hadn't it always been a case of her stepfather handing over some money with the request, 'Get Lyn something from me, will you, darling? I never know what to buy,' and Lyn had been approached the same way to purchase his presents for Tracey.

Some of the happiness left her eyes and she conceded, 'Yes, aren't they?' in a small voice completely devoid of emotion. But not for the world could she say how delighted she had been with Ryan's gift, because any pleasure she derived therefrom had now totally evaporated.

'However, that wasn't all I came to see you about,' Lana continued, and Tracey's eyes flickered over the composed countenance uncertainly. What now? 'You see ... oh, dear, I do have to be careful, because I wouldn't like to hurt your feelings unnecessarily,' she gave a regretful laugh and Tracey nearly mocked, 'That'll be the day!' aloud. 'But I know Ryan's too soft-hearted to tell you himself, so in a manner of speaking, I'm deputising for him. I understand that it's your twenty-first—and nobody's denying that it isn't an important milestone in one's life,' she put in patronisingly, 'but really, Tracey, don't you think you're asking just a little too much by expecting Ryan and me to change our dinner plans so that you can be included as well?' she questioned caustically. 'After all, it was *me* that Ryan brought down with him and, even if I say so myself, I was good enough to give up some of my time with him so he could spend today with you. I think it would be a nice gesture on your part now if you bowed out graciously and at least allowed us some privacy for tonight,' in a voice as sharp as finely honed steel.

Tracey's hands closed jerkily. Was that the reason Ryan had been such pleasant company all day—because he knew he had an enjoyable evening ahead of him with Lana? Oh, good God, what an infatuated idiot she had made of herself! To think she had openly admitted wanting to spend more time with him was so humiliating she wished the ground would open up and swallow her. Suddenly the blood began coursing hotly through her veins again. As much as she disliked the woman opposite her, it was for Ryan that most of Tracey's angry condemnations were reserved.

So he 'envisaged being around this evening too', did he? In that case, she would see that he had a night to remember! She had been spied on, tricked into taking a position where she could be kept under surveillance and finally, heartbreakingly, been made to look and feel a fool! Well, there was one thing Ryan Alexander shouldn't have overlooked—his ward could play games of make-believe just as well as he could!

Now her gaze lifted slowly, defiantly green. 'I'm sorry, Lana, but I don't think I can oblige,' she informed her with not one whit of apology evident in her tone. 'Ryan took great pains to stress that my birthday didn't finish until midnight, and I rather think he found my presence today quite ... pleasurable,' she paused to accent the word suggestively.

Lana's eyes glittered maliciously as she leant forward to charge, 'You always were a precocious brat, weren't you, Tracey?' with a sneer. 'I think your whole vocabulary used to consist of two words, "Want Rine, want Rine!",' she imitated spitefully. 'And you haven't changed one iota, have you? You're just like they reckoned your mother was ... willing to chase after any male just so long as he's presentable!'

With Lana losing some of her carefully disciplined composure, it was easier for Tracey to ignore the derogatory remarks in order to keep the upper hand. 'Well, naturally I wouldn't be interested in anyone who wasn't presentable,' she acceded flippantly. 'But you seem to have forgotten the most relevant aspect, Lana ... it's a well-known fact, it takes *two* to tango!' she smiled annoyingly.

'Now you listen to me, you illegitimate little bitch!' Lana was swiftly on her feet, shaking with fury. 'I've had all I'm ...'

'What was that you said?' demanded Tracey in disbelief.

'I said you were illegitimate ... a bastard, a by-blow, born on the wrong side of the blankets ... whichever you prefer,' Lana jeered and then laughed. 'You must be the only one who didn't know!'

'You're lying!' Tracey retorted fiercely. 'My father died before I was born.'

'Oh, sure, he died before you were born all right!' Lana took delight in informing her. 'The only trouble was, your mother unfortunately forgot to marry him before he departed!'

Tracey's muscles ached with the strain of appearing unaffected by the malevolent disclosure as she walked with unbelievable calm to the door and held it wide open with obvious intent. 'And the trouble with you, Lana, is that your mind is as warped as a waterlogged breadstick!' she announced contemptuously. 'But if you thought the use of your distasteful shock tactics would make me change my plans for tonight, then I'm sorry to have to disappoint you, because I can assure you it was a wasted effort,' she lied convincingly.

Halting momentarily in the doorway, Lana turned back with ruthless design. 'And I'm telling you ...'

'Nothing, absolutely nothing!' Tracey interrupted bleakly, beginning to close the door. 'Goodbye, Lana! I don't suggest you call again—you might find being left standing in the hall after the door's been slammed in your face for the second time somewhat disconcerting!' she advised with a savage thrust on the door which had the other woman scrambling out of its way in undignified haste before it shut with a resounding slam.

As Lana departed, so did Tracey's iron control, and she rushed impulsively into her bedroom, dragging her cases out of the storage cupboard and throwing them on to the rack provided at the end of the bed. To hell with the pair of them! They were welcome to each other! It was the perfect opportunity for her to make good an escape and she didn't intend to let it slip past. By using the back stairs she could be out of the hotel, and their lives, before anyone even knew she had left her room.

It was disquieting though to find that her brain was working at the same furious pace as she was in tossing clothes indiscriminately into her cases. Was she illegitimate? There had been an incontrovertible ring to Lana's voice when she had viciously imparted the information. Tracey shrugged. It hurt to some extent, of course, but as she had never known a time when Ben Alexander hadn't been accepted as her father, it didn't worry her as much as Lana had no doubt hoped it would. Perhaps because it wasn't such a rare occurrence these days and, therefore, the prejudices weren't as strong either.

The idea of Ryan asking Lana to select a gift for her and then not telling her that his girl-friend would be joining them for dinner—or, as was apparently the case, she was to join them—was what hurt the most, and the more she thought about it, the more resentful she grew. She should have known there was something behind Ryan's unusually tolerant attitude. She scowled at herself in the mirror for being so easily won over and affording him some amusement at her own expense. The only consolation was the knowledge that he wouldn't be getting the chance to ever do it again!

The muted burr of the telephone beside her bed had her staring at it indecisively. She didn't really feel like talking to anyone just now, and if she let it ring they might think she was in the shower and couldn't hear it. By the time they tried again, whoever it was, she would be gone. She hurried into the bathroom and scooped out her toilet articles from the vanity unit and dumped them into a corner pocket of the case in haphazard fashion; the contents of one drawer of the dressing table were next, followed by some clothes from the wardrobe.

The click of her sitting room door opening and then closing again had her straightening apprehensively, her heart pounding noisily against her ribs. If that was Lana back again, she was going to regret walking into private rooms without knocking!

'Tracey? Why didn't you answer your phone?'

Ryan! That was worse. She sucked in a deep hectic breath and raced for the doorway in order to head him off before he caught sight of her half packed cases, but she was too late, and he reached it just as she was starting to pull the door closed.

Although he had obviously showered and shaved since she last saw him, he was still only in casual clothes and his hair had an unruly look to it as if he had pulled his shirt on in a hurry and not bothered to comb his hair afterwards. His eyes took in her own unchanged state of dress cursorily and then flicked past her into the bedroom where her packing was in full view.

'All right, Tracey, what's going on?' he asked suspiciously, moving further into the room and thereby forcing Tracey to retreat before him.

The tip of her tongue ran quickly over her dry lips. 'I'm leaving ... and you can't stop me!' she blazed at him mutinously.

'The hell I can't!' Ryan made a grab for her arm, but she dodged elusively out of the way, retrieving a shoe from her case and heading for the comparative safety of the far side of the bed.

'You get out of here, Ryan!' she flung the shoe at him stormily. 'I never want to see you again! Did you really think I'd be happy acting as chaperone for you and your girl-friend?' bitterly.

Ryan smoothly evaded the carelessly aimed missile and rested his hands ominously on his hips. 'You do that again, young lady, and I'll paddle your behind with it,' he threatened.

'Oh, yes, that's right, resort to violence!' she taunted,

sweeping her hair impatiently from her forehead. 'Well, I may be illegitimate, but that doesn't mean I'm illiterate as well ... I can read the writing on the wall without any help from you!'

'Who told you that?' he demanded peremptorily, eyes narrowing grimly.

Tracey didn't bother to pretend not to know to what he was referring. 'Does it matter?' she countered aggressively.

'I happen to think so.'

Widening eyes provoked with a tenacious heedlessness. 'And why shouldn't *I* know?' she retaliated tartly. 'Apparently everyone else does!'

Ryan raked an exasperated hand through his hair and commanded irately, 'Don't be such a little fool!'

'Oh! And why should I stop being one now?' Tracey's expression revealed her self-contempt. 'Thanks to you, I thought I'd played the part rather well today.'

'Meaning ...?'

With Lana's deflating remarks still ringing in her ears, Tracey's temper rose even higher. 'Meaning whatever you damned well please!' she tossed at him insolently. 'I don't care any more ... and I'm getting out of here!' stalking around the bed belligerently and brushing past him.

'That's what you think!' Lean fingers whipped around her wrist and brought her to an abrupt halt. 'You're not going anywhere, honey! So how about you start giving with some answers, hmm?'

Tracey's left hand came up to try and prise her right hand free as she tugged strenuously against the restraining grip. 'I thought you were the one with all of those! Don't tell me you're losing your touch!' she found the breath to goad amid her struggles, triumphantly managing to break away at last—but only temporarily.

This time a firmer grasp swung her about forcefully and toppled her on to the bed before she could strike back, Ryan's greater strength quelling her frantic opposition inexorably, and his weight preventing any further resistance. A hand twined in her hair, immobilising her head, and he smiled ruefully at the eyes blazing so brightly up at him.

'I hope not,' he eventually replied to her last derisive

comment. 'Where you're concerned, I have the feeling it would be fatal,' as his shapely mouth lowered leisurely to take possession of her unconsciously parting lips.

Tracey hadn't intended to respond—she had wanted to remain chillingly unmoved—but Ryan's lips were too persuasively demanding for that, and involuntarily she began returning the sensuous pressure with a fervour that shocked her. All disconnected thoughts disappeared, leaving only a throbbing desire for a more fulfilling intimacy as his hands explored the satin-smooth skin beneath her lacy top and her arms linked lovingly about his neck. Gradually intoxicating lips inched down the side of her neck to linger against the soft curve of her shoulder, the stimulating warmth of his body kindling a fire in her blood which had her arching against him invitingly and murmuring in pleasurable surrender when his mouth imperiously claimed hers yet again.

When at last he relinquished her, Tracey tightened her hold about his neck, drawing his head back down to hers, but with a groan and one last hard kiss pressed against her lips, Ryan moved to sit on the edge of the bed, head bent, elbows resting on his knees.

'Would it make any difference if I told you I loved you, Tracey?' he queried tautly.

An avalanche of joyous emotion overtook Tracey ... then she remembered. 'I don't honestly know,' she whispered despondently. 'I don't think I could bear being second best for very long.'

Ryan twisted round to look at her in astonishment. 'Second best to what, for crying out loud?' he ejaculated.

'Oh, don't play dumb, Ryan!' Tracey propped herself up on her elbows to castigate angrily. 'Who else but your friendly neighbourhood widow, of course!' she jeered.

'And what makes you think you would be—as you put it —second best to Lana?' he enquired interestedly.

Tracey pushed herself up to sit cross-legged, a smouldering look on her face. 'She picked out my birthday present, didn't she?'

'Like hell! How on earth would you come up with a fantastic idea like that?'

The dogmatic denial had Tracey eyeing him doubtfully. 'But when Lana called to see me this afternoon, she said she had,' she explained warily.

'The lying ...!' Ryan smothered a furious epithet and tilted Tracey's head up to his with a compelling forefinger. 'Did you really believe I needed any help in deciding what to give my one and only redheaded ward? Uh-uh, nothing doing,' he answered his own question with a teasing smile. 'I've known for a long, long time exactly what I wanted for you, honey.'

It seemed to Tracey that there could have been a hidden meaning in those words, but although her heart started drumming at a rate which threatened to suffocate her, she nevertheless had to point out accusingly, 'You still arranged to take her to dinner tonight.'

'Did I?' Ryan's eyebrows crooked expressively. 'That's the first I've heard of it.'

'But Lana said ...'

Two hands reached out and settled firmly on either side of her face, his lips effectively cutting off any further revelations for long exhilarating minutes.

'Would you believe, I'm not the slightest bit interested in what Lana did, or didn't, say?' Ryan finally broke their embrace huskily. 'Except that I could wring her neck for having told you you were illegitimate! There was no need for you to know,' he sighed. 'As for the rest she's apparently told you, and presumably for reasons best known to herself, there doesn't seem to have been a shred of truth in any of it,' he dismissed the absent Lana with a disparaging shrug. 'All I want to hear at the moment is a plain old affirmative to a simple question. Will you marry me, Tracey?'

That could hardly be classified as second best, could it? Tracey's eyes shone back her reply so convincingly that the breathless, 'Oh, yes!' she sighed really wasn't necessary as her arms wound around his neck and she confessed shyly, 'You see, I happen to love you very much too!'

Ryan's arms caught her to him proprietorially. 'In which case, you might at least have given me some indication before now,' he teased mock ferociously.

'I did,' she sparkled mischievously. 'I asked if I could go to Satinwood for a month, remember?'

'If only I'd known,' he groaned ruefully. 'God, how I told myself I hated you that day we flew up there. You were so distant—I could have killed you for what you were doing to me!'

'Instead you said you were glad of the respite from my irritations and tantrums, and were looking forward to more compliant feminine company,' came the reproachful reminder.

'In an effort to make you jealous,' he admitted with a wry smile. 'Unfortunately it backfired ... you told me to go ahead!'

'And did you?' she now asked in a small voice.

'Are you serious?' He shook his head in mild exasperation. 'I was never interested in Lana—no matter what she might like to imply to the contrary—not even before she married Philip. No, I spent that month slogging myself to near exhaustion so that when it came to sleep I didn't lie awake for half the night haunted by memories of you sharing my bed!' which brought a stain of colour to Tracey's cheeks. 'An incident which was the motivation for many a blazing row with Justin after you'd left, I might add,' he continued dryly.

'You quarrelled because of me?' Tracey bit her lip sorrowfully for having been the cause of dissension between them. 'I guess he thinks I'm pretty shameless,' she sighed glumly.

'You!' Ryan threw back his head and laughed delightedly. 'Darling, you came out of it smelling like roses ... *I* was the one he wanted in the sights of his shotgun!' He sobered ironically. 'That's partly why I was so cold to you when you returned from Satinwood. Not only did you seem to be slipping further and further away from me, but you'd also created a rift between Justin and myself which was something that had never happened before, and which leads us to the reason for my suggesting we let you live in Sydney. I hoped that in your absence Justin and I could reconcile our differences, and that you—a rather forlorn aspiration at the time, I thought—just might find living here too lonely and want to come back to Nindethana of your own accord.'

Tracey's eyes took in the smiling features suspiciously. 'And is that why you had me installed here? The sole object being to make me miss you?'

'Well, city hotels aren't usually the best of places for making lasting friendships,' he grinned without the least shadow of remorse.

'You beast, you utter beast!' Tracey pulled at two handfuls of dark hair in laughing indignation. 'You were relying on me being thrilled to see a familiar face today of all days, weren't you?'

'But was it successful?' he quizzed deeply.

In answer Tracey moved closer, her lips smoothing a temptation across his own. 'You know it was,' she whispered intensely, and caught an ecstatic breath when his mouth took hers masterfully and he pressed her back against the pillows.

It was some time until the next words were spoken, and even then it was a while before Tracey could arrange her thoughts rationally after Ryan had reluctantly pulled away.

'Are you and Justin still at odds?' she asked, a worried frown furrowing her forehead and a slightly unsteady hand outlining the neckline of his shirt.

'We won't be once he knows you're at last to become a permanent member of the family,' he returned with a smile that instantly had Tracey's pulse skyrocketing again. 'It's what he's always had in mind.'

'Doesn't he mind my—my being illegitimate?' she forced out throatily.

'Oh, Tracey!' He bent over her and brushed the curls from her face with compassionate fingers. 'You never could understand, could you?' he sighed. 'No matter who your father was, from the very first day you arrived on Nindethana as a child—and you already bore our name—as far as we were concerned, you were *ours*! And what we have, we don't let go of easily!' he asserted dynamically. 'All I know is, that if he fathered you, he must have been quite some guy!'

She laughed shakily. 'You seem to be an expert at saying all the right things today, don't you?'

'I'll need to be if I'm going to explain to Justin why you're late for your own party.'

Tracey sat bolt upright, eyes half closing intently. 'Justin? Party? What party?' she demanded.

'Must have slipped my mind,' he grinned tormentingly. 'Didn't I tell you that a few of the family would be congregating downstairs in order to help you celebrate?'

'No, you didn't!' she pulled a laughing grimace at him. 'Did Lyn and Carol come with him?' excitedly.

He nodded. 'As well as Nancy, Clive, Ross, Lance, Noeleen ...'

An incredulous expression had spread over Tracey's face as he began to reel off the names, and now she interrupted with a gasp, 'You mean they all came down expressly for my birthday?'

'We're a very close family,' he teased. 'You should know that by now.'

'Oh, Ryan!' she looked at him tearfully, helplessly, and then suddenly her eyes began to widen with something akin to horror. 'Oh, no! My dress!' scrambling to the end of the bed on her hands and knees to peer at the jumbled mess in her cases. 'It's all crumpled up in there somewhere!' she wailed plaintively.

'Then madam will be pleased to learn that the hotel provides an extremely efficient service which will have her dress pressed and returned to her by the time she's finished having a shower,' he quoted knowledgeably with a quick glance at his watch as he rose to his feet. 'You've got half an hour ... think you can make it?' he smiled.

'I'll make it,' she confirmed confidently, sliding off the bed and wrapping her arms around his waist. Her head tilted backwards so she could look up into his face. 'Are you going to change now too?' she queried regretfully.

Ryan's own hands linked together in the middle of her back. 'If I can be sure you'll still be here when I get back,' he retorted dryly. 'Or do you think I should lock your door from the outside when I leave just to be on the safe side?'

Tracey's head moved from side to side slowly. 'I've got a better idea. How about we lock the door on the inside when you come back?' she suggested with an audacious look from beneath her lashes.

'Don't tempt me, witch,' he kissed her unhurriedly. 'I'm finding it hard enough to leave you as it is. This has been quite a day!'

A loving smile curved her enticing lips. 'I know what you mean,' she whispered in fervent understanding. For her too, it had indeed been *quite* a day!

Harlequin

COLLECTION
EDITIONS OF 1978

**50 great stories
of special beauty
and significance**

$1.25
each novel

In 1976 we introduced the first 100 Harlequin
Collections—a selection of titles chosen from our
best sellers of the past 20 years. This series, a trip
down memory lane, proved how great romantic
fiction can be timeless and appealing from
generation to generation. The theme of love
and romance is eternal, and, when placed
in the hands of talented, creative, authors
whose true gift lies in their ability to write from the
heart, the stories reach a special level of brilliance
that the passage of time cannot dim. Like a
treasured heirloom, an antique of superb
craftsmanship, a beautiful gift from someone
loved—these stories too, have a special significance
that transcends the ordinary. **$1.25 each novel**

Here are your 1978
Harlequin Collection Editions...

Original Harlequin Romance numbers in brackets

ORDER FORM
Harlequin Reader Service

In U.S.A.
MPO Box 707
Niagara Falls, N.Y. 14302

In Canada
649 Ontario St.,
Stratford, Ontario, N5A 6W2

Please send me the following Harlequin Collection novels. I am enclosing my check or money order for $1.25 for each novel ordered, plus 25¢ to cover postage and handling.

☐ 102	☐ 115	☐ 128	☐ 140
☐ 103	☐ 116	☐ 129	☐ 141
☐ 104	☐ 117	☐ 130	☐ 142
☐ 105	☐ 118	☐ 131	☐ 143
☐ 106	☐ 119	☐ 132	☐ 144
☐ 107	☐ 120	☐ 133	☐ 145
☐ 108	☐ 121	☐ 134	☐ 146
☐ 109	☐ 122	☐ 135	☐ 147
☐ 110	☐ 123	☐ 136	☐ 148
☐ 111	☐ 124	☐ 137	☐ 149
☐ 112	☐ 125	☐ 138	☐ 150
☐ 113	☐ 126	☐ 139	☐ 151
☐ 114	☐ 127		

Number of novels checked @
$1.25 each = $ _____

N.Y. and N.J. residents add
appropriate sales tax $ _____

Postage and handling $ ___.25___

                    TOTAL $ _____

NAME _____
            (Please Print)
ADDRESS _____

CITY _____

STATE/PROV. _____

ZIP/POSTAL CODE _____

ROM 2205

Offer expires December 31, 1978